TAANG-LEUK - CHOICES

KRUNG THEP BOOK 3

MARIA KUHN

eBook ISBN: 978-1-8384303-4-4

Print ISBN: 978-1-8384303-5-1

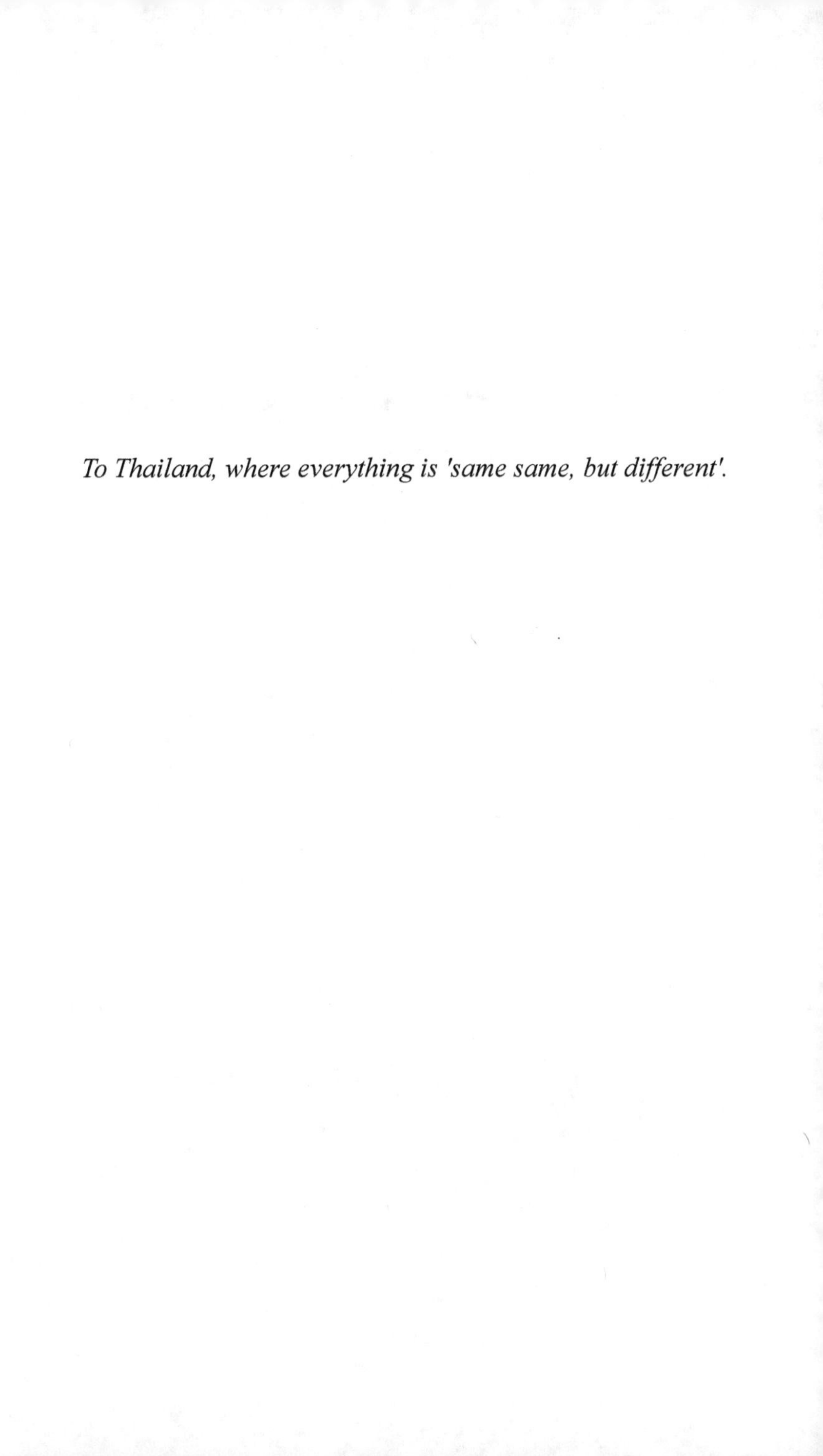
To Thailand, where everything is 'same same, but different'.

CHARACTERS

<u>Taylor Family</u>
Luna – American expat, 16 years old
Luke – Luna's brother, 12 years old
Mark – Luna's dad/Khun Mark
Susan – Luna's mom/Khun Susan

<u>Apichart Family</u>
Nui (Benjawan) – Thai, 16 years old
Duen – Nui's sister, 13 years old
Krit – Nui's brother, 18 years old
Tum – Nui's brother, 11 years old
Mae – Nui's mom
Paa – Nui's dad
Khun Yaa – Nui's paternal grandmother
Khun Bpoo – Nui's paternal grandfather
Aunt May – Nui's aunt
Uncle Dech – Nui's uncle, Aunt May's husband
Panya – Their son, 15 years old
Chaiya – Their son, 13 years old
Khun Yaai – Nui's maternal grandmother

<u>Others</u>
Channon – Veterinary assistant, Krit's friend
Chone – Abandoned husky, adopted by Channon
Yumi – Luna's friend from Shanghai, 16 years old

TAANG-LEUK ทาง-เลือก

CHOICES

Noun:

1. A range of possibilities from which one or more may be chosen.
2. The right or ability to choose.

You have two choices:

to control your mind or to let your mind control you.

Buddha

Bangkok, January
Taylor family condo building

LUNA

You're stalking your own family.

I cringed at the absurdity of the thought. And yet, here I was hiding behind one of the big planter boxes on our pool terrace.

Nui's body was almost six inches shorter than mine, which made it easier to conceal myself. I hoped none of our neighbours would spot and ask me to leave. Mom was reading a magazine on her lounge chair in the shade, mindful as ever of her fair skin. A few years ago, she had declared Wednesday afternoons her *me* time, avoiding meetings or appointments, and simply took the time to relax and do things for fun. Luke and I were told we should only bother her if there was an emergency. At first we'd resented it, but now I could see the benefit of having a mental health day or at least an afternoon. I sniffed and raised my hand to wipe away the tears. Scowling at Nui's hands and darker skin didn't magically change the fact I was still stuck.

This was my first chance to see Mom since she'd returned from Chicago. My last class at BIS, Bangkok International School, had been cancelled as the teacher had called in sick and they didn't have a replacement readily available. Media Studies was one of the few classes Nui and I didn't share, and I slipped away without telling her. Now I wondered if that had been such a good idea, as the sight of Mom made me realise the futility of my situation.

It had been over a week since Nui had point-blank refused to switch back with me into our own bodies, a week that had kept me in a constant state of anxiety. I'd had visions of avenging her betrayal and devising plans to reverse the situation without putting myself into more jeopardy. My last attempt to push Nui out of my body and into her own had backfired big time and showed that brute force was not the way to do it.

A month ago, my biggest gripe had been that we, as a family, moved too much, and I wanted a chance to stay in one place instead of upending my life every two years to follow Dad's appointments as General Manager of five-star hotels. My complaint seemed trivial now, and I didn't care if there were a hundred more moves as long as I could be with my family.

Mom sat up as one of our neighbours approached her to chat. She smiled and nodded, holding her hands up to shield her eyes. I missed her. Sure, she and I'd had our disagreements, but never in a million years had I envisioned myself without her steady presence.

What's keeping you from going up to her, Luna?

I almost stood up to do just that, but then crouched down again. *She won't recognise you. She'll think you're Nui and could be suspicious about why you're here.*

I stifled a groan.

Even if I could convince her somehow that I was really her daughter in Nui's body, how was I going to explain the reason for our switch? *I didn't like the life we were living, Mom, so I switched with Nui to enjoy her life.* Right, that would go over well.

I sat with my back to the planter and locked my hands around my knees. *You really fucked up, Luna. Now what?*

2

NUI

I DIDN'T SEE LUNA AT THE LAST BELL. NORMALLY WE'D walk out of school together, but last week had changed everything. Outwardly, we were still friends, but underneath ran a tense current that made me twitchy with nerves. *Keep your friends close and your enemies closer?* Not that I truly considered Luna an enemy, but right now the scales could tip either way, not least because of what I had done. I'd promised her we'd switch back into our own bodies during meditation, or more specifically, while we were both having an out-of-body experience, but at the last minute I'd reconsidered, and now Luna and I were stuck in a catch-22 situation.

I'd expected her to be openly hostile, but to my big surprise, she'd carried on as if nothing had happened. These days though, we only spoke about school stuff, nothing personal, and most of all we avoided the big elephant in the room. I could only imagine what was going on in her mind, but I suspected she was plotting to get me to switch back with her sooner rather than later. I was getting more stressed every day, trying to figure out what she was up to, and I scrutinised her every word for deeper meaning.

Rationally, I knew I should have upheld my side of the bargain, but I was desperate to visit the States at least one time to find out if the country and people really matched my fantasy. I'd begged Luna to let me go with her family at Songkran, our Thai New Year in April, to look at colleges of her choice, and I promised I'd switch back with her afterwards. Understandably, she didn't trust me to keep my promise. I couldn't really blame her.

Shit, Nui, you've really turned into a selfish person. I ground my teeth and in the back of my mind I could see Khun Yaa, my grandmother, shaking her head at me with disappointment and disapproval.

A hand grabbed my arm as Yumi bounced up next to me.

"What are you doing this afternoon, Luna?" she asked. "Want to see a movie?"

Yumi had been Luna's classmate in Shanghai and had recently moved to Bangkok with her dad after her parents divorced. Obviously, she'd anticipated resuming her friendship with Luna, but I had to keep her at arm's length after she became suspicious of my 'memory lapses'.

"I can't, Yumi. I have to work on my TOK essay. I'm so far behind, it's not even funny."

"Boo, you can always do that later tonight, can't you?" Yumi said with a pout, then dragged me forward, bouncing on the balls of her feet. "Come on, a movie is much more fun."

"Sorry, Yumi. Not today. I need to get this done and Mom said we need to have a family pow-wow tonight."

That thought sent an icy shiver down my spine. I had been waiting to hear from the Royal police about the outcome of their investigation into my blog, which had been banned as potentially anti-monarchist. If the police deemed it derogative, or wanted to use my case as a warning to other foreigners, they could technically sentence me to prison. My nerves had been buzzing all week, and I knew I had lost some weight because I hadn't been sleeping well or eating properly with my life out of whack.

Yumi squinted, clearly not convinced.

"Are you avoiding me?" she asked.

The honest answer would have been yes.

"Don't be silly. Of course not."

"You never want to do anything anymore. What happened? You used to be a lot more fun," Yumi said.

"You know I missed a few days in school. I'm just behind right now, that's all."

I had to smile despite myself. Yumi was super high-energy, to put it mildly, and just fun to be around.

"You're so boring. Fine, but we'll definitely do something tomorrow, no excuse."

3

———

LUNA

I SHOULD HAVE ALREADY LEFT TO GO TO THE ANIMAL shelter, but I couldn't bring myself to move. I wanted to savour every minute I had 'with' Mom. My mind was doing cartwheels, trying to come up with a way out of the situation. I'd been going over the same ideas a million times without coming to a workable solution. A satisfactory solution for me, that is. The only acceptable outcome was to return to my family. I'd even be ready to leave Thailand altogether if it meant getting away from Nui and leaving this mess behind.

What about Channon? I sighed. *Yeah, what about Channon?* He was the only other person who knew about our switch. It had ticked Nui off when I told him, but I was hoping to move our relationship to the next level and I wanted him to know me as Luna. Nui had thrown a wrench into my plans when she refused to honour our deal. *One thing at a time, Luna. You need to get home first.*

As I got up to leave, I heard Luke's voice in the passageway from the elevators to the terrace.

"I don't know, Luna."

I couldn't hear Nui's response, but recognized my voice.

Damn! I'd missed my window and now I'd have to wait for the right opportunity to slip away. I hunched down, hoping they'd be too focused on the pool to look at the planter pot.

Are you three again, Luna? Hoping that if you can't see them, they can't see you?

I swallowed my grunt. Nui and Luke walked onto the terrace towards Mom. Luke wore his swim trunks and had a towel wrapped around his neck.

"Hey, Mom. We're back. I'm gonna go in." Without waiting for an answer, he dumped his towel on the chair next to Mom and ran to the outdoor shower to rinse off. He jumped around like a frog on hot coals, yelping when the cold water hit him, then took a running start and dove into the pool, which he wasn't supposed to do according to the condo rules. A smile tugged at my lips. Typical Luke.

Nui was still wearing the same dress I'd seen her in at school earlier that day. Apparently, she had no intention of swimming, even though that was something I would do on a hot day like this and to give Mom her *me* time. Instead, she sat down next to Mom, sucking up to her.

"Hi Mom. How are you? Having a good day?"

My mother smiled at her and leaned back.

"Yes, thanks, honey. And you?"

I almost gagged hearing Nui treat Mom as her own. Instead, I crept closer to hear better.

"So, what's this big family meeting you want to have tonight?" Nui asked.

"You'll find out. We'll wait for your dad to come home," Mom said. She put her sunglasses back on.

"But why can't you tell me now? Does it have something to do with the police investigation?"

I held my breath. Maybe this was something I could use to make Nui switch back.

"Honey, let me enjoy my afternoon. We'll talk about it tonight. I want Luke to be there. It'll affect him too."

Nui demurred and sat back on her lounger as if she didn't have a care in the world.

"Luna, how come I haven't seen Nui lately? Don't you guys hang out anymore? Is she alright?"

My eyes prickled with tears. Mom always cared about anyone involved with our family; not like Nui, who was only looking out for herself.

"Hmm, we had a bit of a misunderstanding and I think we need to take a little break."

Misunderstanding? I wanted to scream at Nui. This was no misunderstanding. She lied and even admitted to it. My pulse sped up at the sheer gall of it.

"That's a shame. What kind of misunderstanding, honey? I thought you were such good friends?"

I couldn't see Mom's face as she'd turned towards Nui, but I knew that tone. She wasn't happy. Mom hated disagreements and always thought people should be able to work things out.

Right, Nui! What misunderstanding? How are you going to explain your treachery?

"Oh, nothing major. I'm sure we'll work it out eventually." Nui nonchalantly leaned back on the lounger and closed her eyes. I wished I could just walk out onto the deck and confront her right there in front of Mom. I knew I could prove to Mom that *I* was her daughter and then Nui would have some explaining to do. *So would you, Luna.* Dammit. This would not work. A glance at my watch told me I had to hustle if I wanted to go to the pet hospital. I slowly pushed up and shook out my cramped legs and then crept along the wall toward the elevators.

"Nui?" Luke called.

I froze.

4

NUI

Luke's shout jerked me upright. *Luna? Here?* I followed the direction of his gaze, but didn't see anyone.

"There, she was just there." Luke pointed while treading water in the pool. "She was coming out from behind that planter."

Luna's mom sat up and looked towards the passageway.

"Are you sure, Luke?"

"Yeah, I think so."

"Luna, why don't you see if you can catch her? Maybe she wanted to talk to you and make up after your fight," Khun Susan suggested.

As if. A niggle of worry tightened my stomach. What was Luna up to? Why would she be sneaking around here?

"I doubt it, Mom. Luke probably confused her with someone else. Otherwise, she'd have come over."

"Just check."

I shrugged, then got up in slow motion, not really sure I wanted to see Luna or, more to the point, find out what this was about. I couldn't blame her for wanting to see her mom, but why hide and then run away? If it really was her, she was definitely up to something.

5

LUNA

Phew! That was close. I frantically stabbed the elevator button. *Come on, come on, come on.* Typical that they took forever when needed immediately. I glanced over my shoulder towards the terrace, hoping Nui and Mom would ignore Luke's announcement. This was taking too long. One cabin was on the ground floor, while the other was still two floors up. I heard footsteps slapping from the pool area and though I didn't know who was coming, I didn't want to risk having to face Nui.

One more look at the elevators told me I had to get out. I couldn't recall if the emergency exit would set off an alarm, but I'd prefer that over a confrontation right now, while I still felt unsettled after seeing Mom.

I lucked out—no alarm—but just before the door closed behind me, I looked back one more time and saw Nui staring at me. Her eyes were scrunched up with uncertainty, but she didn't call out. The door clunked shut and I hustled down the stairs to the basement. Thank goodness I knew the building well. I had to cross to the garage, then walk past the guard shack into the street. The security guy just nodded at me; he probably thought I was an employee. I walked around the block to the soi leading to the Skytrain. Once I'd pushed my way into the crowded carriage, I finally eased up and let the icy air conditioning cool my sweat. Two stations later, I was shivering, and I shrugged off my backpack to grab a shawl. The train jerked, and I automatically reached up to grab the overhand rail, but Nui's body was too short. I knocked into the people in front of me, and stepped on someone's toes, barely staying upright.

"Oaui!" the guy snapped, and then pointedly stared at his foot with a pained expression. "Rawang noi sii krub". As if I had done it on purpose.

"Khor towd kha," I apologised, but he deliberately turned his back.

For crying out loud. Again, I felt the sting of tears. This day was going from bad to terrible. Stupid little things kept piling on until I wished I'd never gotten out of bed that morning.

You didn't have *to go and see Mom. You knew you'd feel homesick.*

I wiped my eyes. I never expected to miss my family this much, and them not knowing about me being held hostage made it worse. Yes, I got to see Luke in school, but that wasn't the same since we didn't chat except to say 'hi' and 'bye'. Maybe I needed to talk to him to find out what Nui was doing in my place at home.

At Thong Lo station, I left the train and took a moto-taxi to the pet hospital. Technically, I was still under house arrest after accidentally getting drunk with Yumi and lying to Nui's mom. The only reason she grudgingly allowed me to resume my duties was because I needed the shifts for my community credits for school. Paying the driver reminded me I needed to ask Nui for more money. She could hardly refuse to give me some of my own pocket money. *If she can refuse to switch back with you, what's going to prevent her from withholding your money? This sucks!*

Every which way I played out my current situation, Nui had the upper hand. I had to become more creative or daring if I wanted to get back home.

6

NUI

DAMN, IT *WAS* LUNA. WHAT WAS SHE DOING HERE? I ONLY got a glimpse of her exiting through the stairwell, but it was enough to set off warning bells in my head.

I walked back to the terrace and sat next to Luna's mom.

"No one there. I think Luke mixed her up with someone else." I shrugged as if it wasn't a big deal either way.

"Why don't you call her? Then you'll know. What did you say your misunderstanding was about?" Luna's mom was fishing.

"Mom! It's between Nui and me. I'll deal with it, okay?" I shocked myself by using that tone with her, but stacking lies onto lies had left me off-kilter. Khun Susan was usually very easygoing, but the disagreement between Luna and me clearly bothered her, and the pointed look she gave was unmistakable. She expected me to follow through on my promise.

"Fine. Just cut her some slack. She's probably not feeling herself after the hospital scare." She put her sunglasses back on and relaxed back. "By the way, I haven't seen Yumi yet either. Why don't you invite both girls over tomorrow after school for some coffee and cake? It's nice that you have two friends here now."

Let's not! Her suggestion was pretty much my worst-case scenario. Two girls with the potential to ruin my carefully laid plans.

"Erm, sure, Mom. Let me find out what they're up to tomorrow." I softened my tone, but my outburst must have upset her, as she became strangely uncommunicative. When I tried to bring up the planned trip to the States at Songkran, she responded almost brusquely.

"Luna, it's Wednesday! You know better. Swim or do something else." She finally ordered me to shut up. I had no clue why this particular day was so significant, but grabbed my backpack and left in a bit of a snit. First Luna, and now her mom. Why was everyone acting so strange today? *Doesn't matter, Nui. Use the time to do something productive.*

How was I going to manage the girls' visit if they accepted the invite? I briefly considered refusing to ask them, but Luna's mom was bound to insist if not for tomorrow then another day. I was pretty sure Luna hated me now and while she might be okay seeing me at school, it would be different at her home. It would also be her first opportunity to actually talk to her mom since our original switch a month ago. Emotions were bound to run high. How would she react? On top of that, Yumi knew Luna's mom and if they talked about their time in Shanghai, how could I stay out of that? Yumi had more than once voiced her suspicions about my lack of memory. Both girls could create serious trouble for me, especially if they ganged up. Though I doubted that Luna's parents would be easily convinced they had an impostor in the family, Luna and Yumi had enough history and evidence between them that I'd be hard pressed to refute. At the very least, it would make for some very uncomfortable conversations with the family.

BACK IN MY ROOM, THERE WASN'T MUCH I COULD DO BESIDES homework until Luna's dad came home with an update about the investigation. Despite Luna's threat to sabotage my own grades, I wasn't ready to let hers slip, especially if I wanted to use them as a springboard to visit the US, if only for one trip. Five minutes later, I caught myself still staring at the blank screen. I'd completely spaced out, mulling over my battle with Luna. I knew I was being selfish reneging on our deal, but depending on the outcome of the investigation, she might yet thank me for it, especially if the result is a prison term. The thought made me shudder. It would be justified if I had to suffer the punishment for my stupidity, but Luna had said she wanted to be back in her body no matter the outcome, so maybe that would be my way out if the verdict was terrible. My stomach heaved and I dashed for the bathroom and spat into the sink. Even after rinsing my mouth, a bitter tang remained. *That was low, even for you, Nui.* I didn't even recognise myself anymore having those kinds of horrible thoughts.

I splashed some water on my face, then went back to my desk to call Luna, as I had promised her mom. My finger hovered over the call button. Maybe I should test the waters first.

'Hey Luna, when is Yumi's bday and do U remember

what you did for her 13th? She's testing me.' I added an eye-roll emoji to convey what I thought of that. I didn't mention Luke seeing her or the invite for the next day. If Luna responded at all, it would give me a sign of how mad she really was at me and if it was safe to broach other subjects.

7

LUNA

AT THE PET HOSPITAL, I USED MY VOLUNTEER PASS TO GO straight to the adoption centre. Khun Nan was at the reception counter.

"Oh hello, Nui. Sabai di mai, kha?' Khun Nan was one of my favourite people working here. "We missed you. Are you back now? We could use the extra pair of hands and Chone was looking for you." She winked. Everyone at the hospital knew that Chone officially was Channon's dog, but in reality, Chone had adopted me as his primary person.

"I'm allowed to work as of tomorrow, so you can schedule me back in. I just wanted to say hi today and check on Chone."

Khun Nan nodded and returned to her paperwork while I continued to the fenced-in area where most dogs played during the day. It was still pretty hot, and the pack was resting under the trees, but as soon as I walked out, Chone ran over with what I thought was a goofy grin on his face that matched my own. I only had to bend over slightly to hug him. Chone had grown so much that there wasn't much height difference to Nui's body anymore.

"Hey, big guy. I missed you. Come on, let's sit down. I have so much to tell you."

I picked a bench under the roof overhang to stay in the shade and continued to pet Chone. Before I could launch into a recap of my afternoon, Chone turned his head to look at the door. Channon. A flash of awareness zinged through my body. He looked gorgeous as always. His white lab coat stood out against his tanned skin and wavy black hair. We texted almost every day, but I hadn't seen him in a week, and as usual my brain short-circuited whenever he smiled at me.

"Nui!" Channon took me by surprise when he pulled me up into a hug. According to Nui, it was improper for non-related Thais, especially men and women, to greet each other like that, but I hugged him back anyway. His touch felt great, and he smelled delicious, something citrusy or maybe lemongrass. Not for the first time, I idly marvelled at how he kept that smell being around the animals and strong disinfectants each day. The hug was all too short, but when he pulled back, his smile almost made up for it.

"I missed you. I'm so glad you're back. Are you fully recovered?" Channon was the ultimate carer, whether it was for animals or people. It was just one of many things I admired about him.

"I think so, but today I just wanted to say hello to Chone and maybe see the little one."

Before my hospital stay, I got bitten while rescuing a puppy from a soi dog attack.

"You mean you would have stopped by without saying

hello to me?" Channon winked to show he wasn't serious. "Let's sit down. I have a few minutes."

Chone rested between us, soaking up the attention from both sides. I looked over his head and noticed movement behind him. The puppy clumsily crawling forward looked familiar.

I glanced at Channon.

"Is that…?"

"Yup, that's your rescue." Channon grinned. "Cute, huh?"

The puppy was adorable, his big caramel eyes a beautiful contrast to his wheat and white coloured fur. It was hilarious how he was trying to sneak up on us, but Chone was fully aware of him and briefly tilted his head, twitched his tail and emitted a soft woof. The puppy took the invitation to pounce on Chone who gave him a nudge and lick but otherwise didn't move. Traipsing over Chone's body, the puppy stuck his head out towards us, curiously sniffing the air.

"He's too cute for words. And look how wonderful Chone is with him. Did you name him yet?"

"Not yet, but I think I heard one of the staff call him LaTe, which I think works with his colouring." Channon bent down to rub LaTe's ears.

"I like it! It fits. I'm sure he'll be adopted in no time."

"So, how are you? I haven't seen you all week. Did the doctors find out what happened?" Channon asked. "That was pretty scary."

I shrugged.

"They said they'd never come across a temporary locked-in syndrome like mine and want to do more follow-up tests, but what's the point? If they don't know what caused it, how will tests help them figure out what cures it, right?"

Channon nodded. "You know how doctors are. They

always think there's a logical explanation for everything. Maybe they just can't accept that miracles happen."

Again, he smiled at me. I could get seriously lost looking into his beautiful brown eyes. His smile slowly faded, as if he was contemplating what to say next. He rubbed the back of his neck. My romantic daydream took a nosedive.

"So, I was wondering, what is the latest between you and… I mean…?" He stumbled over his words, which wasn't at all like Channon. I could guess what had him tangled up.

"You mean, am I still Luna in Nui's body?"

Even though I'd told Channon about the switch, he didn't know I'd tried to push Nui out of my body, and I would not open that Pandora's box. He'd probably think I was irresponsible, or worse.

"Yeah, that." He nodded, relieved he didn't have to spell it out himself. I couldn't blame him. It still sounded like a delusional story to me too, except I was living proof it had happened.

"It's complicated, Channon…"

"Nui? What are you doing here?" A high-pitched voice cut into my explanation. I looked over Channon's shoulder and saw Yumi marching over. She was wearing her huge red sunglasses so I couldn't be totally sure of her expression, but she sounded shocked, annoyed, or a bit of both? Her camo pants, cropped long-sleeved red top and combat boots made her look ready for battle. Yumi was the poster child for street fashion. Not that she favoured a particular style, but she had a whimsical way of putting clothing together that was uniquely her. She called it her *me* style.

"Uh oh, prepare for incoming missile," I muttered under my breath.

Channon choked, covering his laugh with a cough.

Then Yumi was there, planting herself in front of us and looking me up and down.

"You recovered. That was fast."

"What do you mean? I've seen you in school." That was weird, even for Yumi.

"Yeah, but I thought you weren't allowed to work yet?" She sounded irritated.

Channon stood up.

"Excuse me, ladies, but I've got to get back to work. Nice to see you Yumi, and so glad you're back Nui."

It might have been a trick of the light, but I could have sworn Channon looked uncomfortable. He seemed to jump at the chance to leave, but I couldn't tell whether it was because of our conversation or because he wanted to avoid Yumi. He turned when Yumi put a hand on his arm.

"Wait, Channon, I got something for you. My dad signed the papers. When do I start?" She thrust an envelope at Channon and closed her fingers over his hand. She half turned to me with her chin up, as if in a challenge.

"That's great, Yumi. I'll get it processed." Channon took the envelope, winked at me, and walked away a bit jerkily. Yumi and I watched him go. *Uh oh.*

Sighing deeply, Yumi sat down and rummaged through her backpack. She pulled out two plastic cylinders of brand new tennis balls, four rope toys and a bag of mixed dog treats. Even Chone sat up with interest. LaTe scooted next to Chone to see what the newcomer had to offer.

"Wow, you've come prepared," I grudgingly admitted.

"Well, if I'm going to volunteer here I might as well do it right. Channon said they can always use extra toys and treats. You have a problem with that?" Yumi asked.

Yup, she definitely was challenging me. There was only one reason she would act that way—she was going after

Channon. She'd never made a secret of her interest in him and she had no reason to feel qualms about poaching him from Nui. Ironic that I couldn't tell her who she actually was stealing from. Yumi sounded like she was geared up for a contest. The question was, who would come out the winner?

8

NUI

LUNA HADN'T ANSWERED, SO YUMI WAS NEXT ON MY LIST.

"Hey, Yumi." I could hear barking in the background. "Where are you?"

"Hey, just got to the shelter."

She was huffing, as if she had been running.

"Hang on a second. Let me get those guys settled."

There was a thud when she put the phone down, and I heard her shouting in the background.

'You guys, settle down. You'll get a treat if you behave.'

I grinned, imagining a tiny Yumi facing a pack of dogs and trying to order them around. Given her energy and attitude, it might just work.

"Oof. Okay, they're cool for now. Man, they are so much fun. You should come. Nui is here too." Yumi was still breathing hard.

"Oh, she is?" *Well, well, Luna has been busy this afternoon.*

"I think she came to see Channon." Yumi's voice lowered to a murmur.

"So? You know they've been kind of dating."

"I don't think that's serious, do you?" Yumi whispered.

"How would I know? You said she's there, so ask her."

I had no intention of getting in the middle of *that* conversation, yet suddenly an idea popped into my head. If Yumi dated Channon, then I wouldn't have to explain why *I* wasn't seeing him, plus I wouldn't have to volunteer at the shelter after Luna and I switched back. Could I encourage Yumi to poach Channon from Luna just because it was convenient for me? *Yikes.* My face burned with shame. I had to let them figure it out by themselves. I had enough going on.

"Maybe I will. So, did you get your TOK stuff done?"

"Not yet, but Mom asked if you and Nui want to come over tomorrow afternoon for cake and coffee. She said she'd love to see you."

"What did Nui say? Is she coming?"

"I haven't asked her yet." And I wasn't yet sure I would.

A message from Luna pinged: '26 Jun/Mr X Escape room in Puxi'. A smile spread across my face. *Thanks, Luna.* Apparently, she wasn't so mad at me that she would let me run into a wall with Yumi.

"By the way, Yumi, I forgot to tell you. I remembered your 13th birthday party. We went to the escape room in Puxi."

"Puxi?" Yumi started laughing. "What is Puxi? You mean *Phuksi?*"

Shit. How was I supposed to know how to pronounce Chinese names? Why was it so much harder to get my story right with Yumi than anybody else? Even family life was relatively easy compared to her constantly pointing out things I should have known.

"Whatever. Anyway, satisfied? Now, can you just tell me if you want to come over tomorrow so I can let Mom know?" I didn't have to try to sound exasperated.

"Relax. Yeah, sure I'll come. Want me to ask, Nui? She's right here."

"Just leave it. I'll ask her myself. See you tomorrow."

"Later. Bye." Yumi distractedly signed off.

I wished I hadn't told Yumi that Luna was invited for the next day too, but after she'd responded to my question, I figured I owed her. And with both Yumi and Khun Susan there she was hardly going to make a scene. I sent her a quick text then turned on my laptop. Time to get cramming. If I wanted to maintain Luna's grades for myself, I'd better start working for it. And hopefully, Luna's dad would be home soon with good news.

9

LUNA

W HEN Y UMI SAID P UXI , I KNEW SHE MUST HAVE BEEN ON THE phone with Nui. It couldn't be a coincidence that this would come up immediately after my text to Nui. I bit my lip to keep from laughing. While I'd considered feeding Nui false information, I didn't want to give her ammunition against me or put her in a defensive mode. Besides, it hadn't been necessary. She'd messed up anyway with the wrong pronunciation. At least she couldn't blame me for that. But what had Yumi been whispering about? She obviously had secrets with Nui. If only she knew she was confiding in a traitor and not talking to the real Luna. For a moment I wondered if I should try to turn Yumi against Nui, but that would only backfire on me after we switched back. And Nui and I *were* going to switch back, no matter what. I was not willing to accept defeat, and I was going to fight to get my family back. I wasn't even sure anymore why I'd wanted to leave in the first place. Being in Nui's family had sounded so appealing at first—a traditional family life—but since I was being treated as Nui, it wasn't really my experience anyway. *Should have thought about that before, Luna, and you wouldn't be in this mess now.*

I watched Yumi as she chased the dogs around, throwing balls, tugging on ropes, petting this dog, then another, and having a blast. She issued a steady stream of commands that no one followed because she inevitably broke into laughter at her own theatrics, getting the dogs all revved up. I had to grin despite myself. Yumi had the kind of energy that automatically cheered up everyone in her vicinity. She finally sat next to me, breathing hard but still grinning. She grabbed her bag and pulled out a bottle of water and a towel, wiping her sweaty face. I still didn't understand why she wore long-sleeve tops in this heat.

"These dogs are too much." Half the pack sat at her feet, waiting for treats, the rest retreated under the trees to cool off. Chone sat loyally at my side, leaning against me. I absently scratched his ears.

"They are. I'm so glad I started here, even if I can't do much today. Are you coming back regularly?"

Yumi shrugged. "If we have to do this community service thing for school, I might as well get credit for doing something fun."

"Yeah, me too. Have they trained you yet on what to do?"

Yumi shook her head. "Not yet. I only just got the papers signed. Why? You offering to show me?"

I hadn't thought of that, but it made sense and perhaps I'd be able to find out what Nui was really up to when she talked to Yumi. Also, it would keep her from spending solo time with Channon. A double win for me.

"Sure, I could do that. We can come here from school

together, so that would be easy. Or you could come to my house. It's really close by and we could go from there. You've met my family at the hospital, haven't you?"

"I have, but I think your mom is pretty mad at me."

"Don't worry, I'm sure she's gotten over it now that I'm home."

"So, what was it like to be locked in? I can't even imagine, but it sounds awful." Yumi twisted her shoulders in discomfort.

"Scary." I shuddered at the memory. "I've never been so scared in my life, completely powerless. I think if I'd been in a coma it would have been easier. At least then I wouldn't have been aware of what was happening."

Yumi stared at me.

"Yikes, that's awful. But, how did you recover so fast? I thought the doctors didn't know what to do?"

"They didn't. I figured it out myself." I wasn't sure why I was telling Yumi this, but she was semi-neutral ground and had always been a good listener.

"You did? How?"

"You won't believe me if I told you."

"Try me." Yumi leaned forward in anticipation.

"Well, it will sound weird, but I focused very hard on my breathing and imagined my breath as energy running up and down through my nerves and veins and so on, like in a loop. And then I felt this power surge and my muscles started responding again as if I had switched them back on."

Yumi's eyes stretched as wide as they could go and her mouth gaped open. She snapped it shut with the resounding clack of teeth against teeth.

"Wow. How is that even possible? You mean, you just did this with your mind and focus? How did you even come up with that?"

I could tell she wasn't one hundred percent convinced.

"Yeah, I did. Well, I had nothing else to work with, did I? I was completely paralysed, remember?"

"That's freaking bizarre. I suppose our minds *are* more powerful than we give them credit for." Yumi sounded wistful suddenly.

"Oh, for sure. I mean, I wouldn't know how to explain it otherwise."

"Hmm, I wonder what else we could do? Seems pretty much unlimited if you can reverse paralysis by merely focusing. Imagine if you could turn this in any direction you want. You'd be all-powerful."

"All-powerful? What do you mean? You think you could use that on other people? I doubt it."

"Well, why not?" Yumi seemed excited by the idea.

"Trust me, you can't. I know that for sure." That was a stupid thing for me to say and gave away too much information, even if Yumi wouldn't know the facts behind my statement.

"How? Did you try?" Leave it to Yumi to nail the point.

"No, of course not. But it's logical. If I can do it, so can everyone else, which must mean they can fight it too and you'd be at a stalemate, no*?" Luna stop, why are you even having this discussion?*

"Only if you assume everyone has the same power, right?" Was Yumi was playing the devil's advocate, or did she have some other agenda?

"Why wouldn't they? I don't think this has anything to do with IQ. It's a matter of focus. And why would you want to force someone, anyway?" The discussion, if only hypothetical, was becoming uncomfortable.

"Nah, you're right. It's too scary to think someone would do something to you out of the blue." Yumi finally eased off, but she still had a speculative look on her face. *Uh oh.*

"You know what's funny?" she asked. "This is exactly the kind of discussion I had with Luna when we were friends in Shanghai. We would argue really odd subjects back and forth just for the sake of it. Didn't realise you would do that too." Yumi's gaze sharpened as she looked at me.

Damn. Unconsciously, I'd fallen into an old familiar pattern with her.

I tried to be nonchalant about it. "What's so strange about arguing a topic? Seems pretty normal to me."

"Discussions, sure, but I mean weird subjects like mind control etcetera. Luna and I used to do that. Not so much these days, though."

Yumi's ringing phone saved me from responding. She stared at it with a frown but didn't move.

"Aren't you going to answer that?"

"What?" Yumi shook herself out of whatever trance she'd fallen into and picked up the phone.

"Yes?" she said hesitantly, then switched to a more lively tone. "Oh hey, baby. What's up?"

I knew Yumi too well to not realise she was faking cheerfulness. She got up and walked a few paces, but I could see her face scrunched up. I didn't eavesdrop, but kept watching her while scratching Chone's ears. Yumi wiped her eyes. My hands stilled. I'd hardly ever seen Yumi upset. Angry yes, but crying? She walked in circles, shaking her free arm as if she wanted to rid herself of some tension. A couple of dogs followed, nudging her, but she seemed unaware. My own phone pinged, but Yumi's behaviour distracted me from checking my messages. A few minutes later, she wiped her eyes again, then nodded vigorously and ended the call, dropping the phone in one of her cargo pockets. She breathed in and out deeply, shook her head and finally bent over to pet the dogs sitting at her feet. She looked startled when she saw me and kept her head down before putting her sunglasses back on. She'd definitely been crying.

"Are you okay, Yumi?" I asked.

"Huh? Yeah, I'm fine." Yumi's voice had lost its usual verve.

"Want to talk about it?"

"Nah, just something I have to deal with."

"I'm happy to listen if you need a sounding board." I hated seeing Yumi so sad, even if we weren't best friends right now. It just wasn't like her.

Yumi absently petted LaTe, who had crept closer again, probably looking for treats, but just as happy with getting a rub.

"That was my little sister. She's going through a rough time in Japan. I don't know how to help her from here," Yumi whispered.

"Kiko? What's wrong with her?" I had completely forgotten about Yumi's younger sister. There was a ten-year age gap between them. Yumi had once said her parents tried to use Kiko to mend their marriage. Whether that was true, I didn't know. Kiko had only been three when we left Shanghai, so she hadn't been much on my twelve-year-old radar then.

Yumi whipped her head around. "How do you know Kiko's name?"

I hesitated. "I ... eh... you must have mentioned her sometime?"

"No, I didn't. Why would I? I only talked to Luna about her." Yumi was adamant.

"Well, you're speaking to her now." The thought fell out

of my mouth before I had time to think about it. A blast of heat whooshed over me.

"I'm what?" Yumi whipped around, her eyebrows almost touching in confusion. She lifted her sunglasses to glare at me.

Dare I tell her? She would understand. Decision time.

"I know you'll think I'm crazy, but I *am* Luna."

10

NUI

LUNA'S MOM SENT KHUN BO HOME EARLY SO WE COULD have our family discussion in private. It seemed redundant since Khun Bo spoke very little English anyway. Khun Mark brought takeout from the hotel's restaurant, and we sat down to eat. The mood was subdued and the food tasted like cardboard to me. Luke kept up a steady stream of chatter about school, his upcoming football matches, and some video games he and his buddies had been playing. His parents responded, but I could tell their minds were on something else. I was on tenterhooks to get dinner over with and find out what was going on.

Cleaning up the kitchen felt like torture, ramping up my anxiety, but eventually it was time to have the talk Luna's mom had promised—or threatened. I wasn't sure what to expect, but anything was better than not knowing.

Khun Mark cleared his throat.

"You both know what happened at the police station last

week. Our lawyer called me this morning to give me an update. He heard from Colonel Songpol, and apparently they have dropped the investigation."

My shoulders slumped, releasing the tension in my neck I hadn't been aware of holding.

"But there's a caveat, and it's going to affect us all." Khun Mark trailed off, rubbing his forehead.

What? Why is he stalling? My heart started beating double time.

"Um…" He cleared his throat. "So, there won't be a criminal prosecution, which is great, but they have put a flag on your passport, Luna, for the next five years."

"What does that mean? Flag?" My hands balled into fists, nails digging into the flesh.

"It means that every time you try to enter the country, immigration will run checks for criminal behaviour, warrants etcetera, and they can either allow or deny you entry without a specific reason. It's completely up to them."

"And? I mean, there won't be any of that, so I should be okay, no?" I had the sinking feeling that was not all.

"What it means, Luna, is that we cannot risk leaving the country right now, or at Songkran, or in the summer, unless we're prepared to leave for good. There's no guarantee they would allow you back into Thailand or to finish high school," Luna's mom explained.

"What?" Luke shouted. "We can't leave over Songkran and the summer? That's crazy. No one will be here. And it's gonna be boring and hot. I don't want to stay."

"It also means, Luke, that we can't go away for any weekends here in Asia or anywhere else. We just can't risk getting caught at the airport and Luna being denied entry."

"But, that's only Luna's passport, isn't it? That doesn't mean you and I can't go, right Mom? Dad?"

"Nice one, Luke. Thanks." I glared at him, but my sarcasm fell flat.

"Well, it's not like I did something wrong. You did this all to yourself," Luke countered.

I flinched at his words, but was still too shocked by the news to get fully worked up about Luke's aggressive tone. And of course, he was right. It was my fault.

"Luke, we're a family, and we deal with whatever is necessary as a family." Khun Susan admonished Luke.

"But it's not fair. Just because Luna did something stupid, we don't all have to be punished. Why did you do it?"

"A blog is not stupid, okay?! And my posts were good too. A lot of people liked them. How was I supposed to know they don't have freedom of press here?" My defence was tepid as I *had* known how dicey lese majesté was in my country. My throat hurt from trying to swallow the lump that jammed my breath.

"It still was stupid." Luke was whining now, though he sounded far away to me.

I felt as if I'd entered a time warp, everything around me breaking down to super slow-motion, the family fading into the background, words distorted, gestures weightless like an astronaut floating in space. Even my tears seemed to fall at a snail's pace. Everything I'd done was for nothing. Why was I being blocked at every turn from following my dream? Was it too much to ask for even one trip abroad? I'd already scaled back my biggest wish and promised Luna we'd switch back after Songkran, but now that seemed to have fallen through as well. It was as if the world was conspiring against me. *Maybe it's because you're trying to take what's not yours, Nui?* I hiccupped, trying to quickly tamp down that stray thought.

Khun Susan's hand on my shoulder snapped me back to real time.

"Honey, come here." She pulled me into a hug. By now, I was openly sobbing.

"I'm so sorry. I'm so, so sorry." I wasn't even sure if I was apologising to the family or feeling sorry for myself.

"I know. But it is what it is, and we'll deal with it." Khun Susan rubbed my back as if soothing a small child. Right now, I felt exactly like that. What had I done? Not just to Luna, but to her family as well?

Even Luke had stopped his tirade and was looking down at his hands, probably embarrassed by my tears.

Khun Mark cleared his throat again. "So, we will have to decide if this is indeed the right time to leave the country. Since we already talked about it, perhaps this is the sign that we should consider it more seriously."

Luna's aunt, Jane, had been diagnosed with cancer and Khun Susan had only just returned from Chicago after helping the family cope with the surgery and aftermath. Luna's parents had raised the possibility of a move at the end of the school year in order to support the family. I'd been trying to argue Luna's point that not only would it mean moving a year before graduation, but it would mean moving again for college, something she desperately wanted to avoid. But now, everything had changed again.

What would that mean for me? Would I really be willing and able to leave Bangkok and my family knowing I might not be able to go home for at least five years, if ever?

"Can't we appeal the decision?" I asked. Perhaps I had watched too many TV dramas, but there always seemed to be some kind of loophole for the main character to wriggle through.

"On what grounds?"

"How?"

"You know they are within their rights."

"Do you really think we should risk they might consider changing it to a more severe verdict?"

Khun Susan and Khun Mark talked over each other, but the consensus was clear. Nothing could be done about the flag.

"Oh, okay, I just thought I'd ask." I wanted to shrink and make myself invisible to escape the strained atmosphere and the sight of Luke staring daggers at me.

"I know this is a lot to take in now, and we'll talk more about what our next steps should be." Khun Susan said. "Dad's company knows we want to return to the US towards the end of next year in time for your college, Luna. They're working on finding or creating a position for him, hopefully in a larger regional role. I'm not sure if they can make that happen any sooner or if potentially we should move somewhere else first."

"Move again?" Luke shouted. "We've only been here for six months. This sucks."

"Luke! I know it's not ideal, but you also just said you don't want to get stuck here. So, something has to give. Or do you want to stay in Bangkok for the next year and a half and not go anywhere? These are all options, you know. It's a matter of Luna only being able to travel once." She turned to me. "My concern is we won't be able to look at your university options unless we actually move. I'm not sure if researching them online is enough."

I shrugged. "I'm sure there are ways to do this. I doubt everyone gets to check them out personally before applying." My problem, however, was much bigger than the family could imagine.

"What about Songkran then?" Luke asked.

"We can go somewhere in Thailand, maybe the Golden

Triangle or Phuket or Koh Lanta or something. That's the least of our worries right now," Khun Mark said.

"Anyway, now you know what is happening. I want you both to think about it and sleep on it. We'll talk more tomorrow." Khun Susan went to the kitchen and returned with two glasses of white wine. She handed one to Khun Mark, then looked at us.

"This is new to all of us, and we need a bit more time. Your dad and I will have to think about how it might affect his job, and I also want to talk to Aunt Jane."

I stood on shaky legs, still wiping my eyes.

"I'm so sorry, Mom, Dad, Luke. I really didn't think this could happen."

"I hate you, Luna!" Luke spat at me and stomped off.

I hung my head and followed.

11

LUNA

Late bit Yumi when her grip became too tight. It broke the impasse.

"Ouch!" Yumi jerked her hand away, but immediately resumed her evil eye look.

"What did you just say?"

"I know it sounds crazy, but I can explain." My heart bumped painfully, yet I felt relieved I could talk with someone who knew me *before*.

"You better," Yumi growled.

Chone scooted closer, noticing the tension and wanting to protect me. My hand rested on his head, grounding me.

"Just hear me out before you ask questions, okay?"

Yumi's eyes narrowed, but she stayed quiet.

"It started like this. Nui and I were school buddies when I first moved here. I didn't even like her, but that's another story. We figured out that neither of us was happy with our lives the way they were, but then Nui had this crazy idea. She said that, theoretically, if people can meditate themselves into an out-of-body state, shouldn't it be possible to switch with someone who wants the same thing at the same time?"

Yumi burst out laughing. I held up my hand.

"Wait. You said you'd listen."

Yumi harrumphed and theatrically zipped her lips with her fingers, but her eyes still crinkled in amusement.

"Okay, so Nui and I went to meditation classes at Wat Pathum and, long story short, it worked. Well, to be honest, it was more of an accident, but then we couldn't reverse it and Mom went to Chicago and I met Channon and now Nui doesn't want to switch back. She says she wants to go to the States for Songkran and promised we would switch back after, but I don't think she really means it." I stopped to let Yumi absorb what I'd just told her.

"Is that it? Can I talk now?" Yumi was being facetious and I couldn't blame her. It was a lot to take in.

"Yeah. I get it. You don't believe me, do you?"

"I didn't say that. But can you prove it?" Her expression switched from amusement to confusion to fascination and back again.

"Hmm, you mean like you asked Nui what we did for your thirteenth birthday party just now?"

"How do you know that?" Yumi leaned back.

"Because she asked me and I told her we were at Mr X's escape room in Puxi." I pronounced it correctly to Yumi. "Want me to show you the texts? I didn't tell her there were six of us and we got stuck and had to be let out. Want me to tell you who was there and why you deliberately messed up the clues? Remember you had a crush on George and wanted to stay locked inside? What happened to him, anyway?"

Yumi frowned. "Never mind. You're kidding, right? This can't be real."

"Or how about when you killed one of your mom's precious bonsai trees with lemon juice and she never figured out what went wrong? You think Nui would know this?" I grinned at Yumi's expression. Her mouth hung wide open.

"No way! Absolutely no effing way!" Several dogs barked as Yumi screeched. She waved her hands in front of her as if she had to fend me off.

"Luna could have told you. That's not proof." She objected defiantly.

I thought for a moment.

"Well, what about this? Do you remember when we tried the vodka in Dad's bar, then got sick and Luke almost caught us? And we had to up top up the bottle with water so my dad wouldn't notice? Do you honestly think I would tell Nui that? Why would I?" I asked.

"Oh my God! That was hilarious." Yumi snorted and then laughed out loud. "No one knows that! They would have killed us." She tilted her head. "You're serious, aren't you? How is that even possible?"

I grinned back at her, though it must have been freakish for her to look at Nui's body and face.

"Trust me, it happened, and it's beyond weird."

Yumi resumed petting LaTe but stared at me, shaking her head.

"This is too much. I can't get my head around it." If she continued wagging her head like this, she was going to give herself whiplash. Suddenly, a wide grin spread across her face.

"So, I was right the whole time. There was something off about you two. I knew it. Ha!" She laughed. "But man, I never imagined *this*. Kind of cool, actually."

I shrugged. Yes, it was surreal, but it had gone way past being cool.

"Oh, oh! That explains why you spoke Mandarin when you were mad at me! Now I get it!" Yumi fluttered her hands in excitement, but then frowned. "But how does that work? Shouldn't Nui speak Mandarin too?"

"I don't know. We both picked up each other's language, but apparently it doesn't go further than that."

"So, what do I call you now? It's kind of weird, you know, looking at Nui but actually speaking to you." Yumi frowned and rubbed her temple as if she had a headache.

"You could call me Luna when no one is around, but if it's too confusing, just call me Nui. I'm used to it now."

"Jeez, how am I supposed to keep that straight? Never mind, I'll figure it out. But what I don't get is why you did it in the first place? I mean, what was so bad in your life that you needed to switch?"

I flinched. "Nothing really. I know that now. But I was so sick of moving again after Shanghai, then Hong Kong and then Bangkok. You know what it's like. You never really get to settle in and you always have to start from scratch with friends and everything."

"Hmm, maybe, but I think there are also loads of benefits. Look, how many languages do you and I speak just because we moved around? That's a huge advantage and I am definitely going to use that. Or what about having friends all around the world?"

"But that's all so superficial. Do you honestly remember the people you were in grade four or five with? I don't. Either we or they moved, so most of us didn't even have two years together."

Yumi closed her eyes and sighed. "Why is it that those who have everything are the ones that complain the most?" She sounded pensive. I had the feeling her statement didn't concern me specifically, and maybe was tinged by her earlier conversation with Kiko.

"By the way, what's wrong with Kiko? Want to talk…?" Before I could finish my question, Yumi shook her head.

"Not now. I'll tell you some other time. I want to know more about this switch. So, when did all this happen and did you say Lu… I mean, Nui, doesn't want to swap back with you? Why not? That's crazy."

"We did it just before New Year's. Nui said she wants to go to the States just one time to see what it's like, but her parents can't afford it, and without the money she can't get a visa, so the only way for her to go is as me. But at the beginning she also said 'just one night' and now we're already a month into this, so I don't really trust her. Besides, what would one visit do for her? She still wouldn't be able to study there." I wasn't being entirely fair as I'd been curious enough to extend the switch too, but we'd made an agreement and Nui broke her promise.

"You mean she would actually leave you stuck here while she goes away with your parents? How can she just take over your life? That's so mean. And what about her own family?"

"Exactly!" I jumped up, almost tripping over Chone, who scooted out of my way, whining softly. "Sorry Chone." I bent to rub his ears in apology, but couldn't stay still.

"What am I supposed to do? Stay here with her family and do what?" I started pacing in circles.

"Why don't I talk to her? She must know she's wrong and can't just take over for you," Yumi offered. "And if she discovers that someone else knows, maybe she'll reconsider."

I shook my head. "Nah, that doesn't work. She knows I told Channon, and it didn't make a difference."

"Are you serious? You told Channon? What did he say?" Yumi leaned forward, her eyes lit up. I'd forgotten about her own interest in Channon. This was awkward but hopefully Yumi would back off now she knew she was pursuing her best friend's boyfriend. Okay, maybe not quite boyfriend yet, but still.

"I don't think he really believed me, but he said he'll keep an open mind. He said I should just switch back and we would see where it goes." I shuffled my feet in the dirt. "But it's not that easy."

"Hmm." Yumi seemed unconvinced.

I glanced at her. She was biting her bottom lip.

"What?"

"Don't you think it's strange that he would just go along with that? Or maybe it's a good sign. Maybe it means he's not hung up about looks. Yeah, I think that would be more like him." Yumi nodded to herself.

Her thoughts echoed my earlier musings, but it was best to focus on the main issue.

"Anyway, I'm stuck and don't know what to do. Any ideas?"

"Can you force her to switch back?"

"No, that doesn't work either. We have to be on the same frequency or vibration or whatever it's called. And that only happens when we're both out-of-body during meditation." No need for Yumi to know about my botched attempt and the awful consequences.

"Did you try it?" Of course Yumi would pick up on my discomfort. I stalled.

"You did, didn't you?" Yumi was too smart for her own good.

I cringed and dipped my head.

"Is that how you ended up paralysed? Oh man, Luna, you're just as bad as Nui. Imagine what you could have done to Nui or your own body?"

"Trust me, I know, and I paid the price, remember?" I really didn't need Yumi's reminder of my selfish behaviour.

"Anyway, so what do I do?" I tried to bring her back to my current dilemma.

"Well, if all the other stuff doesn't work, then I guess you have to make her *want* to switch back or give her an alternative or incentive, right?" She made it sound like the easiest thing in the world.

"Right! But how? I've been going nuts, but I can't think of anything."

"Hmm. I might have an idea." Yumi picked up LaTe and kissed him on the head with a wink at me. "I'm not sure it's going to work, but let me think it through, and I need to do a bit of research."

It was my turn to stare at her.

12

NUI

I curled up on Luna's big comfy chair, staring at the ceiling as if a solution might magically appear. I felt like a yo-yo bouncing up and down at the whim of circumstance. Yes, I was relieved to have escaped a prison sentence, but the thought that if we moved I couldn't see my family for at least five years was terrifying. What did I really know about other countries? What if American people were all horrible, and they only made themselves look good for the movies or TV? The news said there was a lot of crime and daily shootings everywhere. Sure, they had free speech and all that, but what if anyone in my family got sick or worse? Five years was just too long.

Khun Yaa's voice played in my head from a conversation we had a long time ago after she caught me eating Duen's candies, a birthday gift from a neighbour.

'What did I tell you about karma, Nui?'

'What? I only ate some candy.' I hated being busted.

'You stole from Duen. It doesn't matter if it's big or small. You took something that wasn't yours.'

'She could have shared. I'll buy her some new candy.'

'That's not the point, Nui. You broke a divine rule and disrespected your sister. It's a matter of Karma. You caused her to suffer and you will reap the consequences in this life or your next or both.'

The criticism had stung, especially coming from Khun Yaa. My flimsy justification didn't stand a chance against her strong moral compass. And now I had broken her rules again in a much bigger way by stealing Luna's life. The consequences were bound to be disastrous. My stomach twisted and my chest felt tight, as if a band of iron prevented air from getting in. I needed to move, anything to distract me.

I jumped when the bedroom door burst open and Luke stormed in. He planted himself on the bed and stared at me. His anger was palpable.

"What do you want?"

"You are so selfish, you know that, Luna? You are the worst sister in the world."

I swallowed. He wasn't really saying anything I hadn't thought myself, even if I had rationalised my actions in my head.

"I'm sorry, Luke. What more do you want me to say?"

My admission didn't stop him.

"I was thinking. You know how Mom and Dad always want us to make joint decisions? So, you and I need to agree right now what *we* want and tell them."

"Yeah, and...?" I asked. He definitely had an idea what that joint decision should be.

"We should move. You owe me."

"Owe you for what?"

"We wouldn't be in this mess if you hadn't been so stupid." Luke raised his chin, daring me to contradict him.

"You've already said."

"It's still true. Did you really think your blog was so important you had to risk everything?"

"And do you think it's right that you can't say what you think?"

"I don't care if it's right or not. They told us we had to be careful. And now we all have to live with what you've done. Is that right?"

I looked at my feet. He had a point.

"So?" Luke asked.

"So, what?"

"Do you agree?"

"But what about your… I mean Dad's job? Mom said he's up for a promotion next year," I said.

"I know that's tricky, but he hasn't even asked yet if there's anything available sooner. He can ask, or maybe there's something open in another city right now. I don't care, I just don't want to be stuck here."

I exhaled sharply, trying to jiggle this new piece into place. Knowing Luna's attitude and her complaints about the family's constant moves, Luke probably thought he'd have a fight on his hands, but right then I didn't know what I really wanted. If I had to stay in Bangkok, I might as well return to my family, and I wouldn't have accomplished anything besides making an enemy of Luna. But I was scared of going.

"But..." I wasn't sure what I objected to; I just needed more time to figure out my best option.

"No but, Luna," Luke said. He jumped up, hands on his hips. "I know you always said you didn't want to move, but you brought this on yourself." I almost jerked back at his tone and posture. This was the first time I'd seen Luke so angry.

"Fine. Chill. I heard you." I tried for nonchalance, but couldn't quite pull it off.

"Besides, Mom already said she wanted to be closer to Aunt Jane, so it makes sense. And you know Dad will agree if that's what we all want. For once, you can do something for us." Luke really was firing on all cylinders.

"Stop patronising me!"

Luke ignored my protest.

"So, when we talk with them tomorrow, we're clear, right?" Luke stretched out his hand as if a handshake would be a binding agreement. Maybe for him it was.

"Fine. Whatever. All depends on what *they* decide anyway." I grabbed his hand.

Luke shook his head. "You know they'll listen, especially if Mom wants to go too." He got up to leave, then tossed back over his shoulder, "Actually, it works out after all. Dad promised to take me to the F1 in Shanghai this year, so he and I would have missed the beginning of Songkran, anyway. I just need to remind him." Luke walked out, not quite slamming the door.

I blew my nose and got up to wash my face. The reflection in the mirror looked pitiful—red eyes, blotchy skin, and pretty much clueless. Even Luna's blond hair looked limp. *Slow down, Nui, slow down.* I forced myself to count to eight, inhaling deeply through my nose and slowly exhaling through my mouth, my eyes closed until I felt the pressure in my chest ease.

What would just one visit have accomplished anyway? If I couldn't stay to study, what was the point? Logically, it also meant I would have to assume Luna's position permanently if I wanted to use my degree. My thoughts were racing, whirling round and round, and sucking up air like a typhoon. I felt lightheaded, barely able to slide to the bathroom floor. I put my head between my knees and waited until the dizziness faded and my breath evened out. A cold sweat covered my entire body.

Unless... The seed of an idea sprouted in my head. Ironically, Luna herself had given me a potential solution when she tried to push me from her body. A tingle of excitement propelled me off the floor. If I could get her to agree, it would solve my problems for now. I smiled at Luna in the mirror.

13

LUNA

I GRIPPED YUMI'S ARM, STUNNED BY HER STATEMENT.

"You're kidding, right? I've been trying to come up with something forever and you have an idea just like that? How? Research?" I threw up my hands in frustration, but feeling a pinprick of hope.

"Well, if you'd kept up with your friends, you would know, too. Check Leslie's Facebook page and you'll see. You can leave the rest to me for now." Yumi grinned, pleased with herself.

I had a million questions for Yumi, but didn't have time to ask. The door to the shelter opened and Khun Nan stuck her head out.

"Girls, it's time to feed the dogs. Can you help?"

It only took fifteen minutes to distribute the food, but I couldn't quiz Yumi as I had to show her where everything was, which dogs had special diets, and how to make notes for the staff's records.

By the time we walked out, I was already late for dinner, which was bound to earn me another scolding by Khun Yaa or Mae. I sent a quick text to Duen saying I was on my way. I'd forgotten about the earlier notification, which was an invitation from Nui for the next day. How weird. We'd hardly spoken to each other in almost a week, instead maintaining an uneasy truce for form's sake. I knew she'd seen me on the terrace earlier that day, but I doubted this had prompted an invitation.

"Want to walk back with me?" I asked. "It's on your way to the train station."

Yumi nodded and hefted her backpack, looking like she was ready for a loaded military training march. I waved the phone at her.

"I got a message from Nui. She said I should come to the house tomorrow after school. What do you think that's about?"

"Oh, yeah, she invited me too. Her, I mean, *your* mom wants to see us both. Not really sure why, but I said I'd go. I think you should come."

It didn't surprise me the visit was Mom's idea and not Nui's. Since I'd overheard their conversation earlier, I was pretty sure Mom was trying to smooth the waters between Nui and me.

"I'm going to call her. Want to listen in?" I offered her one of my headphones. "But you have to stay totally quiet, okay?" If Yumi had any last doubts about the switch, the call with Nui would convince her one hundred percent.

Yumi grinned, intrigued. She picked up the ear bud while I touched the call button.

"Hey Nui, got your message. What's that all about?"

"Hey Luna. Yeah, your mom said you and Yumi should

come. She hasn't seen either of you since she came back. You okay with that?" Nui asked.

"Am I okay to see my own mother? Are you serious?" Next to me, Yumi flinched at my scathing tone. "Of course I'll come."

Nui ignored my snarky comment.

"Okay, good. I'll tell her. We can all take the van together after school."

A beep sounded in my ear. I glanced at the screen and saw one of my five reminders for my rabies shot appointment the next day. Damn. I couldn't miss that.

"I have to get my next shot at Samitivej at five, so I'll only be an hour, okay?"

"Sure, that's fine." Was I imagining it, or did Nui sound relieved?

"Gotta go. See you tomorrow." I hung up and looked at Yumi.

"Wow. That's insane. I mean, I kinda believed you before, but this really takes the cake." Yumi's mouth formed a perfect circle, which morphed into a wicked grin. "Well, well, it'll be interesting tomorrow. Can I be mean and ask Nui some questions?"

"If it plays into your idea, go ahead, but don't overdo it, otherwise Mom will freak out, okay? And I don't want Nui to know that you know. She was furious that I told Channon."

"Not to worry. I know exactly what to do."

"Let's talk later, okay? I want to know more about your idea."

"Have a look at Leslie's feed and see if you can work it out. I'll do some background research."

"Why are you being so mysterious about this?"

"Where would be the fun in delivering it to you on a silver plate? You got yourself into a mess and you deserve some torture." Yumi turned and waved over her shoulder as she pranced down the sidewalk.

"Torture! Ha. I've had enough torture to last me a lifetime."

I exhaled and shook off the blip of irritation. The afternoon had been amazing, and with Yumi on my side I was excited to see what tomorrow would bring.

14

LUNA

JOEY, NUI'S MUTT, GREETED ME AT THE DOOR, HAPPY AS usual. I fended off his boisterous welcome but stopped when a weird sense of unease came over me. Something was off. The house was too quiet. Where was the normal noise and chatter from the kitchen when the family was sharing dinner? I only heard some faint, indistinguishable murmurs.

"What's going on, Joey?" I gave him a last pat, flicked off my sandals and walked to the kitchen.

Even stranger than the hush was the sight of the whole family minus Krit and Tum sitting at the table with only Mae and Paa speaking softly to each other. They looked up when I walked in, but went back to their food without even commenting on my lateness. The grandparents and Duen kept their heads down and stayed silent. Judging by the amount of food on the table, they'd only just begun dinner, which was later than normal. There were takeout containers on the counter and the stove appeared to be unused, no pots waiting to be cleaned. Only the rice cooker sat in its usual spot plugged in on the far side of the sink. Okay, this was downright scary. Khun Yaa never allowed takeout food in her kitchen. She was too proud of her cooking skills and considered it a point of honour to feed her family. I glanced at my watch. I was only a half hour late, and I'd texted Duen to let her know I was on the way. I quickly washed my hands and took my regular seat at the table then looked at Duen with raised eyebrows. She tilted her head towards Mae, who was eating mechanically, barely chewing and probably not even tasting her food. I couldn't read her expression. Something had happened. Why was no one talking to me?

I turned to Khun Yaa.

"Is everything okay, Khun Yaa? What happened?"

She at least looked my way, then motioned for me to pass my plate so she could fill it with food. My good mood and appetite had vanished.

"What is going on? Can someone please say something?" It creeped me out. This was not how I knew the family.

Finally, Paa put down his cutlery.

"Khun Yaai had a heart attack this afternoon. We found out a couple of hours ago."

Khun Yaai? Who was that? I frantically searched my memory for the name, but nothing came to mind. Apparently, it was someone important to the family. How come I didn't know the person? Was I supposed to be upset? Cry?

"What happened?" An innocent enough question.

"Aunt May called and said she'd collapsed and they had to revive her on the way to the hospital. She's now in intensive care and they don't know if she's going to make it," Paa said.

Aunt May? I knew Aunt Varaporn, but didn't recall another aunt. Or was she one of the hundreds of so-called aunties that weren't really related to the family? *Damn. What do I do?*

"I'm so sorry to hear that." I hoped someone would fill in the blanks on what it would mean for the family and me.

"Mae is flying up tomorrow first thing and the rest of us are on standby for either tomorrow night or Friday morning, depending on what Mae finds out. We're waiting to hear if Krit and Tum can come too."

Nui's older brother was finishing up his military draft while Tum was serving as a novice monk in a temple nearby. They would be home permanently again by the end of the month.

Finally, the penny dropped. Khun Yaai was Nui's other grandmother who lived with Mae's sister Aunt May, in Chiang Rai in the Golden Triangle. Khun Yaa had mentioned them once when I asked her about out-of-body episodes. Apparently, the two women had experienced it a few times. But then the second part of his sentence sank in.

"What? But what about school and who will look after Joey and the shop?"

Mae's head snapped up, her eyes red-rimmed. The shock of seeing her like this stopped my inane questions. I didn't know Khun Yaai, so to me it felt like hearing about someone's accident on the news. It didn't affect me personally, but of course I would have to go to see *my* grandmother in the hospital, especially if she was close to dying.

Except… she was Nui's grandma, not mine. Surely, Nui would want to see her. I quickly put my head down, pretending to eat and trying not to show my excitement at the idea. I felt slightly guilty that I would consider a family tragedy a benefit to me. After swallowing some bland tasting curry, I felt composed enough to address Paa again.

"I'm so sorry to hear that. How long will we be gone?"

I hoped I sounded chastised enough to make up for my rash reaction.

Paa looked at Mae.

"We don't know yet. It all depends on her status. Khun Pop will look after the shop and Khun Yaa and Khun Bpoo will stay here to help if necessary and to look after Joey."

I nodded. I had to talk to Nui asap. Though I didn't know how close Nui was to her second grandmother, this surely would be significant enough for her to want to go herself, meaning we had no choice but to switch back. She'd said more than once that it was super important for Thai Buddhists to pay their respects to their elders, especially family. A pinch of doubt remained. Would it be enough for Nui? The reason we were in this situation was because Nui had been railing against the old customs and traditions. Would her defiance stretch as far as dismissing her family? *Don't forget she was ready to leave them behind to go to the States.* My breath caught. Before I could even think of convincing arguments for Nui, Paa spoke again.

"There's something else we need to discuss, Nui. Today, we also got the offer and plans for the cooking school. We haven't had the time to look at it in detail, but the estimate is higher than we expected, and now with the travel and possible funeral expenses…"

My pulse quickened and my fork and spoon dropped onto the plate. Paa didn't have to finish the sentence. I knew exactly what he meant. They'd mentioned before that the tuition fees might have to pay for the project, meaning Nui would have to withdraw from BIS.

If Nui knew she'd have to leave BIS on returning from Chiang Rai, she might refuse to switch. I couldn't tell her that.

"Is that confirmed then?" My voice wobbled.

"No, not yet, but it's a strong possibility. I want you to be aware. We'll talk more about it when we're back and we've had time to look at it more closely," Paa said.

"Okay."

What else was there to say?

15

NUI

THIS EVENING HAD BEEN A MESS. FIRST, THE NEWS ABOUT the flag on Luna's passport, then the argument with Luke, and to top it all off, both Luna and Yumi accepting Khun Susan's invitation. I was nervous about facing them together outside of school, but hoped Luna's mom would provide a good buffer. If I wanted to push my idea forward, I needed to remain on friendly, or at least neutral ground with Luna for now. Her agreement was crucial. But how could I avoid the flag issue? If she found out that her family wanted to move as soon as possible, how would she react? Especially if it killed any romantic future with Channon?

I was tired of thinking in circles. There was nothing to be gained by driving myself crazy trying to anticipate potential outcomes. It all depended on Luna's parents anyway. Determined to concentrate on my reading, I swivelled my chair and put my legs on the ottoman.

My phone buzzed with an incoming call. Annoyed at yet

another interruption, I was tempted to let it go to voicemail, but a quick look showed it was Luna calling again. Immediately, my stomach tightened. We hadn't had our usual end-of-day conversations since I'd failed to switch with her, so for her to call twice in one day could only mean something had happened.

"Hey Luna. What's up? Everything okay?"

"Nui, are you sitting down? I have to tell you something," Luna said. I couldn't quite pinpoint her tone.

"Sure, what's going on?"

"Your grandma had a heart attack. We're…"

I didn't hear the rest of Luna's words. A roar in my ears blocked out every other sound. *Khun Yaa dead?* I dropped the phone, bowled over by what felt like a straight fist to my chest. *No! That can't be true. There must be a mistake.* Luna's voice echoed in the distance.

"Nui? Nui, are you there? Can you hear me?"

My hands were shaking so badly I barely managed to pick up the phone. My mouth opened and closed, but I couldn't form words.

"Nui?" Luna sounded worried.

I had to clear my throat several times before I croaked out a single word.

"How?"

"Your Aunt May said she collapsed this afternoon, and they had to revive her in the ambulance. She's now on life support in the hospital. I'm so sorry."

I carefully put the phone on my desk and rubbed my eyes until I saw spots.

"Nui, did you hear me? Your dad said we're all flying to Chiang Rai either tomorrow night or Friday. Your mom is leaving tomorrow morning."

I finally felt strong enough to speak.

"Luna, I'm going to kill you! I thought you meant *Khun Yaa* had died. You just about gave *me* a heart attack." There wasn't any heat behind my words, just simple gratitude that Khun Yaa was okay. Not that Khun Yaai was any less important, but I didn't know her as well as Khun Yaa, who lived with us.

"Oh God, Nui, I'm so sorry. I didn't even think about that. No, no, Khun Yaa is totally fine."

I could tell Luna was serious about her apology. She loved Khun Yaa as well.

"I know. Sorry, I was just so shocked when you said that. Okay, so what did Paa say? You're flying out on Friday?" I asked.

Luna didn't answer.

"Luna? You there?" I looked at the phone. The connection was fine.

"What do you mean 'you're flying out'? Don't you think you should go to see your own grandmother? Especially if it might be the last time?" Luna asked.

"Oh." I didn't know what else to say. I felt blindsided.

"Oh?"

The entire conversation sounded like a bad farce, but as much as I wished otherwise, Luna was right. This wasn't something I could delegate to her. I hated that no matter how much I tried to tell myself otherwise, I was still hooked on the culture I had grown up in. If I didn't want to create even more bad karma than I already had, it really was my responsibility to pay my respects. Besides, Khun Yaai had always been kind to me and taken an interest in what I wanted to do with my life. We didn't get to see her that often, but Mae had insisted on bi-weekly Sunday phone calls when we were younger, where everyone spoke with her. I often ended up last in line and though initially I had resented it, our conversations became longer and more engaged as I didn't have to pass on the phone. I couldn't remember when we'd last spoken, though. It was kind of sad that we'd dropped the habit, though I had to admit it was mostly due to me once life got busier. The stab of guilt intensified. This couldn't have come at a worst time.

"I guess." I almost had to force the words out against my will. "You're right! I have to go."

"That's what I thought. I'm glad you agree. You think we can switch tomorrow when I come over? Maybe Yumi can keep Mom busy for half an hour?"

"Em, sure. I suppose that's the only window we have, right?"

"Okay, I'll see you at school and we'll switch in the afternoon. Sorry about your grandma, Nui. See you tomorrow. Night."

I flung myself face down on the bed, then rolled over, hugging and biting a pillow to muffle my screams. That Luna sounded almost gleeful only added to the injustice of it. Tomorrow night, I would be back in my own bed. The entire last month would soon become a distant memory, and my dream would remain out of reach forever.

16

LUNA

I SHOULD HAVE BEEN ASHAMED OF MYSELF AT HOW QUICKLY I ended the call to Nui, but I could barely contain my excitement that she'd finally agreed to switch. It was sad that it took her grandmother's illness for Nui to see reason, but since it wasn't something I'd caused, I couldn't feel too guilty about it. Luckily, I had called from the boys' room, as it would have been wholly inappropriate for me to show my cheerful face to the rest of the family.

For a few minutes, I sat on the bed basking in the vision of being home again. I promised myself I would never ever complain or fight with Mom and Dad and Luke again. *Well, maybe not Luke.* I giggled. Yumi was right—you never appreciate what you have until you lose it. Thankfully, in my case that would only be temporarily.

Unexpectedly, my light mood shifted. It hadn't been all bad with Nui's family and I would have never met Channon if not for the switch. What would happen with us now? Did he really mean it when he said he wanted to continue seeing me as Luna? How would we explain that to Nui's family? What would my parents say? The question had never come up, as there had been no one I was interested in. *Or anyone interested in you, don't forget. Ouch. What did that say about me?* I hadn't really considered the potential reactions before and though I didn't think it was anyone's business, a slight unease remained. Before I could tumble down that emotional slide, I picked up the phone to call Yumi and prep her for tomorrow's meeting. Everything else would work itself out once I settled back at home. Yumi answered after two rings.

"Hey, guess what? Big change of plans." I jumped right in.

"Why? What happened? You sound happy," Yumi said.

I quickly brought her up to speed on my conversation with Nui and the plan for the next day.

"So, you need to lay off with the questions and please don't aggravate Nui. She'll have enough to deal with and as long as we switch, it's all good okay?"

"Hmm, sure. How do you want me to explain to your mom that you two need to disappear for a while?"

"That'll be easy. She knows Nui and I had an argument, well that's what Nui called it, so she'll be happy if we go to hash it out between ourselves. I know Mom. She's all for making peace."

"I suppose I'll manage," Yumi said.

"I guess we don't need that idea of yours anymore. What was it, anyway?"

"Never mind. I don't even know if it would have worked. There's a lot of paperwork involved, and I'm not sure if there would have been enough time. This is so much easier. I'm glad Nui agreed."

"Me too. Gotta go. Nui's mom is leaving early tomorrow,

and I don't know if she needs help with anything. I'll see you at school. And Yumi, thanks for being such a good friend. I'm sorry I haven't been in touch since we left Shanghai. I'll make it up to you."

"We'll see." Yumi sounded reserved. I remembered her earlier call with Kiko and how devastated she'd been to leave her sister. Did she feel I'd abandoned her? I promised myself I'd be there for her from then on.

Shaking off the remorse, I went to the kitchen to speak with Khun Yaa. This would be my last evening with her and I would miss her for sure. She was making a list of names and numbers, going through an old-fashioned address book.

"What are you doing?" I'd only ever seen her writing shopping lists.

"These are the people we need to contact in case your grandmother passes away. Your mother won't have time to do it then."

"Oh. Can I help?" It was a pointless offer since I only knew a few of the family friends and neighbours and not even their real names, only their nicknames.

"No thank you Nui. *You* need to pack. If the flight is confirmed for tomorrow, you leave right after school."

What? I couldn't leave until we had switched back. I had to see Nui.

"You mean I have to miss school again on Friday? But I've already lost three days when I was in the hospital."

There was no way I was going to miss the switch back.

Khun Yaa looked up and raised her eyebrows. "You heard what your father said earlier about your school?"

"Yeah, I know, but he also said it wasn't confirmed yet, so I can't afford to drop my grades now. Also, I have to get my third rabies shot tomorrow after school. The appointment is at five. You know I can't miss that." I thought I was playing a trump card, knowing how serious she and Mae were about medical stuff.

"You're going to a hospital in Chiang Rai. I'm sure you can get the shot there."

Damn. That option hadn't occurred to me, yet it was perfectly logical. I opened and closed my mouth a few times but couldn't come up with an appropriate reply.

"Fine. When will we know if we're going tomorrow or Friday?"

"We'll know by lunchtime. The flight is around seven so you come back here to get your bag and Khun Bpoo will drive you all to Don Muang."

"But what if it's not confirmed?"

Khun Yaa sighed and put her pen down.

"Nui, can you hear yourself? This is your grandmother we're talking about. Why are you being so difficult? You should be ashamed of yourself. If you're not doing it for yourself, do it for your mother." She picked up her pen. "I hope you'll show me a bit more respect when my time comes," she added in a low voice.

Ouch. That hurt. I'd have to call Nui again and, if necessary, we'd have to skip a class and find a spot somewhere to meditate.

17

NUI

WHEN LUNA CALLED THE THIRD TIME, I WAS SURE IT WAS TO tell me Khun Yaai had passed away. Instead, we were apparently now in a time crunch and had to switch back during school hours the next day. The pressure in my chest built again. This was all happening too fast for me to digest.

"We can wait until noon, and I'll call Khun Yaa to see if the flight is confirmed. If not, we can go home as planned. If it is, we just don't go back to class after lunch, but I don't know where we could go. I mean, we can't stay at school if we skip a class. Any ideas?" Luna asked.

I still felt too shaken by the whole situation to think clearly, but one option seemed obvious.

"We could go to Wat Phatum. It would be quiet there. And if the sala is not free, we can probably sit somewhere in the garden."

"Great idea. Let's do that," Luna said. "I'm supposed to pack now. What do you need?"

If we were staying at Aunt May's house, I wouldn't need much, just some clothes and toiletries. I ran Luna through the list and where she could find a small suitcase.

"Oh, and…" I swallowed hard. "I need something white in case Khun Yaai passes and we're staying for the funeral. Just remember the temple rules. Nothing off shoulder or above the knees." I finished my instructions.

"You wear white at a funeral? That's weird."

"The family does. What's weird about that? Maybe it's strange that you all wear black, ever thought of that?" I knew I was being oversensitive, but having my plans destroyed left me feeling bitter.

"Sorry, you're right. Anything else?"

"I'll text you if I think of anything or I'll just add it tomorrow. I gotta go, Luna. I want to finish up a few things here." There really wasn't anything to do except lie on my— okay, *Luna's*—bed, and feel sorry for myself. I briefly thought about telling Luna about the police verdict, but discarded the idea. She'd find out soon enough.

"Okay, night Nui. By the way, I was thinking, did you actually meditate this last week? Maybe we need to have our own sessions tonight just to make sure we can still do it," Luna said.

"Hmm, probably a good idea." Maybe it would also help lift my dark mood. Anything would be better than the sense of powerlessness I was feeling.

"Okay then. Night." Luna hung up. She had sounded entirely too cheerful to me. This was all so unfair. Why did she always get everything she wanted? I sighed. I'd been over the same thoughts too many times and I was actually boring myself.

Meditation sounded like a good idea. I locked the door and leaned back against the headboard. Selecting one of our recorded sessions with Ajaarn Anurak, I tapped the play button. His voice sounded calm and uplifting, as usual.

'Inhale to the count of four, hold for four, and slowly exhale to the count of eight. Feel your eyelids relax; let this feeling move down to your face...'

My shoulders dropped and my spine relaxed into the pillow behind me, one vertebra at a time. A smile tugged at my lips. Yes, this was so much better. I was determined not to let my bad mood pull me back down again. *Just appreciate what you've had for all this time. And remember, you made it happen once. Why wouldn't you be able to do it again? If not with Luna, then perhaps someone else.* Yumi's face flashed into my head. I startled and inadvertently broke my meditative state, tapping the stop button.

No, not Yumi. She had all those issues with her family that I wouldn't want to take on. But who did I know who might be adventurous enough to believe a switch was possible?

18

LUNA

PACKING WAS QUICK. AFTER LIFE ON THE GO WITH MY family, I was a pro at it and, of course, Nui's clothing options were more limited than mine. Duen was still sorting through her stuff when I returned to Krit and Tum's bedroom. It was perfect timing that both had been away while I was living in Nui's home. The chance to escape the family occasionally was priceless. I wasn't used to living in such close quarters and I missed my privacy. As of tomorrow, that thankfully would change again. I grinned, then sighed. What a crazy, intense rollercoaster kind of day it had been. First, seeing Mom but not being able to speak with her, then the brief conversation with Channon, and the big talk with Yumi, and now this. My shoulders were tight with tension, but it was over now and tomorrow I would start fresh. I had to figure out how to convince Channon I was still the same person just back in my own body. Yumi had interrupted our conversation and I would be Luna the next time we met. What would I say? Would he believe me? A shudder went through me. *Stop it. One step at a time, Luna. You'll figure it out.*

Determined to put my worries aside for now I decided to take my own advice and meditate. Nui and I could only complete the switch if we were on the same vibrational frequency, and that wasn't something we could turn on or off at will. I usually found it easiest to raise my emotions by not thinking about anything at all. It worked best when I concentrated on my breathing while listening to Ajaarn's voice in the background.

I sat on Krit's bed and scrolled through the recordings. Ajaarn's voice was reassuring as he guided me through the circle of light exercise.

'Imagine a ball of pure, warm light, of love and compassion, just inside your chest. The light is pulsing in time with your heartbeat. Inhale and feel the light expanding, covering your whole body in a white bubble. Feel it expand even further…'

My muscles loosened one by one, and my hands opened as if to receive the universe's gifts. My lower body melted into the mattress like a bubble on a sponge. I knew I was smiling, but kept focusing on my breath. Long inhale, hold, even longer exhale. After a week of being miserable, I finally felt some hope again that everything would work out for me. And yet… startled, I realised this was as high as my vibrational level would go today. I shivered. Why was I being so tentative about this? I should have been ecstatic about the upcoming change. Merely *hoping* that it would work wasn't enough. *Come on, Luna, you can do better than that. You've done it before.* Ajaarn had said that each emotion carried a certain frequency and that love and appreciation were the highest. Hope was down the list, just above boredom. What could I think about that would put me in a better mood?

Maybe if I tried another recording with different mantras? This time, it was even worse. My shoulder muscles knotted and I ground my teeth. This was so frustrating. *You better work the bugs out, Luna, and quickly.* Could I simply trust that by tomorrow I'd be in a stronger frame of mind? *Just sleep on it; it'll be like pressing the reset button.* While that was usually true, I felt nervous I'd left it too long and wouldn't be able to reach the higher frequency without further practise. *You have to. There's no other option. Think of Mom, Dad and Luke and how great you'll feel to be back home.* Putting the pressure on myself only made the tension worse. Irritated, I touched the phone to stop the recording and stretched. Maybe a walk with Joey would loosen me up. I'd try again after.

19

NUI

LUKE AND HIS PARENTS WERE AT THE BREAKFAST TABLE BY the time I dragged myself out of my room. I'd taken an extra-long shower, savouring the luxury of not having to share a bathroom. A small duffel bag with the few things that I'd accumulated during my time as Luna now sat by the front door, ready for me to grab on my way to school. Some books, two pairs of earrings, some lotions and a dress I'd bought in my size with Luna's money. I had debated if I could take extra money from Luna's pocket money stash, but felt that would be pushing it.

"Morning, honey. Sleep well?" Khun Susan asked as she poured me a glass of orange juice.

I nodded, not trusting myself to speak without bursting into tears. The night had been miserable. I'd wanted to stay awake to enjoy my last time in Luna's super comfortable bed, but I kept dozing on and off until my alarm woke me at six. Then, every regular task became a tick on my doomsday list:

last time I'd shower here, last time I'd dress as Luna, last time I'd look in the mirror and see myself through Luna's eyes, last time I'd have breakfast with the family. My vision kept blurring with unshed tears. I desperately tried to hold it together. There'd be plenty of acceptable opportunities to cry in Chiang Rai on the weekend.

"Mom? Luna and I talked last night, and we decided that we both want to move as soon as we can," Luke said.

His parents looked at him, then at me, and back again.

"Really? And you're both okay with that? Luna? You always said you wanted to stay, but now you're okay to go?" Khun Susan asked. "That's enough sugar, by the way."

I looked up and realised I'd been heaping and stirring sugar mindlessly into my tea. I put the spoon down, took a sip and almost spat it out again, pushing the cup away.

"I guess so. Luke's right, it's too difficult to stay here. And you said you wanted to be closer to Aunt Jane, didn't you?"

Luke gave me a tiny nod, pleased that I'd stuck to our deal even if I felt like screaming 'no deal'. *Remember, Nui, today is not about getting stuck or moving, it's about Khun Yaai, it's about family. Besides, it won't make a difference what I want or say.* Resigned, I sat back and buttered a slice of toast.

"You don't sound very convinced, Luna," Khun Susan said.

"No, really, it's okay. It'll make things easier for everyone. I mean, maybe Dad can talk to his people to see if they can figure something out. You said they were already working on something, right?"

The parents gave each other a look I couldn't interpret, but it must have been their own special way of communicating.

"Well, if you're both good with that, we'll see how we can move things forward." Khun Mark pushed away from the table to get ready to go to work.

On impulse, I jumped up to give him a hug as he was leaving the room.

"Thanks Dad, for everything. And I'm sorry I messed up everyone's plans."

He hugged me back and whispered, "Live and learn, Luna. Live and learn." He dropped a kiss on my head and headed for the front door.

"What's wrong, Luna?" Khun Susan asked. "You seem out of sorts. Are you okay? Are Yumi and Nui still coming this afternoon? I want to get a few things from the bakery."

"Can I text you about that? Nui said her grandmother had a heart attack and is in the hospital in Chiang Rai and she might have to fly up this evening. She won't know until noon. Is that okay?"

"Oh, I'm sorry to hear that. Poor Nui, she's gone through so much lately. Hope her grandma is okay. Just call me when you know. But Yumi will come either way?"

I nodded. Despite my best efforts, a tear trickled down my face. *Yes, poor Nui.* I swallowed hard and swiped the tear away. Luke and his mom looked at me, confused by my odd behaviour.

I waved my hands. "It's nothing. Never mind." I got up and rushed from the room. If I gave in now, I'd never stop crying.

20

LUNA

Yumi was waiting for me at the school entrance. Her outfit was a departure from her usual funky style and would have looked good on a catwalk. Skinny black jumpsuit with an open apple-green long-sleeve shirt on top cinched at her waist with a woven black belt. Green high tops, black beret and emerald drop earrings completed the look. Not for the first time, I thought she was the only person I knew who could pull off this style.

"You look great, Yumi. Very stylish. What's the occasion? Oh look, you got your own fan club." Two younger students were trying to be inconspicuous while taking a picture of Yumi, and giggled when she struck a pose for them.

"Nothing. Just felt like it this morning." Yumi casually tugged a stray strand of hair behind her ear. "Where's Lu.. I mean Nui?"

"She should be here any moment. Want to go in?"

"Let's wait for her. So, we're all set for this afternoon? It'll be nice to see your mom again."

"Oh man, I forgot to tell you." I explained the pending travel arrangements. "I'll know for sure at lunchtime."

Goosebumps went down my arms despite the heat. In my third meditation attempt last night, I still hadn't been able to reach the level of certainty I needed for the switch, and my first thought this morning went right back to my fear that something could go wrong. I wasn't even sure why I felt this ambiguity. I knew how to focus. My escape from the locked-in state had proven that beyond a doubt. I also knew I wanted to go home, so why was I feeling so uneasy? Determined to shrug it off, I'd taken an extra-long morning walk with Joey. Nui's parents had already left for the airport, and breakfast with Khun Yaa was sweet but sad, too. I would miss her. Would Nui and I be able to remain friends so I could still see Khun Yaa? Yumi nudged me to bring me back to the present.

"Gee, I really hope you get this all sorted today. You guys are driving me nuts." She rolled her eyes.

"I know. I'm sorry. But even if Nui and I have to skip school to make the switch, I'm still the one going home today, so you can definitely come." The words sounded good; I just needed to believe them. I hooked Yumi's arm through mine. It was great to have my friend back. Why had I ever let her slip away? She had been phenomenal yesterday afternoon, and I owed her for believing me and not being too mad that I'd cut her off after Shanghai. I needed to do something nice for her and also find out what was going on with Kiko and her mom. Maybe I could help her somehow.

"Come on, let's go. And remember to call me Nui now, okay?"

We were already sitting in our home room when Nui showed up. She wore sunglasses and carried one of my small duffel bags, though there was no swimming session on the schedule today. She sat next to me in her usual spot and looked at the table in front of her not even acknowledging me. In the last week, Yumi had somehow manoeuvred her assigned seat to my other side. Nui pulled off the glasses when Mr Adams, our math teacher, walked in. One look at my face showed she'd been crying, her eyes puffy. A combination of sympathy and irritation gripped my stomach. Were the tears for her grandma or because of our upcoming switch? Yesterday, she hadn't seemed too distraught about Khun Yaai's illness. Or was it something else altogether? What did it matter, anyway? We had an agreement. Why should I feel sorry for Nui? She'd almost ruined my life, and jeopardised my family with the police investigation, which she hadn't mentioned at all recently. Was she hiding something else? Again? A twinge of guilt tightened my chest. As much as I tried to justify my position, I wasn't completely innocent either.

God, we are such idiots! Why did we have to mess up our lives like this? I groaned.

"Yes, Nui. You want to say something?" Mr Adams called from the front of the room.

"What? Oh no, thank you. Sorry."

Yumi raised her eyebrows. I shook my head and mouthed 'later'.

Even though I'd made a big fuss to Khun Yaa about maintaining my grades, my brain wasn't cooperating as I counted down the hours before I could call her about the flight. I doubted Nui was doing much better, and I caught Yumi looking at us speculatively a few times, but we all remained tight-lipped.

When the lunch bell rang, I jumped up, grabbed Nui's

arm, and pulled her along to the front courtyard. Yumi trailed behind.

The number at home rang busy.

"Dammit, I can't get through."

"Call Duen. She'll know," Nui said. *I should have thought of that myself.*

Nui glanced at Yumi, but didn't question her presence.

Duen answered on the second ring. I held the phone so Nui could listen in.

"Allo?"

"Hey Duen, did you speak to Khun Yaa?"

"I talked to Paa. He said we're flying tonight, so you need to come home right after school. Khun Yaai is really sick."

"Oh, okay. Thanks Duen. See you later."

Nui squeezed her eyes and bit her lips. Again, a zing of annoyance went through me. It wasn't as if she didn't know what was coming. Why was she being so dramatic? *Stop it, Luna. Maybe it isn't about the switch but her concern for her grandma.*

I turned to Yumi. "Yumi, we need your help. Luna and I have to take care of something urgently. We have to skip the rest of the day."

I tilted my head towards the gate where two guards were checking incoming and outgoing cars for their school permit stickers. Students leaving during the day had to present a pass from their teacher countersigned by the reception lady ticking them off the main roster.

"Can you create a diversion so we can slip out?"

"How?" Yumi asked.

I looked at Nui. She shrugged.

"Never mind, I have an idea." Yumi grinned. "Leave it with me."

She took off one of her big green earrings and palmed it

in her hand. Looking at the ground, she strolled towards the gate. As she approached the guards, she started gesticulating, pointing to her ear, then to the ground, looking distressed. She even wiped her eyes as if she was crying. I couldn't hear what she was saying, but it caught the guards' attention and they moved towards her. I grabbed Nui's arm and sidled towards the smaller side gate. It was locked.

"Oh, shit." I looked around frantically. "What do we do?"

Nui pushed me to the side, threw the small duffel she carried over the fence, and started to squeeze through a small gap between the hedge and the gatepost.

"Help! I'm stuck." She hissed.

It felt surreal to push my own butt and shoulder, but she finally made it through. I quickly followed with little trouble in Nui's smaller body. We both had scratches on our arms, but I giggled, chuffed with our success. In other circumstances, our size difference might have bothered me, but right now it only mattered that we had gotten out. Nui ignored me. I tried to be mindful of her feelings, but resented her at the same time. After all, she'd brought this on herself when she refused to switch. *Come on, Luna, stop it! Forget about the past. Concentrate on now.* Again, I felt my stomach twist. This was so not how I needed to feel. I wanted to be excited about going home and leaving this mess behind. Why did I keep doubling down and rehashing old news? It only got me worked up again, not helpful at all for what we were trying to accomplish.

Inside the gates at Wat Pathum, I stopped and closed my eyes, tipping my head back to take in a few deep breaths. Yes, the temple gardens still worked their magic, calming me.

"Let's go to the spirit house for a minute." We hadn't brought incense or flowers and didn't really have much time, but I needed a moment to settle down. Nui followed, put her hands together and closed her eyes. She'd been passive all morning, as if she had been drugged. Had I missed something?

"What's wrong, Nui? Why are you so quiet?" I had to ask.

"Nothing." *As if!* She didn't even look at me. *Let it go Luna. Don't get yourself worked up again.* I knew better than to probe, but couldn't help myself.

"I thought you wanted to switch. At least that's what you said yesterday."

Nui rubbed her eyes but stared at the spirit house.

"I know. Don't worry, I won't stand in your way," she said.

"My way? You know that this won't work if we're not on the same page. This is not just about me. You really need to want to do it, too."

"Stop patronising me! I know that." Nui's flash of anger caught me off guard.

"Fine. But I'll hold you to that, this time." Damn it. Now I was irritated again too, and I knew full well that I needed to do my part in our session. *Chill, don't let her get to you. Remember, you get to see your family this evening. That's all you need to concentrate on.*

"You had to tell Yumi, didn't you?" Nui asked. The anger was gone, as if it was too much work to maintain.

I didn't bother answering, letting her draw her own conclusions. After our session it wouldn't matter anyway. Besides, I needed to calm the friction between us, not amp it up. We needed to be in sync now more than ever. Nui turned back to the spirit house. I considered telling her that Yumi had an idea that might help her? Perhaps having another option would lift Nui's spirits, but since I didn't know what Yumi had in mind beyond what she called an 'incentive or alternative', it was best not to mention it yet.

I blew out a long breath, then touched Nui's arm and pointed towards the central sala, which stood empty as predicted. We left our sandals at the entrance and picked two rattan mats to sit in front of the Buddha statue at the far end. His palms faced up, resting in his lap, eyes closed, with a serene expression on his face, meditating.

"How do we do this? I don't think we're allowed to make any noise," Nui said.

"Here, use one of my earphones. That won't disturb anyone. Which session do you want?"

"We only ever had an out-of-body with the last one, so use that," Nui said.

"Right. Then let's do it."

I tapped play.

21

NUI

I'D FELT OFF KILTER ALL MORNING, BUT HERE AT THE TEMPLE, I knew I had to put my disappointment behind me and move on. Praying at the spirit house for Khun Yaai had smoothed some of the rough edges of my gloominess except for the brief spat with Luna, but now, sitting in front of the Buddha, I knew I was doing the right thing whether or not I liked it. I exhaled and closed my eyes. It was odd to hear Ajaarn through only one earbud, but the familiar and quiet setting helped. I could feel Luna breathing in synch with me, our arms touching.

'Inhale to the count of four, hold for four and exhale for eight.' Synching my breath to the rhythm of Ajaarn's instructions blocked out random thoughts and I relaxed. The circle of light exercise almost made me want to grab Luna's hand. I was smiling for the first time in what seemed like days.

"What are you two doing here?" A familiar voice broke through my contentment.

Luna jerked, then pulled out her earphone and tapped the stop button. She looked at me before we both turned around.

Ajaarn Anurak stood a few feet behind us, holding a basket with white pillar candles that stood out against his orange robe. We hadn't seen him since our last aborted switch attempt.

"Ajaarn kha, sawasdee kha." I wai'ed automatically. He tipped his head, acknowledging the greeting.

Ajaarn had been our meditation teacher. He knew of our out-of-body experiences, and when Luna told him about the switch, he'd reluctantly agreed to help us reverse it. When at the last minute we both decided not to return to our bodies immediately, Ajaarn thought we were deliberately playing a trick on him. It was ironic that he would show up when we were trying to get back into our bodies for real.

"Nui, Luna, why are you here?" Ajaarn repeated his question. He didn't appear upset, just curious.

"We…" Luna said, then stopped. She too must have felt the irony of the situation.

"We were trying to find a quiet place to meditate. We, um, need to switch back today. I hope you don't mind that we came here," I said.

Ajaarn shrugged. "The temple is open to everyone." He turned to leave.

"Ajaarn kha, I know you don't believe us, but would you be willing to help us one more time?" The question popped out before I could think about the audacity. Last time, he'd been irritated with us, assuming we'd deliberately pranked him, but we had nothing to lose by asking for his help.

A flicker of annoyance skimmed over his face. It still surprised me that he would react like any other person.

Somehow, I always held our religious men to a higher standard. Luna and I waited. He pulled his phone out of his robe to check something.

"I don't guide meditation classes in the afternoon."

Ouch. If he really thought we were tricking him, he had every right to be angry, monk or not.

"But it's not a class, Ajaarn kha. We know what to do. It's just so much easier if you guide us than listening to your recording. We really could use your help, please."

Luna must have been pretty desperate to be so forthright. I wouldn't have dared to demand his help after he refused. Ajaarn looked at her as if he was evaluating her sincerity. He needed more convincing.

"Ajaarn kha, my grandmother is very ill and we think she's going to die soon, and I need to see her and pay my respects. Luna doesn't know her. This is something I need to do myself. I know you understand." If that didn't assure him, nothing would. We Buddhists took the transition between lives seriously. It must have seemed weird for Ajaarn to be looking at Luna's face when I spoke. He looked at his phone again and with a small sigh turned it off, put the basket down, bowed to the Buddha and sat on the platform in front of the statue.

"I am still not convinced you're telling me the truth. As far as we know, no one has ever done it or been able to prove that it's possible. But if it is, I do not wish to stand in the way of you being with your family. You remember what I said last time?"

We both nodded, but he wasn't satisfied with that.

"A crossover of spirits or, in this case a reversal, can only happen if both of you are fully aware, open and willing for it to happen. Your intention and belief that it *is* possible matters most, which means you both must have a strong desire, with no doubts or reservation. Do you understand?"

Again, Luna and I nodded.

"Very well then." Ajaarn closed his eyes and chanted under his breath – his own preparation for meditation.

I nudged Luna and shifted a few inches away to give us more room. I didn't want to be distracted by her movements.

"Now, close your eyes and inhale to the count of four, hold your breath, and exhale to the count of eight."

A smile tugged at the corners of my mouth. It felt so much better hearing Ajaarn speak instead of the taped meditation. It was easier to drift off and stop thinking. Almost immediately, I felt little twinges in my stomach, like worker bees running around a hive, as if my cells were readjusting themselves. With every inhale my mood lifted, and with every exhale I felt more tension slipping away. A tugging sensation in my chest was the signal that my spirit was ready to project away from Luna's physical body. *This* was what I'd been aiming for. I felt completely at ease. I savoured the feeling for a moment and then, just as I had done before, began scanning the web of silvery tendrils around me, trying to identify Luna's spirit thread. *Where are you, Luna?* The other strands represented other living beings' links to the life stream, but they appeared translucent and indistinct to me. If Luna had managed her projection, I should have been able to see and feel her thread, bright and definite, and then it was only a matter of connecting to make the changeover. But nothing stood out. What did that mean? Had she not been able to project herself away from my body?

Distantly, I was aware of Ajaarn's voice. He would bring the meditation to a close soon. *Come on Luna, try harder. You said you wanted to go home. Make it work.*

Again, I looked for her thread but couldn't find it. My concentration slipped. *No!*

"We're now coming out of this meditation. On the count of five, you will open your eyes and feel refreshed and calm. One, two, three, four, five. Take a deep breath in and release. Open your eyes." Ajaarn's voice faded away.

I turned to Luna. She had slumped over, hands covering her face, crying so hard her entire body trembled. I locked my hands together to keep myself from punching her.

"What the…?" I tried to keep my voice low but felt hot anger rising.

It took Luna several tries to control her sobbing enough to speak.

"Why doesn't it work, Nui? I'm scared."

22

LUNA

I SHIVERED DESPITE THE HEAT IN THE SALA; MY TEETH ground against each other until my jaw hurt. My worst-case scenario had come true, just as I'd imagined. I wrapped my arms around myself, trying to hold it together. The lump in my throat felt like a boulder, only allowing a small amount of air to go through. I bit my lip to force myself to concentrate.

"Ajaarn kha, why wasn't I able to lift out of my body this time? You know I've done it before. Am I stuck?" My voice wobbled.

Why did I bother asking him? He didn't believe us in the first place and we'd probably used up all his goodwill with this session.

Ajaarn looked at me quietly, contemplating. He sighed.

"I think you tried too hard to *make* it happen, to force it. This is not how meditation works. I thought you knew that." Ajaarn spoke softly, taking me by surprise. He seemed compassionate rather than upset, contrary to his earlier stance.

"But I really want to switch. I want to go home." My eyes teared up again. Nui pressed some tissues into my hands with more force than necessary. I didn't dare look at her.

"How did you achieve your first out-of-body state? What were you thinking about?" Ajaarn asked.

I tried to recall our initial sessions in the temple.

"Nothing really, why?"

Ajaarn nodded.

"That's right. You quiet your mind and that allows you to release your spirit, or rather it allows your spirit to guide you."

"I understand, but why not this time?" I asked.

"What did you focus on this time? Were you thinking of where you want to go or pushing against where you are right now?" Ajaarn asked.

"Why does that matter if the result is the same?" I sniffed and wiped my eyes.

"Yes, it might seem like the same thing when it's actually like two ends of a stick." He twisted around and picked up one of the smoking incense sticks from a clay pot in front of the altar. "You see, a stick has two ends to it. Let's say this side represents your wish to go home." He pointed to the burning end. "And this side is the opposite, meaning everything you want to leave behind." He nodded towards the handhold. "So which side of the stick were you looking at?"

"I don't understand." I looked at Nui to see if she got it, but she was squinting at Ajaarn, biting her lips.

"Let me explain it this way: one side represents your desire and the other end is the opposite, meaning the absence of your desire. There's a vast difference vibrationally. When you look at what you don't want and you concentrate hard on pushing it away, you're actually moving in its direction and you end up with exactly what you don't want. In this universe, you get what you focus on, whether you want it or not."

The picture he painted was still obscure or I was too stressed to take it in, but it made me pause. Yes, I wanted to leave my current situation behind, and I also wanted to go home. Though the end result would be the same the focus was different. Maybe that's what had created the resistance and kept my spirit in Nui's body? It was also possible that I'd been afraid the projection would end up like my previous attacks on Nui, hurting us both or worse, becoming locked-in again.

"I don't know. I thought I was focusing on it to work, but..." I broke eye contact and lowered my head.

"Are you effing serious, Luna?" Nui almost choked herself trying to keep her voice down. "You were the one who insisted on switching back. How could you have any doubt about it now?" I could feel waves of anger rolling off her and instinctively leaned away. If we hadn't been in a temple in front of Ajaarn, she would have screamed at me, and I'd given her every right to do so. I'd badly misjudged my mental powers this time.

"What about me? I need to go to Chiang Rai today. Come on, we need to try again," Nui said.

"I think you've done all you can for today," Ajaarn said, rising from his lotus position. "This is the second time now that you're claiming to want to switch. If you think this is a joke, I do not wish to be a part of it. You two need to be sure of your motivation before you try anything like this again. And remember, meditation is meant to clear your mind; it is not to be used as a portal for spirit transfers, if that's even possible." Ajaarn's misgivings were understandable. Without another word, he bowed to the Buddha and left.

Nui barely waited for Ajaarn to leave the sala before launching into me.

"Dammit Luna, you can't be serious. What the fuck are we going to do now? I don't care what Ajaarn said, we have to try again."

I felt depleted instead of refreshed by the meditation, more proof that I had split energy about the issue, but for the life of me, I couldn't explain why. What was holding me back? *What the heck is wrong with you, Luna?* My head hurt just trying to think about it.

Nui punched my arm. "Did you hear me? We have to try again. Come on, give me the earphone." She scooted closer.

"Ouch! You heard what he said."

"So what? You just want to accept that? You can't be serious. I've never heard of his stick theory, anyway. I doubt it's even Buddhist teaching. We have to make this work. And you have to do your part this time. Come on."

"I know we can't leave it like this, but I can't even concentrate right now. There's no way I'm going to have an out-of-body experience. Besides, I want to think about what Ajaarn said."

"No, Luna, you can't just leave. *I* have to go to Chiang Rai. She's *my* grandmother." Nui was shouting now, spittle hitting my face. Eww.

"What do you want me to do? Do you think *I* want to go to Chiang Rai? There's no time right now anyway." I tapped my phone. "See, it's already two thirty. We gotta go if I want to make the flight."

"I don't believe this shit!" Nui was livid enough to swear

in the temple, something she had scolded me about before. "I feel like we jumped into quicksand and we're just getting sucked in deeper and deeper." Fuming, she picked up her mat and randomly wai'ed to the Buddha before stomping off.

I dragged myself up and looked at the smiling statue. "You better help us out here, big guy. This has got to stop."

23

NUI

LIFE WASN'T FAIR. THERE I WAS, READY TO SWITCH, AND Luna had messed it up. Deep inside, I knew she hadn't done it on purpose, but that didn't change the fact I was building up a massive pile of bad karma for myself. I wasn't particularly religious or superstitious, but I'd broken at least two of our five Buddhist rules already and, of course, Khun Yaa's own set. Technically, Luna had done the same, but it wouldn't matter to her.

Luna took her sweet time joining me while I paced in front of the sala, letting off steam.

"So, what's your problem? Why are you so wishy-washy about the switch? First, you say you want to move back, and now you're not sure? And this whole time you were saying it's my fault." My anger control wasn't working. Luna flinched at my words.

"I am not wishy-washy. I want to go home and I don't know why it didn't work, okay?!"

"Oh yeah? Every time you say you'll do something, you do the exact opposite of it. It's pathetic!"

"Pathetic? You have got to be kidding me. How convenient for you to put this on me. Are you forgetting that the last time you lied to me, you were willing to leave me with your own family so you could go on your precious trip abroad? I hate you. You started this whole thing." Luna was raving mad, no longer shaky.

"So what? That's old news. We're here because I agreed to switch, and now you're waffling again."

"You can't possibly think I did it on purpose…"

"Why not? You also said you wouldn't tell Channon, and you did. And I'm sure you told Yumi too. You haven't kept your promises either."

Luna stood stock still, her chest heaving, then suddenly slumped like someone had pricked a balloon.

"Dammit, Nui! Let's not do this. This is not getting us anywhere." Her eyes were shiny again with a fresh flood of tears threatening. I never knew my body could produce so many tears, but Luna managed to turn on the waterworks almost at will.

I turned around to count to ten. Luna was right. This fight wasn't helping either of us. I reached thirty and felt somewhat in control again when another thought flashed into my head. What would happen if we couldn't switch and Luna's family moved back to the US? I'd be in serious trouble. Unwittingly, Khun Yaai's illness had made my situation crystal clear – an eye-opener. How could I leave my family behind for a world unknown, especially if I would be stuck outside the country for at least five years? What if it was Khun Yaa who had a heart attack and I wouldn't be able to see her? How could I not be there for her after all she'd done for me? I swallowed hard. What had we done? Khun Yaa had said often 'Every action has a consequence'. I cringed. This was as much my fault as Luna's.

Before I could say anything to Luna to diffuse the situation, I saw a middle-aged monk rushing towards us, shaking his head, looking outraged. He put his fingers to his lips, then motioned for us to go. His gestures were unmistakable. We must have been louder than we'd realised. I wai'ed in apology and grabbed Luna's arm, demonstrating we were leaving.

"Uh oh. I guess we're not welcome here anymore." Getting kicked out of a temple had to be a new low for me.

24

LUNA

FOLLOWING NUI THROUGH THE GARDENS, I TRIED TO THINK about our situation rationally.

"Do you think we've waited too long and now we can't make it work anymore?" I asked Nui.

"No, not really. I don't think it's time related. If I could project, you should be able to do it too. That has nothing to do with timing," Nui said.

I nodded, but it didn't explain why I hadn't been able to focus. In my head, Ajaarn's and Nui's words meshed. Was I being wishy-washy about the switch or, in Ajaarn's words, looking at the wrong end of the stick? Maybe a bit of both. But why? Time to turn the tables.

"What do you actually want, Nui? I mean, yesterday you were still dead set on going away with my family for Songkran, and today you're mad at me for not reversing the swap."

"What am I supposed to do? I want to swap. It is my

family, after all," Nui said, but didn't look at me. She seemed to be torn about the issue too, even if she'd managed to release her spirit today. We both had some serious sorting out to do.

"I promise, as soon as I'm back, we'll try again. We just have to hit it at the same time. I'll definitely meditate while I'm in Chiang Rai. You should too," I said.

"You'll be pretty busy," Nui said.

My breath hitched.

"Oh no. You think she'll pass away? What happens if she does?" I pulled Nui to a stop. "What would I need to do?" I'd been nervous about handling Tum's ordination as a novice monk, but Nui had been there to guide me through.

"Don't jinx it. Don't talk about her as if she's already dead." Nui crossed her hands in front of me, warding me off.

"I'm not jinxing it, but tell me at least who's gonna be there from your mom's side. I know about Aunt May, but who else?"

"Aunt May is married to Uncle Dech. They have two boys, Panya is fifteen, and Chaiya is thirteen, I think. That's the immediate family."

"I hope your grandma will be okay and we can all come back on the weekend. I'll call you as soon as we get there and let you know how she's doing."

Nui nodded. Though she'd been angry, she now seemed equally befuddled by the events of the afternoon.

Nui left at Asok station while I continued to Thong Lo to get ready for Chiang Rai.

I'd been so sure and excited I was going home today, but now everything had turned on its head and gotten much worse. I'd have to act like a distraught granddaughter and face a dying person I'd never met before. My nightmare had only begun.

25

NUI

I WAS WALKING INTO SOI TWENTY-ONE STILL PONDERING THE botched session when I heard a shout behind me.

"Luna, wait up." Yumi was waving wildly, her high-tops slapping the pavement as she dodged around street food carts, her big tote bag bouncing against her side. She looked like she was in a race for her life, and if she wasn't careful, she might well be in danger of getting run over by one of the mad motorcyclists hopscotching around each other at high speed in the narrow street. As if on cue, two cycles honked at her. Where I might have made a rude gesture, Yumi simply curtsied with a big smile. One guy gave her a thumbs up. I rolled my eyes but grinned anyway.

"Hey." Yumi panted as she caught up to me. She wiped her forehead with her shirt sleeve. "How did it go?"

Luna had avoided my question, but I suspected she'd told Yumi about the switch, considering how nonchalant Yumi had been at school.

"It didn't work."

"Oh, so you're...?" Yumi left the question hanging. Luna probably instructed her not to let on that she knew about us. This was ridiculous. Maybe it would be fun to string Yumi along for a bit, but I was tired of pretending and the pressure of the last weeks.

"No, I'm still Nui. I guess Luna told you?" I looked closely at Yumi. "She did, didn't she?"

"Oh!" Yumi repeated, then shrugged. "Yeah, she did. You guys are mad, but at least a lot of things make more sense to me now." She shook her head. "Seriously, I thought I was going crazy and couldn't figure out why you guys were acting so strange. What are you going to do now? I thought you needed to see your grandma?"

I flinched. "Yes, I was ready to go, but Luna couldn't project."

"What does that mean?" Yumi asked.

"Her spirit couldn't leave my body, so we couldn't do the exchange." It was a simplified explanation, but I didn't understand it much better myself.

"Oh no. So, what now?"

"We'll have to try again. I mean, that's the only thing we can do, right?"

"Hmm."

"Anyway. Any issues at school? Did anyone notice we were gone?"

"Don't know. At least the guards didn't, and none of the teachers mentioned it," Yumi said.

"Okay, good. Come on, let's go, but don't freak out when I call Luna's mom, Mom."

"Shoot. How could she not notice anything off?"

"I was lucky. She was in Chicago for most of the time. I

think Luna's dad and Luke probably thought I was just acting weird." My lips twitched.

"You *are* mad, you know that? Both you and Luna, completely mad and utterly stupid." Yumi shook her head.

"Maybe, but don't you think it's kind of cool, too?" I knew I shouldn't feel proud about it, but still.

"I'm not sure I'd call that cool. Did you really think you could just jump in and take over each other's life? How did you do it, anyway? Luna only mentioned you both had an out-of-body experience, then exchanged spirits. But how did you get out of your body in the first place?"

"It's all about focus."

"You mean like what Luna did when she unlocked herself?" Yumi painted air quotes around unlocked.

"She told you that? But yeah, just like that."

"So why didn't she focus like that this time?"

"I don't know. I mean, it doesn't always work, but I thought she'd definitely do it this time."

"What was holding her back?" Yumi asked.

"Now *that* is the million dollar question, isn't it?"

———

KHUN SUSAN WAS IN THE LIVING ROOM TALKING ON HER CELL phone. She held up a finger to signal one minute, so we went to Luna's room.

Yumi looked around.

"Isn't it weird using Luna's things? I mean, I would hate it if someone was wearing all my clothes and using my toiletries. Eww, and you are actually showering Luna's body and using the bathroom for her. That's so gross."

I shrugged. I'd gotten over my initial revulsion.

"Yeah, it was weird at the beginning, but you kind of adapt or try not to think about it too much."

Yumi shook herself.

"How can you not think about that? It's so invasive."

"Well, we had to, didn't we? And she's doing it to my body too, so I'm trying to ignore it."

"Yuck. I can't believe you guys kept this up for so long."

By the time we walked back, Khun Susan was carrying scones, pastries and some finger sandwiches from the kitchen and placing them on the dining room table set for five.

"Yumi! It's so good to see you. How have you been? Look at you, all grown up and so pretty and polished." She walked over to give Yumi a hug.

"Mrs T, how are you? It's been so long. I'm so happy to see you."

"Come, sit down. I want to hear all about you and your family," Luna's mom said. "Luna, call Luke please. I take it Nui couldn't come? How is her grandma?"

"Oh yeah, sorry. Nui is on her way to Chiang Rai."

While Yumi sat down to chat with Khun Susan, I went to Luke's door and knocked.

"Luke, Mom said you should join us. Yumi is here."

Luke poked his head out. "Where were you? Did you skip school? Mom called me and said you weren't answering your phone." He raised his eyebrows, smug at having caught me out.

"Shoot. What did you say?"

"Nothing. I didn't know where you were, but Mom was really worried. You're gonna be in trouble." Luke wiggled his head. I was glad to see he was in a better mood now I had agreed to his demand to move.

"She did?" I snagged my phone out of my back pocket. Sure enough, Luna's mom had called while we were at the temple and I'd forgotten to check my phone afterwards. *Uh oh.*

"So, where were you?"

"Luna and I had to take care of something and we needed to do it this afternoon."

Luke squinted at me.

"What do you mean, Luna and you?"

Dammit. This entire day had been a series of mishaps that left me completely out of whack. *Get with the programme, Nui!*

I rolled my eyes.

"Duh, I mean Nui and I. Forget it. Anyway, Mom said you should come." I turned to walk back to the dining room, Luke tagging along.

Yumi and Luna's mom were deep in conversation, but looked up when we walked in.

Luke waved at Yumi, then picked up a plate.

"Mom, can I just grab something and go back to my room? I'm sure you have more fun without me." He made puppy eyes at his mom.

"You mean you prefer to play video games, don't you? Go ahead and take some food."

Luke didn't need to be told twice. He grabbed a couple of sandwiches and a pastry and rushed back to his room. Khun Susan shook her head, smiling.

"He's right, it'll be quieter this way and we can talk in peace. Coffee or tea, Yumi? I have some mint tea for you, too. If I'm not mistaken, you liked that?"

"Oh thanks Mrs T, that's very kind of you to remember."

Luna's mom and Yumi continued to chat, catching each other up, while I nibbled on a scone. I was still mulling over likely reasons for Luna's blunder, but mainly I felt uneasy about having to let her handle my family crisis. The last time

I'd seen Khun Yaai was over six months ago. She wasn't as outspoken as Khun Yaa who had been looking after us since we were little. Khun Yaai was more introverted, almost spiritual, but still very kind. As far as I knew, she didn't judge anyone, but took every person at face value or at least gave them the benefit of the doubt, something I wished I could do, but never really managed.

"Luna, are you listening?" I jumped when Khun Susan touched my arm.

"What, Mom? Sorry, I was daydreaming. What is it?" The words came out more prickly than intended.

Yumi cocked an eyebrow, amused by my attitude. Luna's mom frowned instead.

"Sorry, Mom. What is it?"

"I said, isn't it great that Yumi and her dad got the apartment on the twelfth floor? So you two can go to school together from here. We should have a welcome party and introduce them to some people."

I stared at Yumi. "You didn't tell me that. When did that happen?" I tried to put a bit of enthusiasm into my voice, but I couldn't keep up with the surprises popping up today.

"I told you my dad was going to ask your mom. Have you forgotten already?" Yumi asked. A smug smile creased her lips. She was having way too much fun with my mental overload.

"That's great Yumi, really great. When are you moving in?" Now that Yumi knew our secret, it wouldn't matter anymore if I messed up her and Luna's shared history, but it still felt a bit too close for comfort to have one of Luna's allies so close by. What if Luna asked her to spy on me or asked her to interfere with her family? *To do what? Luna won't alienate her family against herself. That's silly thinking.* And yet a niggle of worry remained.

Yumi told Khun Susan about her parents' divorce and mentioned several people I assumed had been with her and Luna at school in Shanghai. I listened with half an ear, wondering when I could call Luna to see if she had any news about Khun Yaai. I had to rely on her to keep me up to date since I couldn't call my family directly.

The scone on my plate was all crumbs now, and I used a spoon to pop them into my mouth. It was like swallowing sweet sawdust. Washing it down with a sip of tea, I suddenly flashed back to the idea I'd had yesterday. What if Luna and I tried to 'remote-switch' while she was in Chiang Rai? Hadn't she said she'd found my spirit thread when she tried to push me out of her body? The first time had caused what I thought was a seizure because I wasn't aware of her attempt, and not on the same spiritual level, and the second time Luna locked herself into my body because I fought back mentally. Both times backfired as she did it without my consent. At least we assumed that was the reason. If, however, we both agreed to do this, I thought there was a strong possibility we could make it work and we wouldn't have to wait for her to come back to Bangkok. It was probably too early to call her right now, but I picked up my phone to put a reminder into the calendar for later. I was about to scroll through some notifications when I noticed the silence in the room. Luna's mom looked at me with distinct disapproval. Yumi rolled her eyes.

"Luna, put your phone away. You're being rude," Khun Susan demanded.

"Sorry, Mom. I just had to put a reminder in for something." I turned the phone upside down. "Right, what did I miss?"

"Never mind. I have to get ready and leave soon to meet Dad for a reception at the British Club. There are more pastries and sandwiches in the kitchen, so help yourself if you're still hungry, and Yumi, if you want to stay for dinner you're most welcome. Luna, you can ask Khun Bo to make some food for later or order a pizza or something, okay? Make sure Luke doesn't drink more than one coke."

"Sure, Mom. Leave it with me."

Khun Susan stood. "It was so good to see you, Yumi. Please give my regards to your dad and tell him to call me if he needs anything before the move."

"I will, thanks Mrs T." Yumi smiled up at her.

"And remind Luna, will you? She seems to be a bit distracted lately." Her lips were pressed together.

"I'm right here, Mom. Thanks for the vote of confidence. I will remember."

"By the way, you and I will have a chat later. I got a call from your school."

On that warning note, she walked off to her bedroom.

"Parents!" I groaned, but inwardly I was more concerned than I wanted to admit. Following the blog disaster, I had to build up some trust again with Luna's mom and not add oil to the fire by skipping classes.

"Your parents or Luna's?" Yumi deadpanned.

"All of them. No, actually, that's not true. Luna's parents are really nice. Mine are just... different."

Yumi snorted. "What does that mean? Different how?"

"Well..." I paused. Was there really such a big difference? Both sets had their rules, even if they varied, which was normal because of their backgrounds, but they all wanted what they thought was best for their children. Just because I liked the leeway I had with Luna's parents more didn't make my own parents worse, just... different. This time, I snorted at my own convoluted thinking.

"Never mind. So, what do you want to do? You want to stay or go? Are you still hungry?" I asked.

"Nah, I'm good. I want to hear more about this switch thing."

"I thought Luna told you everything about it?" I asked.

"She told me her perspective, but I want to hear your side and how you actually made it happen. And maybe we can figure out how to reverse it."

"If it was that easy, we'd have done it today. Though, come to think of it... I had an idea. Let's clean up and then you can tell me if it's a good idea or not. Deal?"

LUNA

I ALMOST MISSED MY STATION ON THE TRAIN RIDE BACK, STILL in shock after the afternoon's events, but I had no new insights or ideas about my block. My stomach felt like a bat cave coming to life at dusk and I had to swallow hard twice, afraid of throwing up. What was I going to do? I reminded myself that if Nui and I had switched once, there was no reason we couldn't do it again. If Ajaarn was right, it wouldn't help to focus on the failure, and right now I had to deal with the more immediate problem in front of me.

Duen was chatting with Khun Yaa in the kitchen, her carry-on bag in the hallway, ready to go. I said hello then walked into our bedroom to do a last check of my bag.

"Any news, Khun Yaa?" I asked while getting a glass of water. Joey leaned his body against my leg, demanding a head scratch as I sat down. He seemed to sense that something unusual was going on.

"No, nothing yet. Your Paa should be here shortly, then you can get going. You might hit some traffic," Khun Yaa said.

"Duen, do you have my passport?" I asked.

Her expression was one big question mark.

"Passport? You have a passport? Since when? What for? It's not like we're leaving the country."

Seriously? How could anyone not have a passport?

"Never mind. I suppose Paa has the tickets?"

As if on cue, the front door opened and a moment later, Paa stuck his head around the corner. "You girls ready? Let me get my bag and we can go."

I hugged Khun Yaa, petted Joey and followed Duen out. Khun Bpoo was waiting in the car.

Traffic was heavy, but Khun Bpoo took the toll-way to Don Muang domestic airport, so at least we were moving. Dusk was settling in and the landscape faded away into the string of red tail lights in front of us. The car felt like a cocoon, shielding us against the rest of the world.

"Nui, where were you this afternoon? Your mother said she got a call from your school. They said you skipped classes?" Paa turned around in the passenger seat, looking at me with a deep frown. The headlights behind us painted shadows over his face.

"Uh oh, busted," Duen whispered.

Oh no. I thought we'd gotten away without detection, but we must have overlooked something. It was the first time I'd skipped a class, and I didn't know all their security arrangements.

"We…" I started.

"We? Who's we? Who did you go with?" Paa asked.

"Luna and I went to the temple to pray for Khun Yaai. I'm sorry." I hoped that the location and prayers would appease him to some extent. I'd have to check with Nui if Mom had received a call, too. Nui and I had missed a few days of school recently, so both sets of parents were extra sensitive about attendance right now, especially Nui's, given the high tuition fees.

"And you had to leave school for that? Why couldn't you pray at the school's spirit house or at home? I thought we'd been clear that you needed to show some effort at school. Sneaking out is wrong. Mae has enough to deal with right now. Can't you be more considerate of your family?" Paa shook his head. He didn't sound angry, more disappointed, or perhaps distracted by the upcoming trip. He turned back to face the front. I bit my lips. Playing hooky was definitely supporting their argument for Nui's withdrawal from BIS, but I couldn't feel sorry for going to the temple. The switch was my priority, and I'd deal with any other consequences, or hopefully, Nui would have to.

Duen looked at me curiously, waiting for my answer to Paa's question. I ignored both. We were getting closer to the airport and maybe Paa would forget about it while dealing with the formalities.

Don Muang used to be the main airport in Bangkok, but had been converted to domestic and budget flights only after Suvarnabhumi opened. It looked somewhat shabby compared to the expansive spaceship design of the big airport. Khun Bpoo dropped us at the curb and waited until we got our bags, then drove off immediately to avoid the traffic wardens. Passing through the security check, I automatically looked for the priority check-in and veered left.

"Where are you going?" Duen shouted and waved at me to come back. Paa had already turned towards the end of the line for economy.

"Typical," I grumbled. Given my luck recently, we'd

probably end up at the back of the plane with me in the middle seat. Lately, I was a prime example of Murphy's law. I'd have to pretend to fall asleep so Paa wouldn't try to continue the discussion.

Waiting in the gate area, I quickly texted Channon to explain why I was going to Chiang Rai. He immediately responded with well wishes for Khun Yaai. I sighed. Our conversation was another thing looming on the horizon on my return, and I had no clue how it would turn out.

My prediction for the flight almost came true, but during boarding Duen offered to sit in the middle and give up her window seat to me. I leaned my head against the window and closed my eyes. Normally, I would fall asleep even before take-off but the day had been so hectic I just needed some quiet time to think about the consequences of the failed switch, or rather, how I was going to get myself into the mindset to make it happen. A sharp elbow to my side snapped me out of my deliberation. I glared at Duen who sat to attention and pointed at the flight attendant going through the pre-flight demonstration. Seriously? I probably could have given that demonstration myself given the number of flights I'd taken over the years. I rolled my eyes and ignored Duen's disapproval. Turning away to the window, I sank deeper in my seat and tried to tune out the chatter in the cabin. As soon as the safety demo was over, Duen started talking about *her* cooking school, and the reason for her ceding the window seat suddenly became clear. Was she always this calculating? She must have figured that seventy minutes of Paa's undivided attention was well worth the discomfort of a middle seat.

I sighed and closed my eyes again as we started pushing back from the gate. I really didn't want to be on this plane, but I was even more worried about coming back. If Nui's grandma died, would Nui backtrack on our agreement? Even if Khun Yaai recovered but Nui found out about her withdrawal from BIS, I wouldn't put it past her to renege on our deal, just like she had before. I squeezed my eyes tight, not wanting to consider what that would mean for me. I needed to make sure she didn't find out about school before we switched back. *Better make sure you do your part then.* I breathed out in a slow whoosh, then pressed my tongue firmly against the roof of my mouth, a trick Mom had taught me to avoid crying in public. If all else failed, I would need to enlist Yumi's help to convince Nui. Whatever her idea was, it had to work. *But it still guarantees nothing unless you figure out your own issues.* I bit down hard on my lip and tasted blood.

It was fully dark by the time we landed. Chiang Rai airport was tiny compared to Bangkok's main hub, and it took us all of ten minutes to walk from the gate to the arrival area.

"Uncle Dech!" Duen shouted, as soon as we exited baggage claim.

A tall, grey-haired man was waving at us with a big smile on his face. He hugged Duen.

"How's my favourite niece?" he asked Duen, but winked at me over her shoulder. He had kind brown eyes with plenty of laughter lines. Next, he shook Paa's hand and clapped him on the shoulder and in one smooth sweep pulled me into a hug. "Nong Nui, you look so grown up. It's been too long."

"Hi Uncle Dech, how are you?" He seemed to be less formal than the rest of Nui's family, which was a welcome surprise. Maybe this wouldn't be so bad after all. *Don't forget you're here for Nui's grandma, and she may soon be dead.* Even if I didn't know her, the thought was sobering.

Uncle Dech lead the way to his car in the lot right outside

the doors. The trunk of the older four-door sedan barely fit our three small bags.

"How is Khun Yaai, Uncle Dech? Are we going to the hospital right away?" Duen asked.

He glanced in the rear-view mirror.

"There's been no change and yes, we're heading there now, but just for a short time. We can only take turns visiting her in IC. May and your mom will stay overnight but I bet you're all hungry and tired."

It didn't sound like the matter of life and death I'd assumed from all the talk before. If we could leave to eat and sleep, she must be doing better than expected. It almost seemed anticlimactic after the panic yesterday.

Instead of turning into Chiang Rai town, we left the city behind and drove north. Lit billboards showed images of Doi Tung Palace. Mom and Dad had said they wanted to visit the Golden Triangle at some point, which used to be—some said it still was—the centre of the opium trade with porous borders between Laos, Myanmar and Thailand. Apparently, the Royal family had stepped in and converted the old summer residence into a sustainable coffee, flower and fruit plantation to help offset the loss from the opium trade and encourage the poor hill tribes to grow usable crops. Mom loved their macadamia nuts, especially the wasabi, sea salt and chocolate flavours. Other signs warned of approaching the border to Myanmar with several check-points beforehand. It seemed odd that Nui hadn't been to Myanmar if it was this close to her relatives' home.

Half an hour later, Uncle Dech turned into the driveway for Maechan hospital which was a miniature version of Samitivej. Everything up here was scaled down, almost like a toy town. As we walked towards the entrance, I belatedly remembered Khun Yaa's instructions.

"Paa? Did you bring the paperwork for my rabies shot? I forgot, but Khun Yaa said I should get my shot here?"

Paa nodded. "Yes, I have it. We'll check with them before we leave tonight. They probably only have the essential facilities open right now, so we can do that tomorrow."

"What happened, Nui? Why do you need rabies shots?" Uncle Dech put his hand on my shoulder.

"She didn't mind her own business, as usual," Duen said.

"Just like you, you mean?" I stuck my tongue out at her. Childish, but Duen's sanctimonious talk sometimes really grated on me.

"Girls!" Paa said. "Stop it. Remember why you're here."

Duen and I looked at each other, grimacing at the same time.

"Sorry Paa," we said in unison.

We arrived at the IC unit's waiting room. A small middle-aged woman sat with two teenage boys talking quietly while holding their hands. They all looked up when we walked in. The boys got up and wai'ed to Paa then turned to Duen and me and said hello.

"Hey guys." Duen waved but moved around them towards the woman and wai'ed. "Sawasdee kha, Auntie May. How are you?"

Aunt May smiled at Duen, got up and hugged her. She turned to me and her smile froze, her dark eyes narrowing. She turned her head left to right, then up and down as if she was measuring something.

I looked over my shoulder to see if there was someone behind me but her focus was on me.

"Aunt May?" I wai'ed, waiting for her to either hug me too or at least return the gesture. Instead, she squinted as if she couldn't focus properly and was looking through me, not at me. How weird. I elbowed Duen and raised my eyebrows in question. Duen shrugged, then went to talk to the cousins.

"Aunt May? Are you okay?" I asked again.

"Nui? Is that you?" Her voice was soft and warm, but something was bothering her.

"Yes, of course." I wasn't sure what she was getting at.

"But your aura…" Aunt May whispered.

27

NUI

YUMI SAT ON THE EASY CHAIR AND PULLED UP HER FEET.

"So, tell me, what does it feel like to be out of your body?"

"It's …" I contemplated how to best explain it. "You know those safety ropes astronauts use when they leave their space station so they don't float away?"

"You mean like an umbilical cord?" Yumi asked.

"Exactly. It feels like your body is connected to a safety line that's hooked into an energy stream, so when your spirit leaves your body, you float along that line and enter a different dimension."

"Wow. But how do you then switch over? I mean, it's not like you could cut the cord and then reconnect? Wouldn't that kill you?" Yumi leaned forward.

"No, it's not like that. I'm not sure how it works, but Luna and I linked the cords somehow, and that's how we slipped into each other's body." I shrugged. That was as visual as I could make it. Yumi massaged her neck.

"Hmm, but why exactly did you want to be Luna? How did you guys come up with this crazy idea?"

I swivelled back and forth on the desk chair.

"What did Luna tell you about it?"

"Nothing really. She only said she was tired of moving all the time and wanted to know how it feels to have a settled family. And you? I suppose you wanted the opposite?"

"Pretty much. I mean, what options do I really have as me? No one in my family has ever gone anywhere outside of Thailand and they are all perfectly content to stay where they are. But I want more."

"Can you handle more?" Yumi asked point blank.

I hesitated, then nodded.

"I think I can, or at least I could learn. I mean you guys had to get used to it, didn't you?"

"Not really. That's what we grew up with, so for us it was normal. What I don't get is why you think Luna's life is so much better? Seems to me that both of you had this 'grass is greener' kind of thing going on, huh?"

Yumi had a way of stating issues that made them sound banal. I cringed.

"I suppose. But look at you. You could have gone with your mom to Japan and instead you choose to go with your dad. At least you had an option. Luna and I simply created our options."

"You think that decision was easy? Or that it was great that my parents split up so I could have a choice?" Yumi's tone sharpened.

Put that way, it was a stupid comment from me.

"Sorry. No, of course, I didn't mean it that way. But even

if your parents were still together you'd still be moving a lot, wouldn't you? And look how many languages you speak."

"So what? If you want to learn one or ten languages, there's nothing standing in your way, is there?"

"I guess not," I mumbled, feeling chastised.

"You really thought right from the start that you would fully exchange your lives? I mean, you were willing to give up your families, just like that, on the off chance you'd like the other side better? You are insane!" Yumi said.

"Well, not exactly. I guess we thought it would be a sort of trial run, but then all those things happened and we never got the chance to switch back and then…" I trailed off.

"And then you refused to switch, you mean?" Ouch. Yumi was killing me with her stark assessment. Had Luna put her up to this?

"I… I… Well, I guess we pushed it further than planned. But it wasn't just me. At first Luna wanted to extend too. She had this thing about Channon and her dog. But then everything happened at once and Luna's mom had to go to Chicago and things just spiralled out of control. And now we have a problem reversing it." I suddenly felt teary-eyed and grabbed a tissue from my desk.

Yumi shook her head and muttered to herself, "Mad, just completely mad." She cleared her throat. "How are you going to fix it? I take it you're both now ready to switch back?"

"Did Luna tell you how she tried to force me from her body?"

"You mean when she locked herself in? Yeah, I know. What are you saying? You want to force her?" Yumi looked horrified.

"No, no, of course not. I know that won't work anyway. But I thought that maybe we don't have to be in the same room, and we could try to switch remotely. I mean, it's not like our spirits can't move. What do you think?" I asked.

Yumi opened her mouth then closed it again without speaking. She looked up at the ceiling, around the room, and finally back at me.

"Hmm, maybe. Are you willing to take the risk?"

"Why would it be any more risky than sitting in the same room?"

"Oh, I don't know. What about interferences and other spirits? What do you really know about all this?" Why was Yumi so reluctant about the idea? I thought it was perfectly logical. We just had to…

A knock on the door interrupted my train of thought. Khun Susan stepped in, dressed in an emerald green cocktail dress with matching sandals, her blond hair tucked into a French twist.

"Girls, I'm off. Luna, remember what I said about Luke. We should be back by nine or so."

"You look beautiful, Mrs T. Have a good time." Yumi walked up to hug Khun Susan.

"Thank you, my dear. See, your green shirt inspired me. Come back soon." She closed the door behind her.

Yumi started pacing.

"Where were we? You really think you can make this work remotely?"

I shrugged.

"What have we got to lose?"

"Eh, maybe your lives?" Yumi said, as if it was obvious. "Or what about both of you getting locked in or not re-entering a body at all? What do I know?"

"Oh, come on, don't be so dramatic Yumi. If we switched once, there's no reason for us to not do it again. I thought you wanted us to switch back?"

"I do, and I think it's the right thing. Except, I also think you never can go back to what was before. You're both coming from a completely different standpoint now."

"Don't say that! I don't believe that. We're still both us and we *can* and will go back. Just a matter of when."

"And then what? You're back in your old place and probably even more angry at not having options, right? And you'll resent your family even more. Yeah, I can see that happening."

"I won't! I love my family. And I'll figure out something about studying and all that. There's got to be a way."

I jumped up, suddenly eager to move, then stopped in my tracks when what I'd just said sank in. Without recognising Yumi's subtle reverse psychology tactic, I'd argued myself into a full commitment against my previous wishes. I glared at her, shocked how that was even possible. Yumi winked.

28

LUNA

MY AURA? MY MOUTH WENT DRY AND HEAT FLARED through my body. I stood, rooted, with my hands clenched at my side. A low buzz sounded in my ears and I could feel beads of sweat trickling down my temple. Oh God, what now? A chaotic jumble of panic, confusion and scepticism crashed through my head. I had heard of auras, but of all complications possible with this visit, this had been nowhere on my list. *Please, please let this just be a fluke.* Nui and I had fooled everyone with our appearances, but if someone could read the distinctive energy field surrounding a person, it would be hard to explain, especially if Nui's and mine were completely different. My silence went on too long. Aunt May stepped forward and touched my arm, jerking my attention back to her.

"Nui?" she asked.

"My aura? I'm not sure what you mean, Aunt May. What about it?" I croaked.

She took my hands in hers.

"Yes, your aura. It used to be much darker, and I was really worried about you, but now …" She scanned my body again, or rather the field that no one but her could see. I certainly wasn't aware of what I was transmitting.

"You seem lighter now, more at ease. It's wonderful. Like a veil has lifted." Aunt May smiled approvingly. "What did you do?"

"I am? Do? Eh, nothing. I don't know." I stumbled over my words and definitely didn't feel at ease.

Aunt May nodded. "It's like you're a new person and you're seeing life more positively. Are you?"

The conversation felt surreal.

"I… I don't know. Honestly. What do the colours mean?" I asked, curious despite myself, but mostly to distract her from trying to dig into the reason for the change. "I mean, what was it before?"

I wasn't keen to learn about my aura, even if Aunt May seemed convinced that it was optimistic. Knowing Nui's aura, however, might give me a clue about her real motivation and why she'd been reluctant to resume her own life.

"Well, your base layer is nearly the same, but your astral layer is much brighter now. It was almost muddy before, but it looks like you cleared that up."

"I did?"

Aunt May nodded. "Yes, I was worried about you. It was like you were angry at the world or perhaps jealous. But let's not talk about the past. I am so happy you made an effort to overcome this."

I blinked as if that could clear the confusion in my head.

Aunt May laughed and hugged me. "I'm sorry. I know this can be overwhelming."

"Ah, good, you're here." Mae walked into the room,

interrupting my talk with Aunt May. *Phew, good timing.* I actually felt relieved to see Mae.

"Mae, how's Khun Yaai?" Duen asked. "Can we see her?"

Mae nodded. "Go in with Paa. You can visit for ten minutes but ask the nurse for a mask, and you have to disinfect your hands."

Duen walked off with Paa, and Mae turned to me. I was shocked when I saw her tired face. Her mouth had brackets of deep lines, and her eyes looked almost purplish from exhaustion. She looked as if she'd aged ten years since yesterday.

"Mae, are you okay?"

She sat down heavily in a chair the boys had vacated. Aunt May dropped my hands and went to sit next to her, putting her arm around Mae's shoulder. Mae looked at her gratefully, but I could see tears rolling down her face. My eyes teared up in sympathy, imagining what it must feel like to lose your mother. I shuddered. This hit too close to home as my mom was lost to me too right now. At least I knew, or I had to believe, that I would get her back.

Mae looked up at me and sighed. "What did you do this afternoon, Nui? The school called." She seemed too drained to be angry.

I wiped my eyes. "We went to the temple to pray for Khun Yaai."

It wasn't the full story, but I had said a prayer at the spirit house so it wasn't a complete lie.

She nodded as if it made perfect sense.

"Thank you. But don't do it again, you hear? You can't skip school like that."

Phew, if that was the entire reprimand, I would get off easy this time. I nodded.

Duen and Paa came back a few minutes later and Aunt May got up.

"Nui, come, I'll take you in." She grabbed my arm and walked me to the nurses' station to get the mask and disinfectant. "I'll stay here overnight, but we'll talk more about the colours and their meaning later. I've never seen such a drastic change in just a few months' time. I want to know what you did." She smiled.

Uh oh, how was I going to explain *that?*

29

NUI

How had Yumi backed me into a corner with just a few questions when I'd been waffling around for so long to make the right decision? She returned to her chair, watching me while I paced the bedroom.

"You know, Nui, if you switch back with Luna I might be able to help you get to the US, at least for a while. A friend of mine did it and she didn't have any family there either, or money and stuff."

I stopped in my tracks and turned to her.

"You do? How?"

"I'll tell you after you switch. Deal?"

"You're just saying that, aren't you? Why should I believe you?" It sounded like a trick to me, even though I'd already promised to work on the reversal.

"Why would I lie to you? I've got nothing to gain or lose either way. I just thought it might make it easier for you if you know there are options." She shrugged. "But if you don't want to know, it's no skin off my nose."

"Of course I want to know! Tell me."

"Why don't you talk with Luna first? I thought you wanted to set up a remote switch?"

I snorted, pretty sure Yumi was just messing with me, but then again, she'd never given me reason to think that way.

"Fine. Be that way. I'll text her. They should be in Chiang Rai by now."

I waited for the checkmark that the message had gone through. Nothing happened. Maybe there was a delay with their flight.

"Hmm, it's not going through. I might have to call the house directly, but then I don't know how we're going to time the switch. She can hardly do it in the kitchen with everyone there." I almost smiled at the image of Uncle Dech, Aunt May and the boys looking at Luna sitting on the kitchen floor humming along to Ajaarn's mantras. "I'll have to try later."

Yumi stood up.

"Maybe I should get going. It's getting late."

"Why? Do you have to be somewhere? You can tell me about your idea while I wait for Luna. Are you hungry? Want some pizza? Luke is always up for that."

Yumi checked her phone, then nodded. "Sure, why not?"

"Can I ask *you* a question?"

Yumi raised her eyebrows. "Sure, what?"

"I'm kind of curious about you and Channon. What's going on there?"

My question felt a bit like payback for her earlier harsh assessment of my motivation, but if I'd intended to make her uncomfortable, I again underestimated Yumi.

"Channon? Yeah, he's cute and really nice. I like him. Why?"

"Well, I'm just curious because you know he and Luna have been dating."

"I suppose. If you can call it dating when she's pretending to be someone else. That's hardly fair to Channon, is it? I mean Luna lied to him and now she wants him to forget that and accept her as herself. I think it's actually pretty mean, but don't worry, I'll tell her that myself. I'm not gossiping about her," she said.

"That's all good and fine, but what do you want?" I would not let Yumi off that easily.

"You mean, do I want to get to know him better? Sure, he's very attractive and nice, but he needs to decide first whether he wants Luna in your package or hers or not at all. I bet he hasn't thought it through yet and I'm not getting in the way of that."

I bit my lip. Yumi was right. Luna had gotten herself into a real mess about Channon. I had zero interest in him as a boyfriend, so whether or not he found me physically attractive didn't matter after the switch.

Yumi picked up her thread. "In fairness, I can't blame him for his ambiguity. If Luna hadn't known so many facts from our time in Shanghai I probably wouldn't have believed her either even though you guys were acting strangely. Honestly though, could you imagine dating the same person in a different body? That's just beyond."

Yumi was very accepting of the story Luna and I had thrown at her. I wondered how I would have reacted in her place. Probably would've run fast and far.

Yumi looked at me. "Did it occur to you they might kiss and even do more, but it's actually your lips and your body?"

"*What?!* Did Luna tell you that? She promised she wouldn't!" I felt my entire face pucker up instantly as if I'd bitten into a sour lemon. Actually, Luna had only promised not to sleep with Channon, but we never talked about kissing. "That is so disgusting. She wouldn't do that, would she?" Just imagining meeting Channon afterwards, knowing he'd kissed my lips without me having any memory of it was beyond grotesque.

Yumi shrugged. "I don't know. You're saying that has never crossed your mind?"

"No, it hasn't." I tried to sound certain, but why did Yumi have to put those ideas in my head?

"I don't believe you," she said.

"Even if I did what was I supposed to do about it? Yes, we talked about it at one point, but…"

"But what?"

"I mean, how was I supposed to stop her? Do you really think she'd use my body for… that?" I didn't even want to think about it, much less talk about it. If Luna had broken her promise, the implications were mind-boggling and go way beyond any repercussions from the troubles we had created so far. I shivered.

"You guys really didn't think this through, did you?" Yumi shook her head almost in pity at our naivete. "I mean, fine, I get the switch was more or less accidental at first, but I can't believe you guys extended it. Seriously, what were you thinking?"

Obviously we weren't, otherwise all those stupid mistakes wouldn't have happened afterwards. If I told Yumi about the blog and passport flag, it would only confirm her judgment. She might also feel differently about helping me if she found out I was the reason the family would move again soon, not giving her much time to resume her friendship with Luna. Best to keep my mouth shut.

I checked the phone again. The message still hadn't gone through.

"You know, Yumi, you really seem to have your act together. Is nothing bothering you?" I felt petty poking her, but I was also genuinely curious about how she was so unflappable.

"You think? Let's just say I learned the hard way not to let the small stuff bother me." Yumi turned her hands palms up and lifted her arms towards me, a reminder of her own struggles.

I flinched, recalling the scars on her forearms.

"Do you ever talk about that?" I asked.

"Not anymore. There's no point in repeating stuff when all it does is make you feel bad. You only extend the hurt and build it up to something bigger," she said, clearly having given it a lot of thought.

"Wow. I wish I could do that." I sighed.

"You could if you wanted to. Just a matter of adjusting your mindset. If you hadn't been so bloody focused on escaping Bangkok, you might have found a perfectly legit way to do it, instead of getting into this mess."

"Man, are you a therapist or something?" The mood was getting far too heavy for me, or maybe it just cut too close to home.

"Hardly. Just allowing myself to look for solutions instead of fixating on the problem." Yumi shrugged. "Anyway, let's talk about something else and let's order that pizza."

I looked at my phone again, but nothing from Luna yet.

"Let me check with Luke and I'll tell Khun Bo she can go home. Any preference?"

Yumi shook her head. "I'm good with anything."

When I returned, Yumi was scrolling on her phone.

"Does this building allow pets?"

"Yeah, I think so. I've seen some dogs in the elevator. Why?"

"Maybe Dad will let me adopt LaTe. Did you see his picture? Isn't he the cutest?"

"Oh man, not you too. Why do all of Channon's groupies end up with a dog?"

Yumi laughed.

"Well, they are both very cute. Maybe I can adopt Channon too." She grinned.

30

LUNA

MY FEET WOULDN'T BUDGE. AUNT MAY GRABBED MY ARM, tugging me over the threshold into Khun Yaai's ICU room.

"What is it, Nui? Come on."

How could I explain the barrage of emotions crashing through me?

Until now, Khun Yaai had been a nonentity to me, someone I'd heard of but didn't have any particular feelings or opinions about. Now I was looking at a frail older lady tucked under a sheet, her arms resting on top, hooked up to multiple lines with the corresponding monitors beeping steadily around. Suddenly, she was a real person, not just a figure in a story. The room was chilly with the air conditioning at full blast. The air behind my mask felt steamy in contrast. I shivered from the cold as much as the realisation of how wrong this situation was.

What the heck am I doing here? This is Nui's grandma. I'm just an impostor.

Aunt May tugged again, and I reluctantly shuffled further into the room, standing behind as she bent down to kiss her mother on the forehead through her mask. She turned to me and smiled.

"Come Nui, say hello to your grandma."

Not sure what else to do I wai'ed, the universal Thai gesture that was appropriate anytime, anywhere. Aunt May stroked Khun Yaai's hand, but there was no reaction. Khun Yaai seemed even smaller than Khun Yaa, but it was difficult to judge while she was lying down. Her skin had a greyish tinge, matching her thin braid of hair on the pillow.

I don't want to be here. I'm not supposed to be here. The thoughts kept repeating in my head. And yet, I had no other option than to deal with it. My eyes filled with tears. Sorry for Khun Yaai and myself.

"You can touch and speak to her, Nui. She can probably hear you on some level," Aunt May said.

I walked around the bed and sat down on a stool, tentatively stretching my hand towards Khun Yaai's. Her skin felt dry, papery, and cool. What was I supposed to say to a relative I'd never met?

"Khun Yaai, it's Nui. We just flew up this afternoon to see you. I hope you get better soon."

"Why don't you catch her up on what you have been doing, Nui? You haven't talked with each other in a while," Aunt May suggested. She seemed super composed, the complete opposite of Mae. How would I react if my mom was close to dying? I shuddered, tears finally spilling over. I looked around for a tissue but didn't see a box. Instead, I sniffed and used a sleeve to wipe my eyes.

"I don't know what to say. There's really nothing special going on."

"It doesn't have to be special, Nui, just talk. It's good for her to hear your voice."

"Oh. Well, today, we were at the temple. I mean my friend Luna and I, and we were praying for you, Khun Yaai. Luna and I go to the same school in Bangkok. She's from America and we have become friends. We talked to Ajaarn Anurak who was our mediation instructor. Oh, you probably don't know, but Luna and I have been taking meditation classes at the temple since December and it's really amazing."

Aunt May nodded and smiled.

"And then …" Did I really want to bring up our out-of-body experiences? It probably wasn't smart to volunteer this to Nui's family, but Khun Yaa had said that both Khun Yaai and Aunt May had had them too, so maybe they knew more about this than Ajaarn.

"And then what, Nui?" Aunt May prompted me.

"Well, something strange happened. Luna and I had out-of-body experiences. Khun Yaa said I could ask you about this."

"You did, Nui? How did it feel?" Aunt May asked. "Ahh, so this is how your aura changed?"

I shrugged.

Aunt May tilted her head from side to side, observing me with the same intense focus as when she first saw me.

"Hmm…" she hummed under her breath.

Don't ask, Luna. You probably don't want to know what Aunt May means by that.

I glanced back at Khun Yaai. Who knew what else Aunt May could detect with her special skills?

"So you *and* your friend projected your spirits? You mean, at the same time?"

Uh oh! I should slap myself for having brought up the subject. *Distract!*

"Can you read everyone's aura, Aunt May?" I stole a quick glance at her. She still had that intense look on her face, but then relaxed into a smile once more.

"I believe I can for most people. It was something that developed over time, and like you I meditate regularly."

"What does it mean?" I asked.

"You mean the colours? They have different meanings and usually there are multiple colours, an inner aura and several outer layers," she said.

"Do you always see them? I mean, can you turn it on and off?"

She laughed. "It's not like that. The energy field is always there, of course, but I have to focus in a certain way to see it. And that's a good thing. Imagine you had to walk around all those colours all the time; it would be quite confusing."

"Hmm." I absently stroked Khun Yaai's hand and debated if I should continue to ask questions or let the subject go at least as far as my own aura was concerned.

"Can you see Khun Yaai's aura?" I side tracked.

Aunt May looked slightly to the left of Khun Yaai.

"Hers is changing quite rapidly now. It's mainly white but has been turning more silvery over the past day. I think she is getting closer to making her transition."

I peeked at Aunt May.

"Aren't you sad?" Her calm attitude was extraordinary. I didn't think I would be this poised in the same situation.

"You mean, will I miss her?" Aunt May asked. "Of course I will, but if she decides it's time to go, then I need to accept that."

"You think she has? I mean, decided to go?" If that was

true, it was actually comforting to know that she had the choice.

Khun May stroked Khun Yaai's cheek.

"Maybe she feels she has fulfilled her life's purpose. She certainly has made a lot of difference in many people's lives."

I nodded, pretending to understand. A movement under my hand had me jerk away as if I'd touched a hot plate. The twitch had been slight. Had I imagined it? I waited for another sign, but the hand remained still.

"I think she just moved," I said to Aunt May.

She nodded. "She's been doing that from time to time."

Aunt May brushed back a stray hair from Khun Yaai's forehead, then turned to me.

"I think it's time for you to leave, Nui. Go home, eat, and get some rest."

Relieved, I stood up. "Good bye Khun Yaai. I'll see you tomorrow." I wai'ed again, even if she couldn't see me.

Aunt May put her arm around my shoulder and together we walked out. Her presence was soothing, yet I felt anxious about our conversation. Aunt May seemed to be far more intuitive than normal, and I couldn't afford for her to become suspicious.

31

NUI

I INSISTED ON EATING IN THE DINING ROOM. KHUN YAA always said that watching TV while eating was disrespectful to the cook and food, and though it was only Yumi, Luke and myself, old habits were hard to break. Khun Susan had a similar attitude and didn't allow us to use our phones during meals, a rule I had broken that afternoon. Waiting for Luna's call would have been the perfect time to ask Yumi about her idea, but Luke's presence prevented that.

"Did Luna tell you we're moving again?" Luke asked Yumi.

"Luke! Shut up." I tried to punch his arm, but he ducked out of reach.

"What? It's not a secret, is it?" Luke asked, eyes wide open with fake innocence. He must have known this wasn't something to be discussed outside the family until the parents made the final decision. Was he still retaliating for my mistake that made the move necessary?

"You're moving again? Already?" Yumi sat back, scrunching her nose. "Why?"

"Just ask, Luna." Luke made a face. "It's her fault."

"Luke, damnit it. Shut up. You're such an idiot!" I was seriously pissed off at him. Why did he have to bring this up now?

"What's going on, Nu… I mean Luna?" Yumi asked.

Luke looked at her, his eyebrows pulled together.

"What's going on? Why are you all mixing up names? You're nuts. I'm out of here." He stood and took his plate to the kitchen.

Great, first he drops a bomb and then lets me handle the explosion.

I concentrated on my slice of pizza as if it was the most interesting thing in the world but I could feel Yumi's eyes on me.

"What did you do? Does Luna know about this?" Yumi lowered her voice to a hiss.

I checked the door to make sure Luke wasn't eavesdropping. I tried to swallow my pizza, but coughed when crumbs got stuck in my throat. Yumi refilled my water glass and pushed it closer.

"You didn't tell her, did you?" Yumi shook her head. "Jeez, Nui what the heck are you doing? What happened and why would they move again so soon?" She crossed her arms, giving me a teacher's look of reprimand.

"When was I supposed to tell her? I only found out yesterday myself."

"But why? What did Luke mean by 'it's your fault'? What did you do? It can't be her dad's job. They've only been here for six months." Yumi persisted. Understandably it would be disappointing for Yumi to renew her friendship with Luna only to be left behind again, but I couldn't tell her the real reason since I wasn't sure if Luna had mentioned the blog or the police investigation.

"Yes, no, well, indirectly. It's complicated Yumi. It's also about Luna's Aunt Jane in Chicago. She's sick, you know?"

Yumi frowned. "That's not much of an answer—yes, no or indirectly. What is it?"

I collected the plates to give myself time to think.

"I really can't talk about it. Luke was wrong to mention it. It's a family thing, but I have to speak to Luna first and she needs to decide if she wants to tell you. Besides, it's not even one hundred percent certain yet."

My stomach clenched. I knew I was taking the coward's way out. Not only was I the cause for the premature departure, but to bounce over the explanation to Luna who didn't even know about it was weak and even mean. I suddenly felt a big lump in my throat and tears threatened. Would there be any way to salvage my friendship with Luna or Yumi once we switched back? Even if I hadn't meant for everything to go so wrong, the girls would probably not see it that way. What if Yumi refused to help me? Her loyalty would definitely be to Luna and not to me. I needed to convince her to give me the information before we made the switch just in case.

"Come on, let's go back to my room and you can tell me about your idea."

Yumi stayed silent as we carried the plates and pizza box to the kitchen, but I could almost hear her brain whirling through different scenarios. My phone was charging on my desk and I finally saw a missed call from Luna. I froze, a shot of dread piercing through me. *Did something happen to Khun Yaai?* I had been waiting for Luna to call to talk about the remote switch, but I also needed to know what Yumi had in mind. *Five minutes won't make a difference now, will it? Just talk to Yumi first and then call Luna.* I put the phone face down, pretending that nothing had come in.

"So, what did you have in mind?" I asked.

Yumi sat in the easy chair with her legs curled under her.

"Nothing from Luna?" she asked.

"Not yet." I said. I had become a pro at lying, not something to be proud of. If Khun Yaa knew, I'd be on house arrest for the rest of the year. I cleared my throat.

"Your idea?"

"Okay, so have you ever heard of a J-1 visa?"

"I don't think so. What's that?"

"It's an international student exchange programme. Foreign students can legally study at an American High school for one year, and while there, a local family hosts them. They have to apply through a sponsor company that provides the paperwork to apply for the visa."

My mouth dropped open. Why hadn't I heard about this? *Maybe because you weren't really looking, but took the easy way out with the switch. Easy? Ha.*

"I know about this because when Leslie moved from Shanghai to San Francisco, her family agreed to host one of our classmates from China. She's there right now doing year eleven," Yumi said. She'd mentioned Leslie before, but I'd forgotten the connection and it didn't matter.

"And that works for any nationality?" I felt a sharp jolt of excitement. If I could do this, I wouldn't have to worry about housing or visas and all the other stuff. And just as important, I could go as myself and whatever credits I got there would be mine. I might even revive my blog. My imagination went wild, coming up with more and more ideas for why this could be the ideal scenario.

"… are you listening?" Yumi almost shouted to get my attention.

"Oops, sorry, I was daydreaming."

"Well, don't go celebrating just yet, but like I said, it's definitely a possibility. I don't see why this couldn't work for you too. I guess you'd only have to convince your parents to allow you to go. Your grades need to be of a certain level, but otherwise I'm pretty sure BIS would support it too."

"Oh, my God. That would be so fantastic."

"Well, now you know and you can look into it yourself. I can also ask Dad if there's anyone at the Embassy who has more information," she offered, then got up. "Anyway, I better go. And you should try to reach Luna again. You have to be back in your own body before you can apply you know."

"Yumi, thank you soooo much. This is really awesome. I'll definitely look it up and I'll call Luna asap."

"You better tell her about the move. She has a right to know," Yumi said with a touch of threat.

Ouch. She was right, but I was almost vibrating with excitement to find out more about the J-1 visa.

As soon as Yumi left, I raced back to my room to pick up the phone. *Come on Luna, answer the damn phone. I have things to do and places to go.* I grinned at the silly phrase until I remembered Luna's reason for being in Chiang Rai. My smile shrivelled.

3 2

LUNA

THE WAITING ROOM WAS CROWDED AND NUI'S BROTHERS weren't even there yet. I was the only one who didn't belong.

When Aunt May and I walked in, Uncle Dech said, "Right, everyone here? Shall we get going?"

Aunt May hugged her boys while Mae did the same to Duen and me. I tried not to act surprised at her unexpected show of affection and squeezed her back, understanding she needed every bit of support.

In the parking lot, I hung back to call Nui, but it went to voicemail. Strange. I expected her to be home at this hour. I didn't have time to try again as the others were already piling into Uncle Dech's car. Paa and Uncle Dech sat in front with us four cousins squished together in back. I hadn't spoken to Panya and Chaiya aside from hello, but Duen kept up a steady conversation with them. The three seemed to be in regular touch though Nui had never mentioned them before. The headlights showed empty roads lined by green fields with an occasional road sign lit up. There were no houses or villages; it was basically the middle of nowhere. It felt like a world removed from the nonstop hustle of Bangkok and was actually calming after the upsetting day I'd had. We went directly into the Golden Triangle towards the confluence of the Mekong and Ruak Rivers, separating Thailand, Laos, and Myanmar. It would have been great to explore the province with my family rather than dealing with my current task. Thankfully, the drive took only thirty minutes; I'd twisted myself into an uncomfortable position to make room for the others.

We passed through a village street lined with small open stall restaurants, 7/11 stores and some souvenir shops with barely a soul in sight. It looked like there wasn't much to do after dark in this rural setting and the places closed up early for the night. Uncle Dech turned left uphill and pulled into a driveway. The house stood on stilts like a traditional Thai teak home but was built of bricks. It appeared to lean into the rock wall behind, hopefully just an illusion. A wooden staircase led up to a covered veranda where a strange spotlight created pockets of deep shadows behind the wooden beams. At the top, I turned around and gasped. In front of me, a giant golden Buddha statue loomed over the small village, brightly lit against the night sky.

"I know. It still surprises me every single day. You'd think by now I would have gotten used to it." Uncle Dech chuckled behind me.

"Oh, I forgot about the Buddha on the ship. We need to toss some coins for Khun Yaai for good luck. Can we do that tomorrow?" Duen asked as she brushed by me. Uncle Dech shrugged, then ushered us inside.

The house was larger than I expected. Whitewashed walls stood in stark contrast to the dark wooden floor. I had expected the space to be divided into smaller rooms like in Nui's house, and the open living-dining-kitchen layout surprised me.

"Right, girls, you'll take Chaiya's room at the end of the hall. Narong, you and Lamai have Panya's room and the boys will sleep on the daybed in the living room. Krit can use Khun Yaai's room when he gets here. Welcome to Ban Sop Ruak."

Narong and Lamai? It was weird to hear Paa's and Mae's real names for the first time, on top of all the other names I had to remember. The house would become completely crammed with so many people staying here.

Our room was small with a single twin bed, a dresser, and a small wardrobe. The rock behind the house was almost close enough to touch. An air mattress leaned against the window. Once that was on the floor, there was hardly any room to step. I sighed. At least we didn't have to use Khun Yaai's room. That would have been too creepy. The scene in the hospital was still fresh in my mind. Would Khun Yaai be able to come back home? I crossed my fingers for a second, as if that would make a difference.

"Do you want the bed or the mattress?" Duen asked. "We can put one of our bags on the dresser, then it should work."

"Up to you." The mattress actually looked softer than the bed.

"I'll take the bed tonight and we can switch tomorrow if we're staying." Duen was practical, as always. "Let's eat. I'm starving."

Uncle Dech and the boys had pulled out covered bowls from the fridge and set the table. A wok was on the stove and Duen immediately went over to help.

I sat down next to Paa at the dining table. He was sipping a glass of beer.

"When you were with Khun Yaai, I spoke to the staff and you can get the rabies shot tomorrow morning. Just remind me," Paa said.

"Okay, thanks."

Uncle Dech sat with us.

In the background, Duen bossed the boys around while preparing our food. A good practise session for her own cooking school, no doubt. I almost felt sorry for Nui that it would come at her expense with the withdrawal from BIS. *Well, she was willing to sacrifice your life for her cause. I suppose this is called poetic justice.* While justified, the thought left a bitter taste in my mouth.

"Any word from Krit and Tum yet?" Uncle Dech asked.

"Tum will fly up tomorrow. If I can borrow your car, I'll pick him up in Chiang Rai. I'm still waiting to hear from Krit. I hope he'll be on the same flight. I don't want Tum to fly by himself. He's too young and has never travelled on his own." Paa took a sip.

Has anyone ever travelled in this family? Where did these snide thoughts come from? Yes, I was tired and hungry and unsettled by the hospital visit, but the family was managing difficult circumstances that had nothing to do with my own convoluted situation and I should cut them some slack.

Duen and the boys brought over bowls and platters of food. It smelled delicious and no matter how simple, Thai food was always mouth-watering.

The conversation was lively, but I was in my little mind bubble going over Aunt May's comments. I'd have to look up auras on my phone after I'd talked to Nui and Channon. I had forgotten to let the animal hospital know about this emergency trip and they expected me tomorrow afternoon for a shift. I also wanted to reassure Channon that I hadn't run away from our conversation, uncomfortable as it might have been, though there wasn't much I could tell him given the uncertainty of our switch back. I just didn't want to give the impression I was avoiding him.

After dinner clean up, I finally checked my phone. For a moment, I was confused there were no messages until I noticed I didn't have any reception.

"Uncle Dech? Do you have Wi-Fi here?" He and Paa were finishing their beers at the kitchen table.

"Panya, can you give Nui the log in and show her where the best spot is?" Uncle Dech called to his son.

"Wi-Fi really sucks up here," Panya whispered as he motioned me out the front door. "Give me your phone and I'll connect you. Your best spot is here on the sala. The rock behind us blocks too much of the signal. It's much better down in the village. You can sit over there." He pointed to the bench on the side, which looked comfortable enough with some cushions and even a folded blanket.

"Thanks, Panya. I just have to check in with some friends."

He nodded and walked back inside.

It was chilly on the sala. Night time in Northern Thailand was several degrees below Bangkok's winter temperatures. I pulled the blanket around my shoulders, but still shivered. At least I'd brought my favourite pashmina, the one I always travelled with. Mom had bought it for me in Mumbai during a visit. Duen thought it was a gift from Luna, but I was definitely going to take it back home with me. The only good thing about the cold was that there were no mosquitos trying to eat me alive.

My phone chirped with messages finally coming through. Nui had texted several times, and I owed her an update on her grandmother. I replied saying I was free to talk. My eyes were drawn back to the bright lights of the giant Buddha. The golden statue appeared to be floating over the village. Kind of mesmerising—otherworldly.

"Come on, Nui, where are you?" I quickly texted Channon to say I'd arrived in Chiang Rai and to ask him to inform the shelter of my schedule change. I knew texting was a cop-out, but I felt strangely ambivalent about talking to him about our relationship right now. It had to take a backseat to all the other stuff going on, and my priority was getting home. Besides, what could I tell him? That I was still Luna in Nui's body and that the switch hadn't worked because of me? Deep down, I knew if I had to acknowledge my failure to him it would make it all too real, and for now I had to keep a flame of hope alive that everything would work out with the switch back and Channon.

Shivering, I was just about to give up when my phone finally rang.

"Hey Luna." Nui sounded awfully chipper, considering I was visiting *her* dying grandmother.

"Hey. Why didn't you tell me it's Antarctica up north? I should have brought a puffer jacket." I complained, still cranky and unsettled.

"Don't be so dramatic. During the day, you'll be sweating again. How's Khun Yaai?" Nui asked.

"I honestly don't know. I got to see her for a few minutes, but she was either unconscious or sleeping, and hooked up to monitors, so I'm not really sure what that means, but Aunt May said her aura was changing."

"What's that supposed to mean?"

"Aunt May said she thinks Khun Yaai is ready to make her transition soon."

Nui groaned.

"That is sooo Aunt May. I'm not sure I believe her."

"I think she might be right. You know what she said to me when I first met her?"

"What?"

"She said my aura colours had completely changed and gone from dark to light. She said it was like I was a different person. How would she have picked up on that if it wasn't real?"

Nui sighed dramatically.

"Don't believe everything she says, okay?" Nui sounded more peeved than sure.

"Well, she said it was a wonderful change, and she wants to know what I did."

"Whatever. Don't tell her anything; just pretend you know nothing about it," Nui said.

"I don't, but I'm curious. Aren't you? I want to know why she said my colour now is better than before." It was petty to rub in that comment, but how could Nui completely ignore her aunt's observation?

"Not sure it means anything anyway." Nui sounded like she either didn't care or she was trying to get off the subject. Given all the lying and deception of the past weeks both Nui and I probably shouldn't examine either of our auras too closely.

"Don't you think it's kind of eerie that she'd pick up on something like that? Means there's something to all that vibrational stuff, after all."

"I'd say we've proven that beyond a doubt. We could probably teach her a thing or two about spirit stuff." Nui sniggered, then sobered. "Where are you now?"

"At your aunt's place. We just finished dinner and I had to come out to the sala to get reception. It's hit or miss up here."

"Yeah, I know. So listen, I was thinking. Remember how

you said you could reach my spirit thread when you were trying to force me out of your body?" Nui asked.

I flinched. That wasn't something I cared to remember.

"What about it?" I tried for a casual tone but could hear the strain in my voice.

"Relax, I'm not rehashing that, but think about it. If you could reach me while you were somewhere else, what do you think are the chances we could do a remote switch? I mean, you in Chiang Rai and me in Bangkok? I think you were right and we don't have to be in the same room. We just have to be out-of-body at the same time."

"You want to risk *that*?" How could Nui even suggest that?

"It can't be more of a risk than when we're together, can it?"

"I don't know. But, what if my paralysis wasn't just because you pushed back? Maybe it really can't be done at a distance. I definitely don't want to risk getting locked-in again." The horrifying experience was still vivid in my mind. I shivered.

"But how did you find my spirit?" Nui asked. "I mean, there are billions of threads, so how did you find mine?"

"Oh, that part was simple. I just had to concentrate on it. I'm not sure, but I think there's some kind of connection between the life thread and a particular body." I felt embarrassed by my clunky explanation, but it was the best I could offer.

Nui stayed silent.

"If that is really how it works, then I don't see why we couldn't do it remotely. Look, you could be home by tomorrow. And I would get to see Khun Yaai."

"I hear you, Nui, but I'm not sure." The idea of being

home as soon as tomorrow was tempting, especially after my failed projection today, but the risk was enormous.

"I definitely think we should try it, Luna. If you can't project, then nothing is gonna happen anyway, but if we're both out of body, then distance really shouldn't matter."

Why was Nui suddenly so keen on switching after she'd refused to consider it until yesterday? I could understand she wanted to see her grandmother, but she hadn't been this concerned or definitive about it before. What had happened?

"When would we do this, anyway? I mean, I don't even know what the schedule is. We're supposed to go back to the hospital tomorrow morning."

"Let's try right now while we're both free?"

"I'm not ready. You heard what Ajaarn said about pushing too hard. Let me sleep on it and I'll meditate later to see where I'm at. I'll text you as soon as I have a better idea about the schedule. You'll be in school tomorrow anyway, and I doubt I can just leave the hospital, so I think the earliest we could do it is tomorrow night or Saturday," I said.

"What if it's too late by then? I honestly think it can work if we try now," Nui said.

"I can't even stop shivering. How do you expect me to focus? I really have to go inside now before I catch a cold. Night, Nui. I'll call you tomorrow."

Nui's complete change in attitude was baffling. Maybe I needed to find out what had brought that on. I pulled up Yumi's number and touched the call button.

NUI

Luna's changing attitudes were annoying, if not downright worrisome. First, she was pushing me to make the switch, then she failed to do her part, and now she was too nervous to even try? With that mindset, we wouldn't be going anywhere anytime soon. Why couldn't she just decide and stick to it? *You mean, like you said you wanted to switch then refused to go ahead?* Ouch. Why did my inner voice always have to remind me of my own missteps? Maybe Yumi could have a chat with Luna to set her straight. She seemed to have a knack for getting people to agree with her. I grimaced, remembering how easily she had succeeded with me.

Shrugging off the uncomfortable thoughts, I pulled my hair into a ponytail and opened my laptop. 1,330,000,000 results in 0.48 seconds. I sighed. The sheer volume of information on the J-1 visa was daunting. Why hadn't I known about this option when there was so much data available about it? *Never mind, just dig in.* This programme could change everything for me. If I could study abroad for a year, I was pretty confident I'd find a way to stay if I liked it or at least have the experience under my belt to convince my parents to let me pick something more internationally oriented instead of becoming an accountant or lawyer or whatever they thought was best for me.

I was still taking notes when I heard Luna's parents return. Khun Susan knocked on my door shortly after.

"Yumi left?"

"She went home a little while ago. Did you have a good time?"

"It was nice. A fundraiser for Queen Sirikit Centre. Quite busy."

"Oh good, hope they raised a lot of money. Where was it?" The centre itself was part of Chulalongkorn Medical School as a resource for women with breast cancer. No wonder Khun Susan was eager to support it, now that her own sister was undergoing treatment for the disease.

Khun Susan walked over to the big armchair and took off her strappy sandals.

"I told you. At the British Club." She rubbed her foot, then fixed me with a stern look. I knew what was coming.

"Why did you skip class this afternoon and where did you go?"

"I'm really sorry, Mom, but since Nui had to leave tonight, we met at the temple to talk and make up."

Khun Susan raised her brows. "You had to leave school for *that*? What did you girls do that was such a big deal?"

I squirmed on my chair.

"Can we just leave it at that? We're okay now and I really don't want to go over it again."

Khun Susan examined my face like a human lie detector. I had to fight to maintain eye contact.

"Let me make this clear, Luna! This is the last time you get a pass. You have missed too many days lately and you can't afford to let your grades slip, you know that. I don't care what you girls did. This is unacceptable."

"I know, Mom, and I won't, I promise, but I really didn't want to let Nui go without clearing the air. You know, it's going to be really hard for her with her grandmother." I felt a twinge of guilt at my exaggeration especially since it should have been me on that plane.

I switched gears. Maybe this was not the best time to bring up my idea, but I wanted to plant the seed.

"Speaking of... you remember how I said Nui can't go to the States because of money and visa issues? Well, Yumi just mentioned this official exchange programme for high school students and there are all kinds of organisations that support it. Nui would have to apply, but if she can get it approved, she would stay with a host family."

"And?" Khun Susan leaned back and crossed her arms.

"Well, I was thinking, if we're going back early, do you think we could host Nui? Yumi said her friend from Shanghai is doing it for another student from China."

"Woah, slow down. That's a kind of big decision, don't you think? I mean, we haven't even decided yet when we're going. It all depends on what Dad can do with his job. It's premature to think about hosting someone, Luna."

"But you said you like Nui."

"Yes, I like her, but liking her and hosting her for a year are two very different things. She would practically become a member of our family. Do you really want that? You haven't known her that long, and you already had a major fight, so why would you want her to live with us?" *Damn, I should have thought of that before making up excuses for our behaviour.*

"Has Nui talked to her family about this?" Khun Susan asked.

"Not yet, we only just heard about it from Yumi."

"There, you see. First, she needs to talk to her parents, then apply and get approval, and she has to get a visa too. They probably already have assigned host families, and if not, *maybe* we can look into it." Khun Susan moved to the ottoman, closer to me.

"You know our life is going to be quite different when we move back?"

"What do you mean? Different how?"

"Well, life in the States is a lot more expensive than here and we won't have expat status anymore, so we can't afford permanent helpers like Khun Bo and Khun Pak, which means you guys will have to do your share of chores. Also, we'll have to see what school we can get you in as we'll have to pay for it ourselves; it's not covered by Dad's benefits."

"Oh, but..."

Khun Susan held up her hand to stop me.

"Also, depending on which city we go to, the school may not be as international as you're used to. I'm not saying it's bad, just different. It'll take some adjustment for sure."

Why was Khun Susan so gloomy about the move and why did she imply that life there wasn't as good as I expected it to be? I'd dreamed about living abroad for so long and now she made it sound like it was just a fantasy. The thought scared me and I pushed it away.

"What are you saying? You don't want to go?" *Please don't change your mind! I only just found a potential solution.*

Khun Susan shook her head and sighed.

"No, that's not it. Of course we're going. All I'm saying is we'll have to adapt, so we can't make any promises to your friends, okay? We don't know what our situation is going to be like."

I exhaled loudly, feeling deflated. It would make things so easy for me to stay with Luna's family. I wasn't worried about doing household chores, but Khun Susan was right, there were many variables to sort out before we could talk about them becoming a host. I had to dive more into the details of how to get a sponsorship, and talk to my parents, but most importantly, Luna and I had to switch for everything to make sense. The last big hurdle would be to get her to support my idea of moving with them. She'd been so mad at me she was likely to block the proposal. If so, I would have to find another host family.

"I guess, Mom. It was just an idea." I sighed.

"I'm not saying we're not willing to look at it Luna, but we have to deal with our own situation first, okay?"

She got up and kissed my head.

"And I want *you* to show more effort from now on and no more skipping classes."

"I know and I won't. Thanks, Mom."

"Don't stay up late. Tomorrow is still a school day."

After she closed the door, I debated whether to hit the school books or do more research. Curiosity won out and I went back to my search results.

LUNA

I PUT THE PHONE ON SPEAKER AND TUCKED MY HANDS UNDER my armpits to preserve some heat in my fingertips.

"Hey Lu… I mean, Nui," Yumi said.

"It's okay, I'm alone. I've got you on speaker though. It's so bloody cold up here. My hands are about to fall off." Another shiver went through me.

"What's up? How's Nui's grandma? Did you see her?" Yumi asked.

"Briefly. We're going back tomorrow. How was this afternoon? Did you meet Mom?"

"Yeah, it was really nice. We had a good catch-up."

"I guess Nui told you the switch didn't work?"

"She did. What happened?"

"I don't know. I couldn't relax even when our instructor lead us through the meditation."

"Are you going to try again?"

"Of course. Speaking of… what happened this afternoon?

Why is Nui suddenly pushing for a remote switch when she didn't even want to consider it yesterday?"

"How would I know? Why don't you ask her? You guys have the weirdest relationship ever. I told her about the J-1 visa and how Leslie's family is hosting a foreign exchange student for a year. If Nui can manage it, she can go as herself and doesn't have to use you or your ID. Maybe that's why she's eager to switch now."

"So *that's* your idea? Okay, that makes sense. But what do you think about a remote switch? I'm kinda worried about it to be honest."

"I'm the last person you should ask. I know nothing about spirits and switches, but logically, isn't it like ESP? You think of someone and the next second they call. I suppose that's also spirit stuff or telepathy or whatever. It happens to me all the time." Yumi snorted a laugh. "Who knows, maybe I have some woo-woo skills after all."

Yumi was right. When I had an out-of-body experience, it felt as if I was unrestricted by time or space, so maybe distance really was irrelevant. And if Nui and I agreed, there was no reason for either of us to get stuck.

"Okay, thanks Yumi. Just wanted to run it by you. I better go in. Been sitting outside for too long. I'll call you tomorrow or who knows, maybe if the woo-woo stuff works I'll be back then." I grinned, even if Yumi couldn't see it.

"That would be cool. Oh, guess what? We're moving into your building in a couple of weeks. Dad found an apartment there."

"That's great! It'll be so much fun. We can hang out again."

"I'm not so sure about that," Yumi said.

"What do you mean? Why not?"

"Nui didn't mention it when you just talked?"

"Mention what?" I sat forward and shrugged off the blanket.

"Unbelievable."

"Yumi! Don't freak me out. What's going on?" I stood and started pacing.

"Sor… Lu… I …" Yumi was breaking up so I quickly sat back down.

"What did you say?"

"I can't believe that girl. What game is she playing? Luke said you're moving back to the US soon, but Nui said it's not confirmed yet. But then Luke said it was your—or I guess Nui's—fault? Not sure what he meant by that. I told Nui she has to tell you."

I sat stunned. Dad's normal postings were at least two years. I knew they'd talked about moving a bit earlier because of Aunt Jane, but Yumi made it sound like that deadline had moved forward. Why was it my fault? What had Nui done? And why hadn't she told me? It must have been bad if she'd tried to keep it from Yumi who now knew our biggest secret.

"Luna, you still there?" Yumi asked.

"Yeah, I'm just trying to think why. Did Nui say anything else? She didn't mention it to me."

"No, that was it."

"Damn. Okay, I'll find out what's going on. I better go now. I'll talk to you tomorrow, okay?"

"Good luck."

I glanced at the Buddha again and exhaled, feeling an anxious knot in my stomach. What had Nui done that prompted an early departure? I had the right to know since I would bear the brunt of it. *You mean, just like you're withholding information from Nui?* Dammit. Yumi's news clarified that I had no time to spare to get home. Nui didn't know her parents were planning to withdraw her from BIS, and if that happened she wouldn't be able to do the international student exchange. And if my family was leaving soon, it could be too tempting for her to just move with them. I had no other option than to go ahead with Nui's remote switch idea if I wanted my family back.

35

NUI

Done! The stack of documents was daunting. I glanced at my phone. Midnight. Again, I would get very little sleep, but I felt better knowing I'd taken a major step forward today. I just needed to talk to Luna and set the time for the switch, and if she was still hesitant, maybe Yumi could convince her. I brushed my teeth and crawled into bed, not bothering to shower again.

Hitting the pillow, I popped right back up again, remembering my promise to meditate. I needed to be as prepared as I could be for the next day. The shortest recording of Ajaarn's meditation wasn't the most recent, but I didn't think I could stay awake much longer. I put the phone next to me on the pillow and kept the bedside lamp on as extra insurance.

'Close your eyes and take a deep breath in…'

So much for leaving the light on. I chuckled to myself.

'… exhale to the count of eight.'

36

LUNA

I HAD STAYED ON THE SALA MUCH LONGER THAN EXPECTED and was frozen to the bone. All I wanted to do was sleep and forget about the day, but I knew I needed to meditate to prepare for our remote switch. Where and how we were going to do this was another problem to solve.

Panya and Chaiya were tucking sheets and blankets into the daybed and piled on a few pillows. The fathers were still talking at the dining table.

"Where's Duen?" I asked Panya.

"Bathroom." He pointed towards the back of the house. I hoped there was more than one bathroom in the house, otherwise with eight of us sharing we would need a rota to get ready. *That alone is a reason to switch right now.* I felt punchy from the highs and lows of the day. I was exhausted.

"Night everyone. See you in the morning." I walked back into our room to grab my stuff and get my makeshift bed set up. Someone had brought in extra sheets and blankets and put them on Duen's bed. The space between the bed and my air mattress was the width of a balance beam. Duen and I would trip over each other if we got up at the same time. I kept my leggings on for warmth as the blankets seemed rather thin, but I was tired enough to sleep through all conditions.

I didn't know the layout of the house, but thankfully, Duen had left the bathroom door ajar and light on. Even better, unlike at Nui's home, the doors here had proper locks instead of a tassel. I performed the bare minimum of my night-time routine, then picked up my headphones and crawled under the blankets. My phone had only twenty percent of battery life left, but hopefully, it would be enough to last through a meditation.

"Do you think Khun Yaai is going to make it?" Duen asked.

"I hope so."

"It's so sad that we didn't get to spend any time with her."

"Hmm." This wasn't my conversation to have.

"You know, I'm really sorry if you have to leave BIS. I mean, I want the cooking school, but I wish you could stay in your school, Nui." Duen sounded wistful, not as surefooted as she'd seemed on the plane. I could afford to be generous on Nui's behalf, especially if I was going to be home by tomorrow.

"Yeah, it would suck big time. But it's not really your fault, is it?"

"No, but still. Maybe Mae and Paa can work it out somehow, so you can stay." It was sweet of Duen to hope for that.

"We'll see. Can you turn off the lights? I want to meditate."

Duen shifted in bed, but the light stayed on. I turned my head and found her looking at me.

"What's wrong with you, Nui? We never talk anymore. Are you mad at me?"

I frowned, stumped.

"What do you mean, we don't talk? We're talking now, aren't we? And no, I'm not mad at you. Why would I be mad?"

"Ever since you became friends with Luna, you don't tell me anything anymore. And things have become so weird."

"What do you mean, weird?"

"It's like you're breaking all the rules all the time now. You know, drinking and getting in the middle of a dogfight, and you're snapping at me all the time, and… and it's like Luna has made you forget all about us. It's like you're trying to copy her or be like her." Duen sounded distressed. I sat up to look at her more closely.

"What? What are you talking about? Luna didn't do anything. You don't even know her. I'm not sure where you get that from." I never thought I'd have to defend myself from myself. I exhaled sharply. Duen, of course, did not know the real reason, so I couldn't blame her for making assumptions, but I thought I'd done a better job of pretending to be Nui. Apparently, Duen was more observant than I had given her credit for. I shifted uncomfortably. I wasn't aware that I'd ever behaved badly towards Duen to make her think I was a negative influence on Nui.

"And when you were in the hospital I was so scared." I could see the sheen of tears in Duen's eyes.

What in the world…? Nui had never mentioned that she and Duen had heart-to-heart talks, but Duen, as Nui's little sister, had hardly been on my radar until recently. Maybe she was feeling tender because of Khun Yaai? My heart bumped uncomfortably. I leaned over to touch her arm.

"I'm sorry, Duen. Of course I'm not mad at you. You're

my sister. There's just been so much going on lately, you know that. School, the hospital, the shelter and so on. I sometimes don't know what to do next."

Duen laid back down and spoke towards the ceiling.

"Are you going to marry Channon? I like him. He's nice."

"Marry? Come on, Duen, where did you get that idea? No, we're not getting married."

"Well, you hang out a lot with him at that pet hospital. And you go on dates. And he's got you a dog."

Duen said it as if that was proof of anything. Maybe for her it was. For me? I cringed. My relationship with Channon was so messed up. I wondered if I shouldn't have told him about the switch in the first place, but then there would have been no chance at all to continue seeing him after I was back in my body. This way, at least the potential was there. *Not if you're going back to the States soon.* Duen's mood was contagious. I felt like crying. Every turn I took seemed to get blocked off.

"No, Duen. Channon said he wanted to get a dog anyway and Chone came along at the right time. I don't even know if I'll ever get him home." Duen wouldn't know that I meant *my* home. "Besides, we're not even really dating." *Yet,* I added mentally. Was that still a real possibility or just a dream?

"Hmm. You know I can help you if you want."

"Thanks Duen, it's okay. I think I got it now. But you can still turn off the lights." I teased her to lighten the atmosphere.

She sat up with a huff and flipped the wall switch, plunging the room into darkness with a thin sliver of light shining through a crack in the curtains.

"Night Duen."

A snort was the only answer.

The mattress was surprisingly comfortable and now I'd

warmed up I had to be careful not to fall asleep during Ajaarn's mantras.

THE NEXT THING I KNEW, SOMEONE WAS SHAKING MY shoulder. I jerked upright, squinting against the light.

"Wake up, Nui. We have to go to the hospital." Paa leaned over me, tugging the headphones from my ears. Duen had already pushed back her covers and was leaning over to grab her clothes.

"What happened? What time is it?"

"Just get dressed. We leave in ten minutes." Paa turned and walked out.

"I think it's Khun Yaai. She's probably dying and we want to be there with her," Duen said, pulling on her jeans.

Oh God. I started shaking. *I can't do this. Why do I have to deal with this? I'm not even family.* I really, really did not want to witness someone dying.

37

NUI

MY EYES SNAPPED OPEN, AT ONCE WIDE AWAKE AND SLIGHTLY disoriented. Why had I woken up? I didn't need to go to the bathroom, and I didn't recall having a nightmare, but a vein in my neck pulsed uncomfortably. I heard the soft swoosh of the air conditioning, but otherwise it was quiet. The bedside lamp was still on, but hadn't done the trick of keeping me awake. The last thing I remembered was starting a meditation, but I must have fallen asleep right away. My phone had slipped onto the mattress. Three-thirty in the morning. Weird. I turned off the light but kept my eyes open, still uneasy about something though unable to pinpoint what. *Go back to sleep, Nui. You have a big day tomorrow.*

Just as I was about to drift off again, a puff of air blew across my face carrying the powerful scent of lemongrass, followed by the soft stroke of what felt like a warm hand. I choked on a scream and instinctively curled up. I pulled the blanket tight over my head and scrunched my eyes closed.

What was that? I couldn't breathe, as though my heart was trying to explode out of my chest. Spots swam behind my eyes and I felt nauseous.

Come on, Nui, don't be silly, you're imagining things. I tried to reason my way out of panic. *Hiding under a blanket is stupid. It probably was just the A/C.* Except, I knew one hundred percent that the airflow didn't reach the bed. *And what about the scent? Okay, fine. So, maybe it came from the bathroom. Just turn on the light and look.* My internal pep talk did little to slow down my heart. Logically, I knew there was no way an intruder could be in the apartment. We were on the seventh floor with security and a twenty-four-hour doorman. I poked my nose out from under the blanket. The lemongrass smell had gone. All our talks about remote switches and spirits and portals had opened up an extra dimension of potential otherworldly threats, something I didn't want to think about too closely. Had Luna and I set something in motion with the switch? What we had done was unnatural in itself, so who knew what else we had started? I shivered. *Stop thinking like that, Nui. Use your logic. If someone was there, they'd have already done something. Not if they are waiting for me to lift the blanket.* My competing thoughts weren't very effective in slowing down my terror. If my pulse went any faster, I'd stroke out. *Don't be such a sissy.*

It took an eternity to talk myself off the ledge. I finally got so mad at myself for letting my imagination run away with me I burst out of my cocoon and switched on the lamp. Nothing! No change in the room at all. No one lurking in the shadows. I exhaled sharply and laid down, trying to bring my racing heart back under control.

Khun Yaai. Her face popped into my mind. The smell reminded me of her and how her hand had wiped away my tears when I bumped into something as a child. *Another fantasy, Nui? Khun Yaai is in Chiang Rai, in the hospital.* Despite that, I was absolutely certain it had been her stroking my face.

I grabbed my phone and texted Luna though it was unlikely she'd receive the message, especially not at Aunt May's house with the weak network connection.

'How's K Yaai?'

38

LUNA

Uncle Dech locked the front door behind us as we all filed down the stairs to the carport. The Buddha was still lit up like a beacon, presiding over the village. I glanced at my phone. Why would they waste all this energy at three in the morning when no one was around to see it? Maybe it was some Buddhist thing? I was too tired to think clearly. I had barely brushed my teeth and hair before running out the door. At least I'd remembered to grab my charger. Power was down to five percent. We bundled into the car in the same configuration as before, but no one spoke until Uncle Dech offered an explanation.

"May called. They think Khun Yaai is not going to make it through the night. She thought we all wanted to be there to say goodbye."

No, I really, really don't! I bit my tongue to keep myself from shouting it out loud. Right now, I really hated Nui for putting me in this situation. I'd never been close to a dying person. What if it was really horrifying? Would she be in pain and I'd have to witness it? I wiped my clammy hands on my leggings, feeling ill-equipped and too weak to go through the experience.

The car fell silent again as Uncle Dech drove us back to the hospital. This time, the trip was much faster with no traffic to speak of. We walked into the intensive care unit and a nurse directed us to Khun Yaai's room. Normal visitation hours didn't apply, nor did we have to wear masks.

I hung back, wishing I could beam myself anywhere, preferably to my bed at home. Could I pretend to faint? *You're in a hospital—they'll see through that immediately.*

Mae and Aunt May stood on either side of Khun Yaai's bed, holding her hands. The lights were dimmed, the tubes had been removed and the monitors turned off. It was eerily quiet except for the soft murmur of Aunt May talking or chanting to her mother. Mae had a tissue in her free hand and kept wiping her eyes. The six of us grouped around the bed, watching silently. Oddly enough, now I was there, I no longer felt afraid. Khun Yaai looked peaceful, her chest barely rising with soft breaths. She looked like she was resting, not on the verge of leaving the world. There was a stillness and serenity emanating from her that slowed my own heartbeat and breath. *It was going to be okay.*

Several minutes passed, and I nearly fell asleep on my feet, eyes open but unfocused as if I were in a trance. Duen's hand slipped into mine and gripped it tightly, bringing me back to full awareness. Without it, I would have missed the next moment.

Mae and Aunt May bent over to kiss their mother's cheeks. Khun Yaai's hands visibly tensed around her daughter's fingers. Was she saying a last farewell? She then took a much deeper breath and exhaled all the way, puffing the last bit of air out. I waited for her to inhale again, but nothing happened. Was this it? I turned towards Duen to check, when, out of the corner of my eye, I caught a pinprick of light hovering over Khun Yaai's body. I blinked, wide awake now. It was still there, gently stretching and reaching towards the ceiling like a filigree strand of silver being pulled from her body by invisible hands. I was tired, but I didn't think I was hallucinating. Did the others see it too?

I looked at Duen. Her chin was quivering and a single tear rolled down her cheek. I squeezed her hand in support, but felt compelled to turn back and watch the cord rising. *I wish Nui could see this. It's so real.* The thread reminded me of the links I could sense when Nui and I had hooked up. It looked like a tentacle being retracted, growing thinner and more translucent until the final bit of light dissipated and passed through the ceiling.

It wasn't scary at all, but somehow peaceful and magnificent. Was this Khun Yaai's spirit going home? If so, it was dignified. My concerns about the spirit world and transitions had been ridiculous. Why would I ever worry about something so beautiful and natural? One moment a body is hooked into the source energy stream and the next, it unplugs.

Just before the light dispersed, I felt a soft puff of air touch my face and I knew it was Khun Yaai saying goodbye to me, even though I wasn't her granddaughter. I exhaled, smiled and closed my eyes, totally at peace. I almost felt sorry that Nui had missed this moment.

Duen tugged my hand sharply. She was frowning through her tears and shook her head. Had she not seen or felt the same? I felt as though I'd stepped outside a theatre after watching a movie, surprised that the normal world still existed. I composed my face into a more serene mask but was still too much in awe to fake tears.

Mae was openly sobbing, and both boys kept wiping their faces. They must have been much closer to Khun Yaai than Duen or Nui, as they lived in the same house.

Aunt May turned around and motioned us closer.

I followed the boys and Duen, no longer afraid of a dead body. Everyone wai'ed to Khun Yaai, but we didn't touch her. Aunt May looked at me curiously, as if she knew what I had just experienced. I realised that she and I were the only ones in the room looking at ease, almost joyful. She dipped her head… in acknowledgement?

39

LUNA

WE STAYED ANOTHER TWENTY MINUTES WITH OUR HEADS bowed before Uncle Dech walked out to inform the nurses of Khun Yaai's passing. From then on, things moved quickly. A doctor came in to pronounce her dead officially. We all had to stay at the hospital until the monks from Khun Yaai's temple could transfer her to the shrine for the vigil where she'd remain until her cremation. Mae and Aunt May were going to wash and dress Khun Yaai in new clothes while the rest of us sat in the waiting room.

It was still too early to call anyone, but at least I could charge my phone. I didn't think it was necessary to wake Nui at this hour, but as soon as I looked at the screen I saw a text from her which she'd sent at three-thirty, less than one hour ago. Odd. My breath hitched. That was the exact time Khun Yaai had passed away. Coincidence?

Should I call or text her? It would be kinder to relay her

grandmother's death in person, but she'd probably gone back to sleep. I took the middle ground and texted.

'Call me when you get this.'

Paa and Uncle Dech were at a table, looking at some papers and making notes. Duen and Panya were talking softly and Chaiya had put his head back against the wall and was snoring lightly.

My phone vibrated and I almost dropped it in surprise. Nui. I looked around the room and moved to the far corner to plug in my phone. There was only a little battery life left, so I couldn't walk outside. I didn't know if Aunt May's family spoke English, but hopefully that would provide a safety buffer when talking to Nui.

"Luna? You're up early." I whispered before Nui could say anything. I turned my back to the family and shielded my mouth and phone with my hand. Nui didn't respond immediately, but caught on quickly.

"Is my family there?"

"Yes. We're at the hospital."

"Tell me," Nui said. I could hear the undertone of apprehension.

There was no good way to soften the news.

"Khun Yaai passed away a little while ago." I felt I should add *I'm sorry*, but that would seem odd to the others if they were listening.

"Oh no. I knew it." Nui didn't seem surprised. *Weird.*

"What do you mean?"

"The strangest thing happened. I woke up an hour ago and I could have sworn Khun Yaai was here with me, touching my face. It was scary at first, but then I realised it was her."

"Are you serious? I had the same experience. So it really happened." For a moment, I forgot to keep my voice down. I was glad my experience hadn't been in my imagination. I turned to check on the family and caught Duen frowning at me. I ignored her and went back to whispering.

"She was totally at peace. I could actually see her spirit leaving her body. It was mind-blowing, not scary at all."

"Aww, I wish I could have been there. I felt she wasn't mad at me at all. Somehow she knew I was thinking of her," Nui said with a slight hitch in her voice.

"I thought it was strange that I could see her spirit thread when I wasn't out-of-body myself. I didn't expect that at all. I think Aunt May saw the same thing. She gave me this look after it happened."

"Nothing surprises me anymore." Nui sighed heavily, but with her next question switched back to practicalities as if nothing major had happened.

"Do you know what the plans for the funeral are?"

I didn't know what kind of relationship she had had with her grandma, but I would have expected her to be more distraught.

"I only overheard Uncle Dech saying the monks will pick her up this morning and the cremation will be on Sunday mid-morning," I said.

"Wow, that's fast. I thought they'd want at least a week of prayers before the funeral."

"I can try to find out more, but Uncle Dech said Khun Yaai didn't want a long, drawn out ceremony."

"That makes sense. She never wanted to spend anything on herself. But oh man, what are we going to do, Luna? I really need to be there, especially now. Can you find a place somewhere so we can try to switch?" Nui asked, the first genuine note of emotional upset creeping into her voice.

"I doubt it, at least not anytime soon. They said we have to go to the temple for prayers and I don't know how long that'll take."

Nui didn't respond. I looked at my phone. The call was still live and the phone still charging.

"Nui? I mean Luna?" I quickly glanced around to see if anyone noticed my faux pas, but no one was paying attention.

"I'm here. Just thinking. Do you think I could convince your parents to let me fly up for the funeral? I could get there on Saturday and be there for the ceremony. I wouldn't even have to miss school. We could switch while I'm there then you could go home to your family."

Now it was my turn to pause. Why hadn't I thought of that? It was a brilliant idea that would tick all the boxes.

"Yes!" Oops, again I had gotten too loud.

"Nui! Seriously!" Duen hissed her reproof from across the room. I wanted to stick my tongue out at her, but cleared my throat and dropped to a mere murmur.

"You definitely should ask. Knowing Mom, you need to play up that you want to be here for me, especially now we made up, and that it's a new cultural experience for you and all that. She'll buy that."

Nui hummed.

"I'll ask her first thing this morning and I'll text you later, okay?" She seemed re-energised despite the early hour.

I glanced up to see Aunt May walking into the room, gesturing for us to follow her.

"Gotta go. Aunt May is here."

"'Kay, talk to you later. Bye." Nui hung up.

I let out a long breath. It was only just past five o'clock, and I had a long day ahead of me, but if Nui could convince my parents there was at last light at the end of the tunnel. *Except, you still have to work on your projection, Luna. Without that, nothing changes.* I pushed away the thought for now. I needed to be alert for what came next.

40

NUI

WHAT A STRANGE NIGHT—FIRST, FREAKING OUT ABOUT ghosts, and then Luna's description of what had happened. I wished I'd been there to say my farewell, but deep down I was relieved that Khun Yaai wasn't angry or, possibly worse, disappointed with me. Why had I even assumed she would be upset? Khun Yaai was a very forgiving and compassionate person. She never insisted on us kids accepting everything on her say so, but simply demanded that our actions were well-meaning and respectful towards others always. That was good enough for her. Khun Yaa was much more locked into tradition, including what she considered appropriate behaviours and her frequent warnings about karma. Which side of the family beliefs did I follow? I felt heat rising in my face. What I had done to Luna didn't measure up to either standard, but hopefully I could make up for it, at least to some extent. I jumped out of bed, determined to get started. *You just don't want to look closer at your motivations, do you?* When had my inner conscience become so blunt, or had it always been there and I had ignored it?

I had almost finished my cup of tea when Khun Susan walked into the kitchen. She looked at me as if she'd never seen me before and theatrically rubbed her eyes.

"What happened to the real Luna?" She asked, pouring herself a cup of coffee.

I jerked back, sloshing tea on the table.

"What's that supposed to mean?" My question came out sharper than intended and made Khun Susan turn around slowly. She squinted at me.

"That was a joke, grumpy head. Maybe you *shouldn't* have gotten up so early." Khun Susan's tone took on an edge.

"Well, it's kind of mean. You make it sound like I never do anything here. You're welcome for the coffee." I didn't know what possessed me to start an argument. Plain stupid and counterproductive. Yes, I was tired and off centre, but I needed her approval and not to put her back up.

She stared at me with a look that only mothers, including my own, could pull off to induce guilt.

"Excuse me? What louse ran over your liver? Sounds like you need coffee instead of tea. When did you make that switch, anyway?"

I definitely had soured her mood. Shit. I needed her. *Shake it off.*

"Argh. I'm sorry, Mom, but I got a call earlier from Nui."

Khun Susan raised her eyebrows.

"Her grandmother passed away early this morning."

"Oh! I'm sorry to hear that. Is she okay?"

"No, not really. Nui said the funeral is on Sunday morning, and I want to be there for her. Can I go? I want to support her."

"Wait. Slow down. I haven't even had my first cup yet." Khun Susan sank onto the bench by the kitchen table.

"Sorry! Do you want me to make you some toast?"

"No thanks, not right now."

I wiped the spill and turned on the kettle to make myself another cup of tea, mainly to hold myself back and not prod her again.

"I know you made up with Nui, but I don't think it's necessary for you to fly to Chiang Rai. She'll be busy with the funeral anyway and you don't even know that side of her family. You can send flowers to the temple or to her house or whatever else is appropriate," Khun Susan said. I turned around slowly, wondering if she'd said no because I snapped at her or if she really meant it.

"But…" I didn't get any further.

"No, Luna. I really don't think it's a good idea. You have plenty of stuff to do here and I'm sure you have things to make up for since you skipped class yesterday. You're lucky I didn't ground you. You stay here."

"But, Mom, you always said we should experience and respect the local customs and traditions."

"Do I really need to remind you that you broke the local law only two weeks ago? Is that what you call respecting the local culture? Besides, until yesterday, you didn't even speak to Nui because you had some sort of gripe going on. No Luna, you can't go. Like I said, send her some flowers, and that's it."

So much for Luna's assessment of what would sway her mom in our favour. Khun Susan's voice was unusually sharp and I couldn't even pretend that I didn't know why she felt that way. I had brought that on myself. Dammit.

I considered making a last ditch effort and opened my mouth, but Khun Susan pre-empted me.

"Whatever you were planning to say, save it. Don't test my patience. This discussion is over." She stood up, refilled her mug, and walked out of the room.

Ouch. I had never seen her like this. Why did she have to act this way now? Luna and I finally had a solid plan and now we couldn't execute it. We were back to the remote switch idea if I wanted to be there for the funeral. With a heavy sigh, I grabbed my phone and texted Luna.

41

LUNA

The monks would arrive at seven, but I was starving and seriously coffee deprived, a pounding headache forming at the base of my skull. The combined effect of the middle of the night wake-up call, the intense experience of Khun Yaai's transition and the conversation with Nui were all catching up with me. I knew I was crashing from an adrenaline overload and I would need some caffeine soon to make it through the rest of the day. We stood around the hospital bed quietly, waiting.

Khun Yaai was now dressed in a traditional maroon coloured Thai sinh skirt and long sleeve cream silk blouse. Both looked brand new. Mae or Aunt May had combed and braided her hair and placed her hands in a prayer position holding a white lotus flower. She looked peaceful, as if she was taking a nap. Paa and Uncle Dech moved about with their lists and phones. I assumed they were calling people and making funeral arrangements.

I looked around the room. Mae was sitting with her eyes closed, but tears were rolling down her face and she had several tissues balled up in her hand. Aunt May seemed calm in comparison. A zing of anxiety shot through my belly. Maybe she had forgotten about the different aura colour but what would happen once Nui and I switched? Would Aunt May notice and if so, would she question it? If she'd picked up on my aura so easily, there would be no way to hide a sudden transfer like we'd planned. What could we say if she asked? If Nui was coming to the funeral, we wouldn't be able to avoid being with Aunt Mae at the same time.

I turned to Duen and whispered, "Do you think it would be okay to get some coffee and something to eat? Are you hungry?"

"Shh. We have to wait until she goes to the temple," she hissed back. That didn't really make sense to me. Why did we have to sit here if Paa and Uncle Dech could move about? Not that I didn't want to pay respect to Khun Yaai, but I had seen her leave her body, and it seemed unnecessary to watch an empty shell, even if everyone else thought this was Khun Yaai. I gulped. Unless anyone else had experienced what I had seen, it was better not to talk about it. Few people would be open to this viewpoint and would probably crucify me if I told them about the spirit thread. Would Aunt May know? She seemed very tuned in if she could see the energy field of people.

I glanced at my watch. If the monks were on time, it shouldn't be long now. I yawned, light-headed from lack of sleep, lack of coffee and an overload of confusion.

Duen elbowed me and shook her head, scowling. *Man, she's such a goody two-shoes.* I wanted to elbow her back, but at the last second remembered why we were there.

The door opened and Paa and Uncle Dech motioned for

us kids to step outside. Mae and Aunt May moved to the wall, their hands raised in a wai. As soon as I walked into the corridor, I saw four orange robed monks waiting in line to enter the room. I wondered why there were only four but knew enough to simply wai and move aside. Two of their lay helpers rolled a gurney into the room, then came out again and waited with us. The monks walked single file into the room and a minute later I heard chanting. It was quite moving, despite the wall between us. When the chanting stopped, the helpers walked back into the room and rolled out the gurney with the monks walking on either side. They'd covered Khun Yaai with a white sheet. The hospital staff bowed their heads and wai'ed, paying their respects to the monks or saying goodbye to Khun Yaai. Mae and Aunt May fell in step behind the monks, their husbands following and us kids bringing up the rear, a solemn procession towards the rear exit. A hearse was waiting by the doors to take Khun Yaai away. The monks met up with their other helpers waiting outside, picked up their alms bowls and continued on their morning rounds.

"What happens now?" I whispered to no one in particular.

Aunt May took charge.

"Dech, is everything confirmed for the temple?" she asked her husband. He nodded.

"They are all set. Why don't you and Lamai go home first, shower and eat something so you can go to the temple as soon as everything is ready?"

"I'll wait here. I need to book a rental car as soon as they're open to pick up Tum and Krit this afternoon," Paa said.

"Don't bother, Narong. You can use mine while you're here." Aunt May rummaged in her purse and handed over a set of keys. "Let's all head home. That makes more sense."

Mae nodded listlessly. This was so different from her normal demeanour that I couldn't help but feel sorry for her. I didn't think I would have been able to stand upright after being awake all night like she'd been, and apparently she wouldn't be getting rest anytime soon, either. Maybe keeping busy helped to dull the pain of losing her mother. I turned sideways, feeling a sudden ambush of tears, homesick for my own mom.

"Panya, Chaiya and Duen, go with your mothers. Nui still has to get her rabies shot and I need to handle some paperwork with the hospital. We'll follow you when we're done," Uncle Dech said. Jeez, I'd forgotten about that. Thank goodness someone else was on top of things.

"Can we get a cup of coffee first? It's still too early, no?" I asked.

"I could use a cup myself. Narong?" Uncle Dech asked.

Paa nodded and the three of us headed back inside to the imitation Starbucks coffee shop.

Taking that first sip felt like heaven even if it wasn't particularly good coffee. I nibbled on a stale blueberry muffin just to get some food inside me before the rabies shot. Paa and Uncle Dech talked about their lists again.

"How did you arrange everything so quickly this morning?" I asked.

Uncle Dech smiled. "Khun Yaai was pretty specific about what she wanted and gave us instructions."

"Do you think she knew she was going to die?" Dying seemed the wrong word after what I had seen. More like a transition or a move into another sphere. Nothing to be afraid of. Maybe the reversal of that thread movement was how we got here in the first place? I smiled. *Kind of deep thoughts so early in the morning, Luna.* Nonetheless, it made sense to me.

"I'm not sure she *knew,* but I think she had a sense of it

and was preparing herself. She was meditating a lot more than normal and she made an effort to meet all her friends in the last few weeks. Maybe she wanted to say goodbye." It surprised me how openly Uncle Dech talked about this. His entire family seemed to be more broad-minded than Nui's immediate family. Even now, Paa was frowning at me. I tried to ignore him. This was too good a chance to find out more about the schedule for the coming days and consequently our window for the switch.

"What exactly did Khun Yaai want for her funeral?" I asked.

"Well, she said she didn't think it was necessary to spend too much time or money on formal ceremonies. Don't get me wrong, she was deeply spiritual but didn't follow all the traditions. I wish you'd gotten to spend more time with her. She really was a great grandma to the boys and a great mother-in-law to me."

Paa turned away. Maybe he regretted that his family hadn't been as involved with Khun Yaai. Was this why Mae was so much more distraught than Aunt Mae? Did she feel guilty for not having spent much time with her mother? How could she while running a business in Bangkok? Despite my previous misgivings about her rigid attitudes, I felt sorry for her.

"Yeah, I wish so too." The more I heard about Khun Yaai the nicer she sounded.

"This afternoon we go to the temple for prayers. Narong, what time do you have to be at the airport?" Uncle Dech asked.

"Their flight lands at two. Plenty of time," Paa answered.

"Are we going to be at the temple all day?" I asked.

"We'll take turns. Don't worry, you won't have to sit there the whole time." Uncle Dech winked at me. Paa harrumphed. I shot him a quick look. Maybe it was better not to aggravate him more, though I didn't really know why he would be upset at my simple questions. Wasn't it natural to want to know? *Nui would probably know everything. Or maybe not, if Khun Yaai didn't insist on formal ceremonies.*

I checked my phone. I had a message to call Nui back, but she would be on her way to school now.

"Why don't you go ahead and get your shot? I'll meet you back in the lobby after I finish the paperwork," Uncle Dech said.

Paa and I walked to the main reception area and they directed us to the department for infectious diseases. The doctor was kind and handled the jab quickly and, better yet, almost painlessly. One more to go and unless something went wrong, Nui would be the one to get poked next time. We went back to the lobby to wait for Uncle Dech, and shortly after that we left.

Paa and Uncle Dech talked quietly in the front while I stared out the window lost in thought. As soon as Nui arrived, we'd need to find a place to meditate together and switch. If I had to sit vigil in the temple, I would have plenty of time to practise on my own with or without Ajaarn's lessons. *Remember how you got yourself unlocked?* If I managed that without verbal instructions, then mediating in the temple and even releasing my spirit from Nui's body should be easy. *Should. It should also have been easy at Wat Pathum.* Dammit! My thoughts were pin balling around my head. *And there you have it, Luna. That's exactly your problem. Why aren't you sticking with one line?*

I almost groaned out loud. Knowing how it worked was one thing, but doing it was something different altogether. Why did I have so little control over my own thoughts when it counted most?

42

NUI

I HADN'T EXPECTED KHUN SUSAN TO FLAT OUT REFUSE TO let me go to the funeral. Of all times, why did she have to put her foot down now? *Maybe because you've pushed a few too many buttons lately, Nui?* I huffed as I climbed into the school van. Luna and I were back to the remote switch idea and she would just have to find a time and place where she could be alone.

The van passed a travel agency with colourful posters in the window. I'd gone past this place hundreds of times, but today one poster caught my eye. A photo of the Golden Gate Bridge in San Francisco with the city shrouded in fog behind it with only a few skyscrapers poking through the mist. A long forgotten memory popped into my head: Khun Yaai had been the first person I confided in about my dream to study abroad and, to my surprise, she hadn't dismissed my idea outright. Instead, she asked me where I would go and what I would see, which developed into a game where she asked me to describe the places I wanted to visit in so much detail she eventually could say, 'Ah, now I see it.' In hindsight, I think she often pretended not to understand what I described, so I had to think harder about it and become more creative in visualising a life abroad. It had been so much fun fantasising about tasting beignets in New Orleans or climbing to the top of the Empire State Building or riding the cable cars in San Francisco. I smiled at the memory. Mae hadn't been too happy about the phone bills, but since I was talking with her mom, she tolerated it, even though she didn't know what our conversations were about. Khun Yaai probably enjoyed the daydreaming as much as I did. We played the game for almost a year, but after I talked my parents into letting me go to BIS, I'd become too busy, or if I was honest, I simply didn't want to take the time anymore. I bit down on my lip and wiped at a stray tear. The guilt was back and had settled in more heavily. How had Khun Yaai felt about that? Did she miss our chats? Did she feel I abandoned her? *Shit!* One stray tear quickly turned into a stream. I grabbed my backpack, hoping I'd left some tissues in one of the pockets. I slipped on my sunglasses and bit down on my tongue to pull myself together before we arrived at school.

Yumi was already waiting inside the gates. Every morning I expected a new fashion statement from her and again she didn't disappoint. Today she was going for elegant, wearing black Palazzo pants with a basic tight black tee shirt on top. Layered over it was the most gorgeous maxi length black silk Kimono wrap with vibrant flowers and bird shapes embroidered across the back and long sleeves. She had knotted the inside tie loosely, letting the coat sweep behind her like a royal robe. Instead of her usual trainers or boots, she wore black ballerina slippers complementing the outfit. Her hair and make-up were subtle by comparison. I sighed, looking down at my plain cream linen pants and loose black top. Clearly, neither Luna nor I had Yumi's dramatic flair.

"You look amazing, Yumi. Is there anything normal in your closet at all?" I asked with a slight tease.

"Sure, but by whose standards?" Yumi grinned. "So, did you look into the J-1 stuff?"

"I did, and it looks promising. Thanks again. I'll definitely apply. I have some sad news though. Khun Yaai died last night. I talked to Luna this morning."

"I'm so sorry, Nui." Yumi pulled me into a hug. My chin wobbled again, surprised and overwhelmed by Yumi's sympathy. Did that mean she didn't see me as an adversary anymore, someone who was keeping her best friend away? Yumi's gesture affected me more than I expected. Luna's mom, of course, hadn't known Khun Yaai was my grandmother, so had offered no consolation. I sniffed, trying to not completely fall apart. I wasn't a crier by nature, but unexpected kindness had a way of getting to me. To outsiders it must have looked just like two old friends embracing.

"Thanks Yumi. I talked to Luna's mom this morning about the funeral. I really want to be there, but she said no."

Yumi rolled her shoulders, not quite a shrug.

"What about your remote switch, then? Why don't you try that tonight? I'm sure Luna would trade places in a heartbeat," Yumi said.

"I know. I need to call her, but they are probably at the temple right now. I'm not sure she'll have time today. This is all so screwed up. I don't know what to do." I tilted my head left to right, front to back, and heard my spine cracking, relieving some tension in my neck.

"You could always go anyway, couldn't you? I mean you have enough money and you got Luna's passport. There's nothing stopping you," Yumi said.

I stared at her, shocked enough to stop feeling sorry for myself.

"You mean, go even though Luna's mom said no? But..." There were so many buts that I didn't know where to start.

"Well, if it's that important to you, then go," Yumi said.

"But..." I stopped again.

"See? You're doing it again. You're always looking for excuses why you can't do something. If you really want to go, then just go. It's your choice. Maybe Mrs T will be upset, but it's better to ask for forgiveness than have regrets, don't you think? Besides, if you switch, you won't have to deal with that, anyway." Yumi lifted her head, daring me to object. She exuded confidence. I suspected Yumi had even more freedom than Luna, but suggesting to travel without parental permission seemed bold even for her. My mouth opened and closed a few times like a koi out of water. While I wasn't averse to breaking a few rules, going on a trip against the parents' wishes was a much bigger deal. If it was my family, I wouldn't even contemplate it.

"Isn't it kind of mean to do that to Luna?" I asked, trying to at least keep some semblance of fairness.

"More mean than when you refused to switch back?" Yumi asked. "Besides, I doubt she'll care about that once she's back home."

I cringed. Yumi's statement was a slap in the face, more so because it was justified. Her tone suggested she wasn't even being sarcastic about it, just matter of fact.

"I..." There was no good comeback.

Yumi narrowed her eyes, assessing me. I forced myself to stand still, but I couldn't hold her gaze. What did she see? Yumi had proven several times that she was way more perceptive than Luna and me, and it was almost uncanny how she picked up on thoughts or feelings that I thought were private.

"It's not really about Mrs T is it? You're afraid to travel on your own, aren't you?"

"Don't be silly. Why would I be afraid?" My knee jerk reaction was to deny it, too proud to admit it.

My denial didn't dissuade Yumi.

"Are you sure? Have you ever gone anywhere on your own?"

How in the world could she possibly pick up on that? I shrugged sheepishly.

Yumi shook her head and puffed out an exasperated breath.

"For crying out loud. If you're worried about going by yourself, I'll come with you. Dad has some golf stuff anyway on Saturday."

I froze, a shiver running down my spine.

"Are you serious? You would do that? But what do I tell Luna's parents?"

"Maybe you shouldn't say anything until you're on that plane, so they won't ask you to cancel."

"Will you tell your dad?"

"Of course. He'll be fine if he knows we're going together," Yumi said, like it was no big deal.

"But, what if he talks to Luna's mom?" I asked.

"Why would he do that? I told you, he has a golf tournament and if we leave Saturday afternoon, he'll be out on the course and won't have time to talk to them."

The first bell rang, startling us both. We'd been so caught up in conversation we now had to rush to make it to our home room before the teacher arrived.

"Let's talk about this during break and maybe we can look at flights at lunch," I suggested.

Yumi shrugged as if it was a done deal. Was I making too big a fuss about this? What if this was the only option? I had no guarantee yet that Luna would find the place and time to meditate or that she could project her spirit. *Don't forget you have to do the same thing.* If I was at the funeral in person, even in my Luna guise, at least I could be there to pay my respects to Khun Yaai. Definitely worth considering.

The morning went by in a blur. I might as well have skipped classes with my attention span at zero. Instead of taking notes I scribbled a to-do-list in my notebook. Every so often, I had to push aside a stab of fear and guilt. *Luna wants you there, so you're only making sure you are. She'll be okay. Will she? You still haven't told her about the premature departure to the States, either.* I almost moaned. I never meant to change Luna's life the way I had. Would mine be different too?

43

LUNA

WE WALKED INTO WHAT SMELLED LIKE A RESTAURANT. THE dining table and counters in the kitchen were heaving with dishes, bowls of noodles, fried rice, curries, vegetables, fruit, colourful sweets and some stuff I couldn't identify, but everything smelled delicious, especially after the stale muffin at the hospital. There were at least twenty people, mostly elderly women and men, eating and chatting noisily. Mae and Aunt May had changed into traditional Thai dresses and were now moving between their guests talking, nodding and even smiling. I didn't see Duen, but the boys were cleaning away empty plates and making sure everyone had what they needed. This wasn't at all what I expected to happen when someone died. The mood was more cheerful than sombre, like everyone was celebrating at a neighbourhood party. It was actually a relief, and given my experience at the hospital I thought it completely appropriate to commemorate Khun Yaai's life like this. Since I didn't know any of the people, I figured I could escape to our room for a while and maybe even call Nui.

Duen was wearing a midnight blue long Thai wrap-around skirt and buttoning her blouse when I walked in.

"Did you get your shot?" she asked.

"Yeah, all good. Who are the people out there?" I asked.

"I don't know them all, but most of them were here for Khun Ta's funeral as well, remember?"

Shit. It hadn't even crossed my mind that there had been a grandfather, too. Depending on how long ago he'd passed away, I could walk into a minefield where people expected me to remember them. Best to lie low for as long as possible. I was itching to ask when we would leave for the temple, but I didn't want to give away my ignorance.

"I guess I'll go shower and change."

"Hurry. Mae said we have to help," Duen said and walked out.

I looked at my air mattress, which was back against the wall, and sighed. A nap was definitely more enticing than facing a crowd of strangers.

The noise level had increased by the time I'd showered and dressed in a Thai skirt and blouse as well. Not quite trusting my wrapping skills, I secured the skirt with a few safety pins.

I took a deep breath. Time to assume grand-daughterly duties.

More people had arrived and it had warmed up considerably from the previous night, just as Nui predicted. Panya, Chaiya and Duen looked like a well-coordinated team moving around the rooms, replacing cutlery, paper plates and refreshing soda drinks and water.

"Do you guys need help with anything?" I asked Panya.

"No, I think we're good. Just talk to some people." He

tilted his head towards an older woman sitting alone against the wall, watching the crowd move around her, occasionally dabbing at her eyes.

Uh oh, was she someone I should know? Could I ask Panya? What was I supposed to say to her? *Just wing it, like everything else.*

I swallowed, grabbed a little red plastic stool and walked over. She was watching me with keen interest and a tentative smile.

I wai'ed to her.

"Sawasdee kha, Khun Paah. Sabai di mai kha?" Luckily, Thai language allowed me to address any older woman I didn't know, as 'aunty'.

Her face crinkled into a million wrinkles with a smile, showing some very uneven, yellowish teeth. Oddly enough, it enhanced her genuine air of warmth like a well-worn sheepskin glove. She patted the stool I had put down.

"Nong Nui? Is that you? Are you well? I haven't seen you in so long. Look how grown up you are. Come sit and talk to me." Damn, so she was definitely someone I should know.

"I am well, thank you. And you?"

"Oh, let's not talk about this now. I just lost my puen sa-nid, but I suppose we all have to go at some point. Tell me about yourself. Have you kept your promise?" She winked at me. Ahh, she was Khun Yaai's best friend. I let out a small sigh of relief not having to guess the relationship. But what did she mean by promise?

Khun Paah frowned, her eyes almost disappearing inside the wrinkles.

"You forgot?"

"Forgot what?"

Khun Paah tilted her head, squinting as she contemplated me.

"You promised to make Khun Yaai proud and study hard. You forgot how you begged Khun Yaai to convince your mother to let you go to that fancy school of yours? Why do you think she sold her fields?" Khun Paah said. Her tone held a note of rebuke.

I tried to keep my expression neutral, not sure how successful I was in hiding my confusion. What kind of deal had Nui made with her grandma? And what did fields have to do with BIS?

Khun Paah pursed her lips. "She paid for your school and now you don't remember?"

She tsked and shook her head, disappointed.

I was glad I was sitting down, my legs suddenly felt wobbly. My stomach cramped. I felt guilty on Nui's behalf.

She looked at me inquisitively. "You didn't know?"

"I...I...." I searched for words. She didn't wait for my answer, but suddenly chuckled.

"You can send me that postcard from Noo Jowk that you promised, and I'll put it on her altar."

New York? Khun Yaai had paid for Nui's BIS admission? Did Nui know this? She must have if she'd promised postcards from America, though I was pretty sure Khun Yaai hadn't meant for her to assume someone else's body in order to do so. But wow, it hadn't occurred to me how serious the financial constraints were if Khun Yaai had to sell valuable property to fund Nui's schooling. Another lightbulb clicked on. Was that why Nui had insisted on attending the funeral herself, instead of waiting for me to come back to Bangkok to make the switch? She owed Khun Yaai big time. But something didn't add up. Nui had said that the school fees were a burden on her parents. How could her parents threaten to use the money paid by Khun Yaai for Nui's education to build the cooking school?

"I'm so sorry, Khun Paah. I'm exhausted. We were at the hospital all night."

She patted my hand. "I understand. We all have to adjust to life without her now, don't we?" She picked up her tissue and dabbed at her eyes.

"Can I get you anything? Some food, something to drink?" I needed to escape before she could corner me on other commitments I knew nothing about.

"You go. I'll just sit here and remember our good times," Khun Paah said.

I wai'ed and detoured back to our temporary room, not even bothering to grab a plate of food. My appetite had vanished.

It was one thing for Nui to attend the funeral, but I couldn't allow her to speak with her family before our switch. If she heard about the withdrawal from school, the double hit of leaving BIS and therefore not being able to apply for the J-1 visa to study abroad might be too much for her to accept. It definitely would be safer for me to go ahead with the remote switch idea before the funeral. My head throbbed. I only had a day left to reclaim my life.

44

NUI

Yumi and I reconvened in the cafeteria for lunch. She got food for both of us while I tried calling Luna then texted her to call me as soon as she was free.

"Ok, let's divide this up," Yumi said, sitting down with a tray and putting a sandwich, yoghurt and a bottle of water in front of me.

"I'll check flights. You handle hotels. Do you know where the funeral will be?"

"Khun Yaai used to go to Phra That Doi Pu Khao. I assume the funeral will be there as well, or at least the vigil, but I'm not sure if they have a crematorium."

"Pra what?" Yumi asked, then wiggled her hand. "Never mind. You know where that is so just look for a place close by, okay? We're flying into Chiang Rai, correct?" Yumi asked, already tapping and scrolling on her phone.

"Yeah, Chiang Rai, but Ban Sop Ruak is still an hour north from there."

"And? You know how to get there, right?" Yumi stopped scrolling long enough to frown at me, making me feel inadequate.

"I've been there, but I never had to book anything. Paa or Mae handled everything and Uncle Dech or Aunt May picked us up, so no, I don't know." I threw up my hands, resentful that I had to rely on Yumi for support, then feeling guilty for resenting it.

Yumi shook her head again. "Geez. Fine, we'll figure it out. I assume they have Uber there?"

"It's called Grab here, but same-same." I grinned. Yumi had answers for everything and it actually was kind of fun to plan a trip with a friend—especially a secret mission. A second later, the reason for the trip hit me and my mood shifted again in a flash.

"Shit, I keep forgetting why we're going." My voice wobbled.

"You'll have plenty of time to think about that later. For now, let's just get it sorted."

Clearly, Yumi was more experienced than me with travel arrangements. I wondered if she'd expect to stay in a fancy hotel. I wasn't even sure how much money was left in Luna's account since I'd used some for the blog. We were both quiet for a while, scrolling on our phones.

"Okay, I have some flight options," Yumi said. "We can leave at one thirty, or four or five. It takes about one and a half hours and you said it's another hour to that village so I think it's best we take the earlier flight. We should get into the hotel by around four or five, which is perfect." Yumi was talking to herself, working through the different options rather than asking my opinion. I felt a pang of envy at how easy this was for her.

"That sounds good. I guess that means I need to leave the

house around eleven or eleven thirty. What do I tell Luna's mom?"

Yumi barely suppressed an eye roll. *She's helping you,* I reminded myself. *Stop being so testy and simply be grateful for Yumi's expertise.*

"Just tell her you're meeting me for lunch. I'll pack a sandwich and we can eat on the way, so you won't be lying about that at least. Shall I book it?" she asked, with her finger poised over the phone.

I held my breath, then exhaled sharply. "Do it."

45

LUNA

How long could I hide in Chaiya's room before the family would come looking for me? Though it felt safer here, I risked another telling off for shirking my duties as Khun Yaai's granddaughter if I stayed too long. Besides, the room was tiny like a monk's cell, and didn't leave any option other than to sit on the bed. My phone was fully charged, but I still had zero connectivity, so couldn't even use the lull to call Nui.

Bracing myself, I pasted a smile on my face and went back to the living room, wai'ing to random people. *This is no different from one of Dad's cocktail parties. Just pretend you're listening, nod a few times and you'll be fine.* Better yet, if I could keep busy, I wouldn't have to talk at all. Though Panya had said they were managing, I volunteered to wash empty bowls and platters for people to take home.

After what felt like forever, the visitors finally started to leave, as if by some unspoken signal. Had I missed something? I snuck in a few bites until Duen slapped my hand away.

"Stop it. We don't have time for that."

Time for what? What did they all know that I didn't?

She covered up leftovers and put them in the fridge. The boys cleared the last of the plastic cups and paper plates and took two full trash bags outside. Mae and Paa came from their room with jackets over their arms.

"Girls, we're leaving in ten minutes," Paa said.

"Almost done," Duen called from the kitchen.

I mentally slapped my head. Prayers, of course. My short-term memory was clearly not up to speed after the restless night and morning.

I dashed into the bathroom, then grabbed my shawl, phone, and backpack. By the time I got back, Nui's parents were standing on the sala looking towards the Golden Buddha. The sun reflecting off the statue was almost blinding. Damn. I'd missed my window to call Nui. Paa had his arm around Mae's shoulder, steadying her as she took deep breaths. It felt wrong to disturb them when they clearly needed a minute to themselves. Did Nui have any idea what her family was going through? I felt annoyed with Nui and equally guilty for pretending to have a stake in Khun Yaai's passing. Unexpectedly, I felt myself tearing up. The call to Nui could wait a little longer.

Paa followed Uncle Dech in what turned out to be a fairly quick journey, bypassing the giant Buddha statue, which looked even more colossal up close and dominated the entire river front. Life-sized carved wooden elephants stood sentry in front and behind, facing south along the Mekong River.

The temple was up on a very steep hill. Two five-headed stone Nagas protected the staircase leading up to the temple grounds. The serpents' faces were truly terrifying, as if they were about to strike. I had seen similar sculptures at Angkor Wat in Cambodia when I was younger and still remembered how scared I had felt. Their bodies rippled up either side of the steps, a constant reminder of their powers as one climbed.

"One hundred steps," Duen grumbled under her breath.

"You counted them?" I asked.

"You didn't?" She snorted, then took a deep breath and started moving. "Nueng, song, saam, see…"

My first step almost had me nose plant onto the staircase. Long skirts weren't meant for climbing. Lifting the hem high enough to walk, I was huffing by the time I reached the top. Maybe the point was to arrive breathless, though I had to admit that Aunt May's household seemed to be fitter than the Bangkok branch of the family. I turned around to see the broad muddy ribbon of the Mekong flow south towards Cambodia and Vietnam. Several long-tail boats were racing up and the down the river. When revved up, their diesel engines sounded like angry wasps on attack, and I had considered using earplugs when Nui and I took them in Bangkok to cross the Chayo Praya river. Their buzz could even be heard up here.

I looked over my shoulder and saw several buildings in the square, similar in setting to Wat Pathum. Aunt May lead us to a sala with glass sliding doors. We left our sandals at the door as usual. A simple closed casket stood in front of a Buddhist altar with big flower arrangements surrounding it. At the foot of the coffin was a low table and urns filled with sand and burning incense sticks. An easel with Khun Yaai's portrait framed by flower garlands stood to the right. This was the first time seeing her open-eyed and from the look and smile on her face, I thought I would have liked her. There was a faint resemblance to the face I saw every morning in the mirror. A shiver went through me. This morning she had still been in the hospital bed and now her body was in that box. Creepy. Next to it was a smaller easel with a clock face set at one thirty for the first round of chants. Two laypersons were busy placing talapad ceremonial fans, a roll of white string, and water bottles on the dais for the monks. Impressive that they had arranged everything so quickly.

Mae and Aunt May went to the incense table and lit some sticks, praying silently with their heads bowed. They then walked to the coffin and wai'ed again before returning to the two centre chairs. We followed their example in pairs, Duen probably not realising that I stayed half a step behind so I could copy her lead.

I sat down and closed my eyes. There was nothing to do but wait quietly. It was so peaceful that I had to caution myself not to fall asleep.

Slowly, I became aware that Aunt May was talking to Paa and Panya to Duen. If that was okay, it was probably also alright for me to text. It seemed that Thai memorial rituals were less formal than I had expected.

I grabbed my backpack from under the seat, turned away from Duen, and cautiously pulled out my phone just to see if I had a connection. Yes! Two new messages from Nui.

I quickly texted her.

'At the temple. Chant in ½ hour. Tum and Krit OTW. You coming?'

Nui would be in class now, but she might respond. I needed to know if Mom had agreed to let Nui come for the funeral, or if I had to find a way to escape this evening to do the remote switch somehow, somewhere.

At one-thirty sharp, four monks walked into the sala and took their places on the dais. I had attended a few Buddhist ceremonies during our cultural awareness training when we first moved and hoped this wouldn't be so different.

Otherwise, I'd have to rely on Duen to take the lead in any rites we had to perform.

One monk unrolled the spool of string and tied it to the coffin, then wrapped the thread loosely around his wrists before passing it on to the next monk, who did the same until it connected all four to the coffin. The string was supposed to combine the power of the monk's prayers. During one of our temple visits, a monk had tied a string around my wrist and I could not remove it until it fell off naturally. I still didn't know why there were only four instead of the usual nine monks I had seen at other ceremonies. Nine was considered auspicious, so maybe four was for mourning? I'd have to ask Nui about it at some point.

The chanting was mesmerising, rising and falling in pitch similar to an ocean swell, surging, and retreating. I held my hands in a prayer position and felt myself swaying back and forth with my eyes closed. It didn't last long though, and suddenly, people got up and walked outside.

"That was quick," I said to Duen as we slipped into our sandals.

"What do you mean, quick? We've got three more to go. And the same this evening." She looked me up and down. "What's with you these days? You sound like you've never been to a funeral."

Well, I haven't. I almost snapped back, but choose to ignore Duen.

A refreshment station sat around the corner with water, juices and some bite size snacks. People were standing around, drinking and chatting.

This definitely was unlike any funeral I'd ever heard of. The family was mingling with Khun Yaai's friends. Looking across the open courtyard, I saw a sign for toilets.

"I'm just going to the bathroom," I said to Duen. "Be right back."

I needed to call Nui and find out if she was coming for the funeral. Should I ask her about her deal with Khun Yaai? Maybe it would give her ammunition to negotiate with her parents about the withdrawal. But what if Nui was the only beneficiary of Khun Yaai's generosity? Would her parents use it as a counterargument to teach Nui fairness with her siblings? Either way, I'd be better off keeping my mouth shut until we switched back either here or remotely. *If you can manage, Luna.* I groaned. *Stop imagining the worst-case scenario.* The battle inside my head was raging strong, the complete opposite of how I was supposed to feel.

NUI

Yumi and I huddled in the courtyard after the last bell. We only had a few minutes before I had to get in the van to go home with Luke.

"Okay, I've got the flight confirmation and I'll do the online check-in for us tomorrow morning. Did you book a hotel?" Yumi asked.

"Not yet. Luna texted. I need to let her know we're coming. At least we won't have to worry about the remote switch tonight."

"Is there a dress code for a Thai funeral?"

"Just wear something dark or white, but make sure your shoulders and knees are covered because we're in a temple. And don't take this the wrong way, but nothing flashy," I said, almost feeling the need to apologise to Yumi.

"Trust me, I figured that much." Yumi snorted.

"Can you meet me at Central Embassy Mall? The toll

way entrance is right there, so it'll be easy to grab a taxi and go. Shall we say ten thirty or eleven?"

"Sure, that'll work."

"Luna, let's go!" Luke called from the driveway.

I waved to him.

"Let's talk later. I'll call you when I've booked a place, okay?" I walked away, but turned around one more time. "Thank you, Yumi. Really appreciate your help."

"Never mind. Just make sure you guys are getting it done right this time."

LUNA'S MOM WASN'T HOME WHEN LUKE AND I ARRIVED, which gave me time to prepare for the trip. The Imperial Golden Triangle was only ten minutes on foot from the temple. It was a three star resort, but I thought it would be acceptable to someone used to Yumi's or Luna's standards. We were staying only one night, anyway. My family would be crammed together in Aunt May's house, so I'd definitely be more comfortable at the hotel.

Yumi probably wouldn't like the steep climb to the temple, but if necessary, we could use one of the *songthaews* trucks that ferried people up the hill. Ban Sop Ruak was tiny, and as far as I knew, only existed because of its proximity to the Ruak and Mekong Rivers, the very heart of the Golden Triangle. To Yumi, this would seem like a complete backwater, but she'd surprised me more than once with her easy-going attitude. Maybe she'd consider it an adventure. I had to remind myself again that this was not a leisure trip for me.

Though Luna didn't have any traditional Thai outfits, packing was easy as I knew where I was going, the acceptable attire and who would be there. Besides, no one would expect a *farang* to show up in a *pha sinh* skirt.

I checked the wallet to see if I still had enough cash. My stomach twinged when I saw Luna's Hong Kong ID. Could I use a foreign ID for travel? Not likely. I needed her passport to be on the safe side. Looking through the drawers in her desk, the nightstand and even in her closet, I came up empty-handed. Did Luna's dad give me her passport after our trip to Bali, or had he stored them away together? If so, where? I had no reason to ask, especially after Luna's mom had said I couldn't go. Did they have a safe? I felt iffy about invading their bedroom and wanted to look in Khun Susan's office first. A quick check through the drawers of her desk revealed nothing but standard office supplies. A small filing cabinet sat under the desk, locked. Dammit. I was riffling again through the drawers, looking for a key, when the door opened and Khun Susan stepped in. She looked up in surprise.

"Hi honey. What are you doing?"

"Eh, nothing. I was just looking for ...." I looked down. "For some highlighters." I picked one up as evidence, but felt myself blushing.

"Okaaay." Khun Susan drew out the word and raised an eyebrow. "You alright?"

"Fine." I stood there trying to figure out if I could just ask Khun Susan for the ID when a thought hit me out of left field. What if the government confiscated the passport to put that flag in it and hadn't returned it yet? I'd be screwed. But wouldn't they do that electronically in this day and age? I simply didn't know.

Think Nui. Maybe Luna knew where her parents keep official documents. My stomach tightened. Why did everything have to be so complicated? All I wanted to do was go to my grandmother's funeral. Was that too much to ask?

"Anything else, honey?" Khun Susan asked.

I had completely spaced out.

"Ah no, or actually yes. I'm going to meet Yumi tomorrow at eleven at Central Embassy."

"Does it need to be tomorrow? Dad is off, and I thought we could go to the Tiger Temple. Luke said you wanted to go too so we can make it a family day."

Seriously? It seemed the entire universe was conspiring against my trip.

"Why don't you go ahead, Mom? Yumi is on her own tomorrow. Her dad is playing golf, so I want to keep her company." Lately, most of my conversations with Luna's mom seemed to develop into a fencing match, constantly blocking and regrouping.

"Yumi is welcome to come along if she likes. I can call Jake to make sure he's okay with that."

No!

"Em, Mom, actually Yumi and I just want to have some girl time, maybe do some shopping, have lunch and see a movie, you know?" I was scrambling.

Khun Susan sighed. "Fine. Maybe we'll do something else then and go to the Tiger Temple another time."

"Oh, I think you should go ahead. I'm not that keen on it, anyway." If the family left the house early to make the five hours round-trip, that would give me plenty of time to get ready and leave.

"We'll see. We can talk tonight," Khun Susan said.

I retreated to Luna's room before she could come up with new ideas that would prevent my trip. My stomach felt sour from flat-out lying. I'd have to confess to Luna that I'd gone behind her mom's back, so she could prepare herself for any fallout.

I sent her a text message to call me as soon as she was

free. My message had barely gone through when the phone rang.

"Oh, thank God. I'm so glad I caught you." Luna said in a hushed voice. "I can't talk long. We're at the temple and there's a quick break between chants. Tell me, are you coming?"

"Perfect timing. Yes, I just confirmed the hotel for us and…"

"Us? Who's us?" Luna interrupted.

"Yumi wanted to come too, so she booked the flights. We should get in around three-thirty and by the time we get to the Triangle, it'll probably be five o'clock."

"What did Mom say? Was she okay with that?"

"Em… not exactly." I stalled.

"Meaning?" Luna asked.

"Well, she said I should send some flowers, but didn't think it was necessary for me to fly up. But you know I have to be there."

"Thanks a lot, Nui. Now I'm really looking forward to going home." Luna's sarcasm could have cut ice.

"I know, and I'm sorry, but I didn't know what else to do. I mean, we could try the remote switch, but when?"

Luna sighed.

"No, you're right, you should be here. I think it'll be safer to do it when we're together."

"Agree. Hey, do you know where your passport is? It's not in your desk."

"Mom has all documents locked away in her filing cabinet. The key is in the jug with the pencils on her desk."

"Phew. Okay. I think I'll manage that. What else is going on up there? Do you know the schedule yet?" I asked.

"Your paa is picking up the boys right now. There'll be another prayer session tonight at six or seven, but I don't know what happens overnight or tomorrow. I need to find out and text you. Where are you staying?"

"At the Imperial. It's close by. Maybe you could come there tomorrow night and we switch then?"

"I'll text you as soon as I find out. I gotta go. People are coming back. I think the monks are starting again."

"Okay, just text me when you can, and I'll see you tomorrow. Bye."

"Wait, Nui. Yumi told me Luke sa…"

I bit my lip and closed my eyes, shame twisting my insides. I knew exactly what Luna wanted to know, but I tried to convince myself that I had already tapped the end button *before* she asked. The tension in my body told me otherwise. Everything was coming down to the next twenty-four hours.

47

LUNA

DAMMIT! NUI CUT ME OFF BEFORE I COULD ASK HER ABOUT Luke's accusation. Deliberately? What did she do that made an earlier move necessary? I didn't have time to consider the question, but rushed to take my seat.

The ebb and flow of the chanting pulled my mind away. Would I be able to sneak out tomorrow night to see Nui and Yumi at the hotel? Would we be able to complete the switch? If so, should I stay for the funeral or leave immediately? Mom would be furious with me for going against her orders, but I was willing to take the punishment as long as I was home.

The police! My whole body jerked. I almost knocked into Duen, but she had her head down, eyes closed, and missed my reaction. In all the upheaval around Khun Yaai, I had completely forgotten to ask Nui about the outcome of the investigation. If Luke held me responsible, then *that* was the only reason we would have to leave the country quickly.

What exactly had the police concluded, and how long had Nui known about this? It must have been bad if it had made her change her mind. And, of course, now Yumi had given her an out with the J-1 visa, she didn't need my body anymore, but could let me suffer the consequences of her actions. At this stage, I wouldn't put anything past her—the snake. What other crimes had she committed and kept from me? How dare she upset my life like this? Once I was back home, I'd find a way to punish her. *Ha! You won't have to. If she loses her place at BIS, that would be her just rewards.* I came out of my vengeful fantasies when people got up to move outside. *I'm sorry Khun Yaai.* I wai'ed in apology for the ill-timed tantrum.

Nui's paa and brothers arrived during the next break. Tum was in his novice monk robes. He had to finish another week of service before going back to school. I was curious to see what his role would be at the upcoming funeral. He looked sad, in need of a cuddle, but he wasn't allowed to touch his mom or aunt or any female during his training.

Krit hugged both his mother and Aunt May. Mae leaned into him as if she needed Krit's strength to stay upright. Since I'd known her, she had never been overtly affectionate, but seemed to rely on stricter methods to run her family. Now, however, she appeared positively vulnerable.

Krit turned to me with a smile and pulled me close.

"How have you been, sis?"

"I'm fine, Krit. Welcome back. Sorry it has to be for this." I tilted my head towards Khun Yaai's coffin.

"I know, sad." Krit nodded.

"How long can you stay?" I asked.

"I'll come home with you guys, but I have to do one extra weekend soon to make up for the days. And then I'm officially free." He grinned. Relief over the end of his service trumped the sadness of the occasion.

"And then?" I asked.

"We'll see." Krit shrugged. Maybe as the oldest son, he had more leeway than Nui to choose his own direction. I almost felt sorry for Nui—almost.

The sala became packed, every chair taken and even people sitting on the floor in the back. Krit grabbed my arm and pulled me toward the seats reserved for the family up front.

"Come on, we'll catch up later."

I was glad he hadn't asked about Channon. The two had met and become friends when they overlapped during military service. Unless the family had told Krit, he wouldn't know that Channon and I had gone out a few times or that we worked together at the animal shelter. Given the current flux between us, there was no need to bring it up just yet.

The chanting was hypnotic and again lulled me into a slight trance, letting my mind wander. I hadn't seen Krit since New Year's Eve when he and Channon had taken me to their friend's party where I ended up kissing Channon. Though it had happened more by accident than design, I had been thrilled. But now Channon and I were at crossroads and I dreaded what he would do after Nui and I switched back. I wasn't sure if we'd built up enough of a rapport during our limited time together. Sure, I had met his mom and there was Chone, but what if Channon was simply humouring me? Maybe he was using my implausible story as an excuse to distance himself. *Stop, stop, stop.* This endless internal commentary was driving me nuts. Why couldn't I just choose a line and stick with it? My thoughts were so tangled up in hypothetical scenarios and mind games I didn't know anymore which outcome would be best or worst. I groaned, my shoulders stiff to the point of being painful.

Sure, Nui had said she wasn't attracted to Channon, but what if he felt differently and Nui appealed to him physically more than I did? My hands locked in a tight grip, the knuckles turning white. *Stop imagining things, Luna.* Even if Channon backed away, it was better than continuing a charade that could go nowhere with me in Nui's body. And if he wasn't interested in me after we switched back, then it was better to know. I exhaled sharply. *Right, that's better thinking. Now pay attention.* Krit looked at me with a question mark on his face. I shook my head and smiled sheepishly. Did everyone space out during prayers, or was it just me? I silently apologised to Khun Yaai again.

By four o'clock we were done. Khun Yaai's friends were offered more drinks and food, but the majority left, promising to return for the evening prayers.

Mae and Aunt May would stay until evening prayers and ordered the rest of us to go home and rest. I felt bad for them sitting around on uncomfortable chairs and grieving for their mother, but maybe it was their way of processing it. Poor Tum had to stay at the temple too with the monks. I could tell he was trying to be brave about it, but I saw him biting down on his lower lip. It seemed like an unnecessary hardship for a twelve-year-old, but who was I to judge?

Duen yet again organised the kitchen with Panya and Chaiya. Krit settled into Khun Yaai's room and the fathers went over more lists at the dining room table. Everyone was busy but me. What was I supposed to do with myself?

Isn't this what you wanted? A big normal family? Well, yes, but I hadn't realised how much close contact it required and that no one would have any privacy. The only escape was the sala, which was also the sole spot for the internet connection. While I needed to have a conversation with Channon, I wasn't ready for it and couldn't risk being overheard by the family, especially Krit. Besides, there was nothing new to say. Either the switch worked or it didn't and until then, nothing had changed. *Convenient, Luna, isn't it? Admit it, you're not really sure anymore what you want. You like the idea of having a boyfriend, and Channon was handy.* I froze on the spot. Oh my God, where did these thought come from? My throat tightened. It wasn't fair to Channon to think that way. He had been nothing but nice to me and yet... If I didn't really believe that he and I had a chance to make this work I could have saved myself a lot of trouble. Which brought me back to Nui. What had been her motivation?

I was still too angry to call her again. It would be better to wait for her arrival tomorrow. And why did Yumi want to come to Chiang Rai? She had even less reason to be here than me. *Maybe she wants a ringside view while Nui and I battle it out.* I scoffed at my childish crabbiness, but calling Yumi now somehow required too much effort.

Maybe I needed to take a nap. The early morning alarm and crisis were catching up with me and we would go back to the temple soon. I never realised that funeral traditions were so busy. *You could meditate to make sure you're up to speed for tomorrow.* Another jab of worry went through my body. I almost resented having to do the practise, but I knew it was necessary to get myself in the right frame of mind. Maybe a miraculous solution would present itself while I was 'under' or 'out of it'. I squirmed at the dubious notion. No one was paying attention to me, so I slipped into our room and sat on the mattress, leaning my back against the wall. I didn't want to fall asleep, but needed to be comfortable enough to fully relax.

Headphones in, I selected one of the earlier versions of

Ajaarn's recordings. Maybe if I went back to basics, it would work. Most importantly, don't even think about the switch. *Yeah right. How do I not think about something I don't want to think about?* I needed a distraction and hit play.

Ajaarn's voice was soothing.

'Breathe in to the count of four, hold for four and slowly exhale to the count of eight.'

I could feel myself relaxing, shoulders dropping. A pleasant current ran through my body as if someone had plugged me into an electrical outlet to recharge. It reminded me why I liked meditation so much. My only aim was to hold the current and possibly deepen it but not push for an out-of-body-projection.

<h1 style="text-align:center">48</h1>

<h2 style="text-align:center">NUI</h2>

KHUN SUSAN'S OFFICE WAS RIGHT NEXT TO THE KITCHEN, SO I would have to wait until after dinner to sneak in and get the passport. Khun Bo had left for the day but prepared a som tam salad and egg-fried rice with stir-fried chicken vegetables for dinner. If I was careful, I might even sneak in a few bites of chicken while pretending to separate it from the veggies. After tomorrow I could eat Khun Yaa's delicious curries again without having to hide my tastes. At least that was something to look forward to.

Luna's dad arrived early by his standards and we sat down to eat immediately.

"TGIF. Cheers everyone." He raised his beer in salute.

"Mark, I was thinking we could go to the Tiger Temple tomorrow. Luna said she promised to meet up with Yumi, so maybe we should go another time," Khun Susan said.

Luke snorted. "Of course! What Luna wants, Luna gets."

I wondered how long he would hold the grudge against me, or rather Luna.

"Luke. Be nice. We can still go if you want to. I just have to let Khun Pak know. Mark, what do you think?" Khun Susan asked.

Luke interrupted before his dad could reply.

"Dad, did you talk to your boss yet? Do you know where we're going?"

Khun Mark put down his cutlery.

"I did. It's a bit more tricky than I had hoped. They are looking into it, but right now there are no immediate vacancies in the US at my level. So either I'll do an interim posting or look at another company. But that would mean giving up my seniority and starting fresh." He sighed.

I ducked my head. *Oh God, Luna will not like this at all.* It also meant that if they were not going to the US, I would not be able to live with them once I got my exchange student application approved.

"Are you happy now, Luna? See what you did?" Luke spat at me.

"Luke stop. We had this discussion before." Khun Susan chided him. "I know it's not ideal, but we'll work it out. Where do they have jobs right now, Mark?"

Khun Mark took a sip of his beer.

"There are a few new openings coming up, but the one that's most urgent right now is for the opening-GM for Langkawi."

"Langkawi? But that's tiny. I bet they don't even have a proper soccer league there," Luke complained.

"Langkawi? Mark, do you really think that's a good idea? I mean, it's a beautiful island, but do they have any international schools there?" Khun Susan asked. "We don't want to live in KL when you have to be on the island."

Khun Mark scrubbed his hands over his face.

"No, it's not ideal for sure. Maybe someone from the States gets transferred to the island and that opens up a new position in the States, but I don't know. I'm going to put my feelers out to some head-hunters as well and see what's available right now." He sighed and picked up his glass.

I put my spoon on the plate, my appetite gone. I didn't know what all those acronyms meant, but I hadn't realised how much trouble I had caused for Luna's family with my reckless actions. Would the family have to separate because of the job location? Luna would never forgive me for that. And even if that was only an interim solution, it would entail yet another two moves for her, which was the exact opposite of what Luna had wanted. The frequent transfers were part of the reason we came up with the switch idea in the first place, as she had never known a stable base. I should shoot myself now, as Luna was bound to strangle me once she found out.

"I suppose we could move back to Chicago while you open the place so the kids can go to school there while we wait for an opening," Khun Susan said, but then shook her head. "No, that's silly. If we have to separate, you might as well stay here while we move ahead. Do you think they would cover the move even if we didn't leave at the same time?"

Khun Mark shrugged. Neither parent looked thrilled at the idea. To be separated would definitely not be my idea of family life either. The predicament I had put the family in really hit home. Did other expats have to decide something like this all the time? Maybe that status wasn't so appealing after all. On the other hand, how many kids would force their parents to make a move like that? I felt bile in the back of my throat rising fast.

"Excuse me." I jumped up and dashed to my room,

pressing a napkin in front of my mouth. I was dry heaving into the toilet when Khun Susan walked in.

"Are you okay, honey? What's wrong?" She went to the basin to wet a hand towel and pushed it into my fist. I sat on the toilet lid and wiped my face.

"I'm so, so sorry, Mom. I didn't know this would create so many problems. I wished I had never thought of it. I'm really sorry." Tears started to flow.

"I know you didn't mean for this to happen, Luna. We'll deal with it one way or another." Khun Susan brushed her hand over my head. Her kind words were killing me. It was even worse than if she'd been shouting. Would she be this forgiving if she knew I wasn't her own daughter? Luna was super lucky, but then again, Luna most likely wouldn't have done the stupid things I had.

"I won't, Mom. I promise." Even as I spoke, I felt like throwing up again. I already knew that tomorrow I would break another promise. The parents would never trust Luna again.

For the first time, I wondered if Luna and I shouldn't just come clean and explain everything to the parents.

49

LUNA

I KNEW I WAS SMILING, BUT KEPT MY EYES CLOSED TO SAVOUR the moment. For the first time in days, I had quieted the rollercoaster of thoughts and was strictly focused on the flow of my breath. What a relief. If I could hold that state, I was confident I could get back to a full out-of-body experience as well. There was no way to push that. Either it came naturally or not at all. I had to be satisfied with the status quo for now.

"You awake?" Krit asked. He moved to sit on the bed beside my mattress, but I kept my eyes closed to feel the afterglow of the meditation a tad longer.

"I am now." I tugged off my headphones.

"What are you doing?" he asked.

"Meditating. I'm done though." I opened my eyes. He'd look cute once his buzz cut had grown out a bit. Did Channon have to shave his hair like that too while he was doing the compulsory training? I much preferred him with wavy hair.

"How have you been, Nui? What's happening?" Krit asked.

I shook my head. "Same old, same old. What about you? What are you going to do now?"

Krit shrugged. "Haven't thought too much about it yet. I have a few months before I start Uni and I'll figure something out. Take some time off unless Paa needs help in the store. I heard they are planning on expanding the shop. That'll be cool."

Not for Nui, if it meant leaving BIS. Maybe Krit didn't know that yet.

"Were you there when Khun Yaai passed away?" Krit asked. "I wished I'd made it in time to say goodbye."

"Yeah, we were, but we didn't get to talk to her. She was in a coma the whole time and then just moved on. At least that's what it felt like. It was actually very peaceful."

Krit sighed and rubbed his face.

"I'm glad she didn't suffer. She was such a special lady."

"Hmm." I suspected she was, given what her best friend had said to me. I was curious if Krit or the others had received similar favours from Khun Yaai, but figured it was best to not poke that hornet's nest in case only Nui had benefitted.

"So, what is this I hear about you and Channon?" Krit grinned at me.

"Channon? What about him?" I tried to sound casual.

"Are you guys dating? I heard you went out a few times. He's a really great guy." He playfully nudged my thigh with his toe.

I rolled my eyes to avoid looking at him, but felt a blush creeping up my face.

"Where did you hear that?" I hedged.

"Oh, you know… a text here or there."

"And they say women are gossips." I threw my hands up as if exasperated, but was curious as to what Channon had told Krit. *As long as he didn't bring up my story about the switch.* I trusted him enough to know he wouldn't do that.

"Who said it was Channon who texted me?" Krit teased.

Not Channon? That was a little deflating. I doubted Mae or Khun Yaa would have said something unless they wanted Krit to intervene? Duen! Who else would gossip like that? That girl always needed to get her two bits in. No wonder she had asked me about Channon last night.

I sighed.

"Yeah, we've gone out a few times and we work together at the animal shelter, but who knows? I'm not really sure what's going on."

"Well, you could do worse. Come on, let's eat."

Krit stood and reached out a hand to help me up.

"Oh, and you can ask him yourself tomorrow." Krit winked.

My hand slipped out of his hand and I sat down with a heavy thump.

"Channon? He's coming here?" I croaked out.

"Yup." Krit turned and walked out without looking back, but I could see his shoulders twitching as if he was laughing at me.

Channon, Nui and Yumi, plus the entire family in one place. *Shoot me now.*

50

NUI

I SPENT THE REST OF THE EVENING IN MY ROOM, HIDING FROM the family by claiming sickness. My backpack for tomorrow was packed, and all I had to do was get the passport from the office after the parents went to bed.

I walked around the room, touching things here and there as if I needed to commit them to memory. This would be my last evening here. In just a few weeks, my life had been completely turned upside down. *No, Nui,* you *turned your life upside down. That was all your doing.* I shivered. Having seen first-hand the consequences of my actions on Luna's family, I found it increasingly difficult to pretend that some unseen force was responsible for what had happened.

I can't deal with this right now! Can't or won't? It felt as if during the last hour, a hidden door to my most negative feelings had cracked open, and more and more horrible emotions were creeping out. Yumi was right. I had acted like a spoilt brat to get what I wanted, never considering the effect on anyone else. To compound the guilt, I wouldn't even have to deal with the consequences, but that would fall on Luna. I could still apply for a J-1 visa and achieve my goal with no one's help. Somehow, that thought didn't taste as satisfying as it had before. Sure, I'd go ahead, but the cost to the others made it a pretty shallow victory. *Stop this right now. Wallowing in regret won't serve any purpose. Just get through tomorrow and then you can make a fresh start.*

The hectic day and interrupted sleep last night was catching up with me. I set the alarm for midnight to grab the passport and sat back on the bed to read a few pages.

The frigid air woke me up. I hadn't pulled up a blanket to avoid getting too comfortable, but still must have hit the snooze button a few times, as it was already one o'clock in the morning. The apartment seemed quiet, but with the doors closed, it was difficult to tell if people were still awake. I grabbed the water glass from my night table and slowly opened the door. The hallway was dark except for a nightlight shining from the kitchen. I tiptoed towards the kitchen then turned left into Khun Susan's office right next to it. For a second, I debated leaving the lights off, but if I closed the door, I figured it would be safe with everyone tucked away in bed.

The key was right where Luna said it would be. After a few fumbles, I pulled out the third drawer and found nine passports rubber bound. *Phew. Mission accomplished.* Flipping through them, I found one with Luna's old photo that was full of stamps and visas from all over the world. I couldn't resist taking a closer look. Thirty-two pages covering God knows how many countries. I saw visas for Egypt, India and Kenya, stamps from France, Spain and Italy, Mexico and Peru, Vietnam, Malaysia and Australia. Was there anywhere she had not been? How could she possibly complain about this kind of life? Determined not to let myself get morose again, I slapped it shut to continue my search without success. Luna's parents had three passports and Luke had two.

Shoot, where was Luna's current one? Had the police taken it? I didn't think so, at least not while they were at the house. Did Luna's dad bring it to the police head office when we went for the interview? I couldn't remember much about that day as I'd been too terrified of being thrown into prison. *Come on, it's gotta be here somewhere.* I started again from the top drawer, carefully going through all the documents and paper folders one by one, when I heard a small sound in the kitchen. The ice/water dispenser made its distinct gurgling sound. *Shit.* I froze for a second, then lunged for the light switch. Khun Susan normally left the door ajar, but there was nothing I could do about it now. Had the light been visible under the doorframe? I crossed my fingers that whoever was in the kitchen had been too tired to notice anything.

Pressing my ear to the door, I couldn't hear anything, but I didn't dare look just yet. I wouldn't be able to explain what I was doing in Khun Susan's office in the middle of the night.

After counting to one hundred, I slowly eased the door open. The kitchen was dark and empty, no one lurking to catch me out.

I was ready to abandon the entire idea of travelling, but Yumi had already paid for the tickets and I owed it to Khun Yaai to be there. *Okay, five more minutes and if you haven't found the passport, that's a sign you're not supposed to go.*

Turning back to the filing cabinet, I went through each drawer and folder again. In the end, it was stupid luck. Luna's passport had gotten stuck backwards inside Khun Susan's passport, which had been on top of the pile after she returned from Chicago.

One quick glance to double check I had left the office with no tell-tale signs of my trespassing. I filled my glass with water at the fridge, went back to my room and fell into bed. It took a while for my heart to slow down, but exhaustion pulled me under.

51

LUNA

THE EVENING PRAYERS WERE PRETTY MUCH THE SAME AS IN the afternoon, except they lasted longer and more people showed up. Khun Yaai must have been really popular in her village. We eventually made it home around ten, everyone exhausted. Mae and Aunt May had gone to bed immediately. Krit and I had sat outside on the sala for a little while, mostly in silence, just unwinding while watching the Giant Buddha light up the sky. He told me about a few of his favourite memories of Khun Yaai, which again confirmed how wonderful she had been. I sadly had nothing to contribute to her memorial. I felt privileged to see her transition, and that she had acknowledged me, but that wasn't something to be shared.

The house was quiet as a tomb after everyone settled down. I was too tired to even contemplate meditating again. I had to trust that everything would work out once Nui got here, then start reclaiming and rebuilding my family life. The separation made me realise how much I had taken for granted, and I vowed to be a better daughter and sister.

DUEN SHOOK ME AWAKE AS THE FIRST LIGHT SPILLED through the window above my head.

"Morning. Better get up soon. The bathroom is free now. I'm gonna help Aunt May make breakfast." She walked out. Duen's industriousness certainly came in handy sometimes.

I stretched and smiled. Not only did I feel much better after sleeping well, but today was also the day I was going home again. *And you'll see Channon.* My heart picked up a beat. Krit and I hadn't talked about why Channon was coming to the funeral; maybe they were closer friends than I had realised. *Maybe he's coming because of you?* I smiled at the idea. Regardless, if he was here and things went well with Nui, I might get my answer where he stood with me right away. I felt the push-pull of competing emotions and tried not to let my worries about the switch drag me down again. *Enough of this, Luna. Just think positively.* I threw back the blanket, prepared to tackle the day.

The dining table was too small to hold us all, so the boys and Duen ended up eating breakfast on the daybed. Mae looked much better this morning, and her eyes weren't as red. I wondered how Krit managed to sleep in Khun Yaai's room. Despite everything I had seen yesterday, that idea still creeped me out. The good thing about being embedded in a large family was that I didn't have to talk, only listen and nod occasionally. Apparently, the plan was to go to the temple early, but I couldn't quite figure out if there we'd be saying prayers or simply sitting vigil. If all the monks had to complete their morning alms round in the village, break their fast, and hold the prayers, there wouldn't be enough time to do it all.

It turned out to be much more practical. Because Khun Yaai hadn't wanted an extended mourning period, the number of prayers per day had increased to three. The family had food delivered to the temple for the monk's lunch and that left at least some of them free to conduct the funeral prayers.

We were back in the temple by nine o'clock and already there were people waiting. I recognised Khun Yaai's best friend whom I had talked to yesterday, and she'd been given a prominent place right behind the family.

The sequence was the same as before—prayers broken up by brief intervals where people could talk, eat, and drink. There were no rituals for us to perform, so all we had to do was sit and listen. It almost felt like a version of *Groundhog Day*, one of Mom's favourite movies, or perhaps, more aptly, the calm before the storm. The fairly relaxed atmosphere left way too much time for me to let my thoughts wander, running through scenarios of how the day would unfold. I tried to be patient for Nui and Yumi to arrive and finally getting some answers to what was really going on with my family. At the same time, I worked hard to push away any doubts that Nui and I wouldn't accomplish the switch. Maybe Khun Yaai could help us since she was now in the spirit world and aware of her real and make-believe granddaughters.

5 2

NUI

ON SATURDAYS THE FAMILY NORMALLY SLEPT IN, BUT I heard movement in the apartment at eight in the morning. I'd been awake for a while, tossing and turning after my midnight mission, not being able to shake the feelings of guilt and shame over the mountain of lies that seemed to be self-perpetuating. My plan was to linger in bed, mainly because I didn't want to risk the parents changing their minds about how I should spend the day. As much as I liked Luna's family and would have loved to have more time with them, I couldn't afford to not be on the plane that afternoon. Given the chaos I had put them through, a day spent apart was probably a good idea, anyway; it would give Luke a chance to calm down before Luna got home, even though I would have to explain a few things to her first. I squirmed at my pathetic reasoning, suddenly eager for a distraction.

The parents and Luke were having breakfast when I walked in to get some tea.

"Morning. You're up early," I said.

"Morning, honey. Are you feeling better?" Khun Mark asked.

"I am. What are you guys doing? Are you going to the Tiger Temple?" I steeped a tea bag in my mug.

"No, we're going to Khao Yai instead. It'll be nice to get out of the city for a bit and it'll be cooler up there. We'll have lunch, maybe hike or ride bikes for a while, and I wanted to check out some wineries. I've been meaning to do that," Khun Mark said.

Luke rolled his eyes. The plan, clearly, wasn't his first choice.

"We should be home by six latest. Depending on how tired we are, we can go out for dinner then. I'll text you when we're heading back," Khun Susan said.

Khao Yai national park was about two hours northeast of Bangkok. My parents had taken us kids on a day trip once when we were little and I had loved the green hills, forests and waterfalls. We'd even seen some wild elephants, but I hadn't known there were wineries up there too.

"That sounds great. Enjoy." If they were leaving soon, it would give me plenty of time to get ready and meet Yumi. For once, things were going according to plan.

"What were you doing last night, Luna? Where were you?" Luke asked, eyes narrowed.

"Huh? What do you mean, where was I? In bed. Why?"

You jinxed it. So much for things going smoothly. My hands tightened around the mug to stop the trembling.

"Your door was open, but you weren't there," he said. "I even called you, but you didn't answer."

"No idea. I didn't hear you. I got some water and went straight back to bed."

"But I didn't see you in the kitchen."

Just pretend he's making it up, trying to stir up trouble.

"What do you want me to say? Obviously, I was here. You must have been sleepwalking." I shrugged as if it was of no consequence or mysterious at all. Apparently, he hadn't noticed the closed office door. Thank God for small favours.

"Why didn't you look for her, Luke? You knew Luna hadn't been feeling well," Khun Mark said.

"I called her, didn't I? Who knows what she was doing? I don't care anymore. All she does is make trouble."

Ouch. That hurt. Where was the sweet guy who had looked after me when I tried to swim, and during the seizures? I missed my own brother. Krit would have had my back no matter what.

"Luke, that's enough now. You've made your point." Khun Susan snapped at him. "Go to your room and get ready. We leave in half an hour."

I jumped up to get myself out of the firing line. If his parents started digging, there wasn't any way to explain how Luke could have missed me in the apartment.

"I'm gonna shower. Have a great time and I'll see you later." Even though my stomach was empty following the bathroom episode last night, I had to swallow hard to not gag again. Why did I have to keep lying to the family? They had done nothing but support me and I felt rotten for having paid them back in the worst possible way. My eyes started tearing up. *Come on Nui, when did you become such a cry baby?* The lump in my throat was like a boulder, but I was determined not to fall apart again.

By the time I returned to the kitchen, the family had left. For some perverse reason, I felt abandoned, and decided to take a private farewell tour of the apartment.

Looking down on the pool terrace from the living room balcony reminded me I now knew how to swim. Would I still be able to do that after I switched back with Luna? What about our language skills? Would they return to a more basic level? If so, we'd have to come up with some good excuses, though it would be more difficult for Luna to explain why she couldn't speak Thai anymore. At least I was fluent enough in English to carry on.

"Damn it. Enough already." I spoke out loud to assert myself. "Get moving."

I went back to Luna's room to grab my bag and make sure I had her wallet, passport and the booking confirmation from the hotel. One last look around and I pulled the front door firmly shut behind me.

I ARRIVED EARLY AND TOOK A SEAT AT PAUL BAKERY ON level one at Central Embassy. Having skipped breakfast I ordered an almond croissant along with a chai latte. I was idly scrolling on my phone when a thump brought me back to real life. Yumi had dumped her bag next to my seat and plopped down on the chair opposite.

My lips automatically curved upward.

"You know we're going to Chiang Rai, not Phuket, right?"

She had dressed for a regatta—dark blue Capri pants with a navy/white striped long-sleeved t-shirt, white canvas slip-ons, a blue neckerchief with tiny red and white anchors and to top it off, a white Dixie sailor's cap that I'd only ever seen in old movies. Yumi pulled off her sunglasses and tossed them on the table, glanced at my plain jeans and white T-shirt, but otherwise ignored my comment. With her level of confidence, she didn't have to justify herself or her style.

"Any problems at home?" Yumi waved over the server.

"Not really. They all went to Khao Yai this morning. But Luna's mom said they'll be back by six and may want to go for dinner. I'll have to figure out what to tell her."

"Let's see how the day goes." Yumi shrugged and ordered a cappuccino and a slice of banana bread.

"I've checked us in for the flight so we can go straight through to the gate," Yumi said.

"Great. You need to tell me how much I owe you."

"I'll sort it out with Luna when she's back. It comes from her account anyway, I suppose."

I didn't think Yumi meant to imply that I wasn't good for the money, but the remark stung nonetheless. Lately, every throwaway comment hurt, though that was probably just me being super sensitive about money and other issues.

"Did you tell your dad where we're going?" I asked.

"Yeah. He said it's fine as long as I'm back tomorrow afternoon and to call him once we get there," Yumi said.

"I texted Luna the flight details and I'll call her when we're on the way to the hotel. I hope she can meet us there."

Yumi nodded, busy chewing on her cake.

"What's wrong, Yumi? You're so quiet."

Yumi looked as if she had to decide what to share with me.

"Come on, spit it out."

"If you must know, I've been thinking, but I can't decide whether you guys were incredibly stupid or incredibly lucky to have done what you did."

I raised an eyebrow, encouraging her to continue.

"When you think about it, how many people can actually prove that their body is not who they are but that it's all about the mind? Most people think it's the same."

My jaw fell open. Yumi used her finger to tap it shut so hard my teeth clacked together.

"I… I never thought of it that way," I finally managed, then cleared my throat. "Was that the stupid or lucky part?" I was half-serious, but Yumi snorted.

"Stupid was to try it in the first place. Sounds like neither of you has a very good opinion of yourself if you were ready to give it up so easily."

Ouch. Once again I felt run over by Yumi astute observations. Were Luna and I really this shallow or unsure of ourselves?

"Am I the only one you share your wisdom with or do you lecture Luna too?" I knew I sounded defensive and cranky, but Yumi seemed to hit a raw nerve every single time I talked to her.

"Oh, I intend to," Yumi said, then looked at her phone. "Shall we?"

The ride to Don Muang airport took all of thirty minutes, plenty of time to go through security and find a seat near the gate. Yumi had asked a few questions about the funeral protocol, but otherwise we'd hardly spoken on the ride. I didn't know if I should be angry or grateful to Yumi for pointing out the core issue so bluntly. Maybe Luna and I needed to sit down and have an open conversation to fix any ill feelings and misunderstandings between us. That most likely would also help with the reverse switch. I was still contemplating what I would say to her when I heard Yumi's voice.

"Channon? What are you doing here?"

I looked up and squealed in surprise. Khun Yaa had her hand on Channon's arm as he escorted her towards the gate.

53

LUNA

THANK YOU KHUN YAAI. SO GLAD YOU SHORTENED THE ceremonies. If the repetition of prayers, breaks and socialising continued for much longer I'd go mad. Of course, I knew that for many people the traditions were comforting, but I was too antsy to sit still and pretend to be praying. *Sorry Khun Yaai, I really don't mean any disrespect.* I had the inkling that if Khun Yaai could have had her way, there would have been only one day of prayers followed immediately by the funeral.

After the morning session, we had to serve an early lunch to the monks, as they had to eat before noon. There was music playing in the background and I wasn't sure what to make of this celebratory atmosphere that didn't seem to mesh with what I knew about western funerals. I had been too young when my American grandmother passed away and remembered little except for people crying. Here, everyone seemed to be positive, if not cheerful, about Khun Yaai's transition. Even Mae appeared to feel better now. Perhaps they were on to something and I was just feeling contrary because of my own issues.

A hand on my shoulder made me jump.

"Nui, are you okay?" Aunt May looked at me with a soft smile. "You seem distracted or worried."

"I…" I stopped to clear my throat. "Em, I… I've got some things on my mind."

"I know. Your energy field keeps shifting, like you're trying to figure something out, but it's making you miserable."

My mouth dropped open. How could I have forgotten that she was sensitive to people's auras? With Khun Yaai's passing I would have thought her to be too pre-occupied to notice. Did an energy field really change that quickly?

"Wow." It was all I could manage.

"Can I help you?" Aunt May asked. Her offer appeared genuine. She must be a truly amazing person to be thinking of me at this time and to even have noticed my turmoil.

I spontaneously hugged her. Immediately, I felt more peaceful, as if she had wrapped a cosy blanket around me. Though I couldn't see her energy level, it had to be really high to affect me like this with a simple touch.

"Thank you so much, Aunt May, but I think it's something I have to figure out myself."

"Alright. But I'm very happy to listen if you like." Aunt May didn't pressure me, but I was tempted to take her up on the offer. How could I phrase what was on my mind without giving away the underlying issue?

"Aunt May, do you ever wonder why we are here and what we're supposed to be doing with our lives?" I knew it sounded grandiose, like some deep philosophical question, but I really wanted to know.

Aunt May burst into laughter. "Don't we all, Nui?"

She tilted her head, looking at me curiously. "What made you ask this now? This has nothing to do with Khun Yaai, does it?"

I knew I was playing with fire, but if Aunt May could provide some answers, it might settle the mess in my head.

"No, it's not about Khun Yaai, but I can't really talk about it. Can we just leave it at that?" I pleaded.

Aunt May nodded, then took my hand.

"Well, the way *I* try to make sense of the world is that I believe we all have the freedom of choice."

"Could have fooled me. I don't think I have much choice over anything," I grumbled.

Aunt May smiled.

"You may think so, but consider this: you get to choose what you think, how you act and most importantly how you feel—happy or unhappy. No one can take that from you."

"But what choice is there when Mae or Paa tell me to do something I don't want to do?"

"Ah, but those are just conditions. The choice is in how you react to them. You can either resent them, or decide to make the best of it. You see, I think our purpose in life is to experience joy and uplift others."

"Tell that to my parents." I wasn't sure what she was getting at.

"Ahh, you see that's a choice they made too. They think what they are asking you to do is for your best. Can you at least give them the benefit of the doubt?" Aunt May asked. "Eventually you may decide to pick something different, but in the meantime why not think of it as exploring your options? How can you decide on your future if you don't know what you don't want? You need to know about both sides to make a decision, right?"

"Hmm, okay I kinda get this. But if it's really about

choice, what about all the bad stuff? Like being poor or sick or, or… oh, I don't know. Are you saying that's a matter of choice, too?"

"The choice is in how you react to that. You can either learn from difficulties and open up new opportunities or complain about them and see yourself as a victim. It's up to you. Imagine you were getting a divorce. One side might say it's a big loss and the other might say it's liberating. Wait, maybe that's not a good example for you. Let's say you score a B on a test. If you're used to Cs, a B would be a great success, but if you're used to As then it will seem negative, no? The event itself doesn't matter. It's only when you judge or compare yourself to others or think something or someone is keeping you from being happy that things get difficult."

Aunt May's smile was radiant. I could almost imagine a sunny aura around her.

"It's really quite simple. It all depends on your point of view and only you get to pick what you want to see."

I slowly nodded, not totally sure I understood what she'd just said.

"There's one more thing, Nui. I also believe that everything in this universe acts like a mini magnet. You draw to yourself what you send out into the world. I don't know about you, but I prefer to be happy." She winked at me.

"I guess. But then what's the point of it? I mean, fine, we get to choose if we want to be happy or not, but why?"

"The point is…"

"May! Come on, we're starting." Uncle Dech waved from the sala.

This time Aunt May hugged me, then looped my arm into hers.

"Let's go. We'll talk later. Just remember: freedom and choices."

"Wait." I pulled her to a stop. "How do you know all this?" I asked.

She smiled and tugged my arm to get moving.

"Lots of studying, meditating and life experience, Nui. I can tell you what I know, but until you look back on your own experiences and make that connection, it may be hard to simply accept my words."

As I sat down, it hit me. Hadn't Nui and I done exactly what Aunt May had pointed out? Nui saw her family life as a negative, while I figured she had the better deal and vice versa. I felt like slapping my head. Duh. We were so ignorant. All we had to do was change our viewpoint. *Maybe, but that still doesn't help with the mess you're in right now.* If Aunt May was right about choices, maybe she was also right about the magnet thing and all we had to do was send a message to the universe that we wanted our old lives back.

I almost giggled, feeling much calmer and lighter and welcoming the prayers as a chance to mull over Aunt May's points.

5 4

NUI

I SHOULD HAVE KNOWN KHUN YAA WOULD INSIST ON attending Khun Yaai's funeral. Why hadn't that occurred to me before? But what was Channon doing here? Why was he escorting my grandmother? Had Luna called him? I couldn't imagine her asking him to come to Chiang Rai when we were trying to switch back tonight. Maybe he was there as Krit's friend.

Channon led Khun Yaa to where we were sitting. Yumi jumped up to offer her seat. Oops, I should have done that but instead simply wai'ed to her. It was good to see my grandmother and a timely reminder that I would be home again tomorrow.

"Khun Yaa, sabai di mai kha?"

"Sabai, sabai." She patted my hand and smiled. "Are you going to the funeral as well?"

"Yes, we are. We want to be there for Nui."

"That's very kind of you. Krit asked Channon to escort

me. I think he was afraid I would get lost." She chuckled. That answered that question.

Yumi moved to Channon's side and started a rapid fire conversation, more one-sided than reciprocated from what I could tell. I tried to cover up a smirk. *Stop it. Just because you didn't like Yumi's earlier comment doesn't mean you have to be smug now.* I turned my back on them.

"How have you been, Khun Yaa? How's your heart?"

"I'm fine, Nong Luna. How about you? What have you been up to? I haven't seen you in a while."

"Oh, not much. School, you know. It doesn't leave much time for anything else."

Except creating havoc wherever you go. The voice in my head simply wouldn't shut up.

"Ah yes, school. Did Nui tell you she might not be able to continue?" Khun Yaa asked.

My heart skipped a beat, and I felt a whoosh in my ears like a wall of water crashing over my head. I was glad I still had my seat, as my legs had gone weak.

"What do you mean, not continue?" My voice shook and sweat dampened the T-shirt against my back.

"Her parents want to expand their shop, and your school is very expensive." Khun Yaa started fidgeting with her hands, looking around the gate area pretending she hadn't just dropped a bomb into my lap. I instantly recognised her dilemma. As a rule, my family never ever discussed finances with outsiders and she was embarrassed having revealed this much. Khun Yaa turned back to me, sighed and patted my hand.

"But it's not decided yet. And you can still be friends and I hope you'll come and visit us. I'll make you more kanom krok." She smiled a bit stiffly.

Luna's favourite coconut pancakes were great, but not on my top-ten list of Khun Yaa's dishes.

"Of course." I leaned back and exhaled slowly, trying my best to not cry. This couldn't be happening now. Had long had Luna known and kept it from me? If I couldn't be at BIS, would I still be able to apply for the J-1 visa, or would this be the end of my dreams?

55

LUNA

KRIT AND PANYA WERE OLD ENOUGH TO LOOK AFTER TUM and Chaiya if needed, so the four grandsons would sit vigil at the temple between the midday and evening prayers. I ended up in the car with Aunt May and Uncle Dech while Duen rode with her parents. I hoped there wouldn't be any more visitors at the house. An actual break would be nice, and maybe I would have time to talk to Aunt May in more detail.

When I reached the top of the stairs, I turned to look at the Giant Buddha, but my eyes immediately diverted to the mountain of flowers, garlands, candles, incense sticks, framed photos and envelopes on the sala. Where had all this come from? We were only gone for a few hours, but from the sheer number of gifts it looked like a lot of people had stopped by.

"Ah good. We have time to organise all this," Aunt May said.

Even Mae smiled when she caught sight of the gifts.

I wanted to ask what this was all about, but figured it would show my ignorance.

"Anyone still hungry?" Aunt May asked.

I rolled my eyes at the thought of more food.

"I'd love a cup of coffee though, Aunt May, if you don't mind. I'll make it," I said.

"Good idea. I could use one too. Thanks Nui. Let me drop my bag and we'll get started."

Aunt May picked up a notepad and handed it to Uncle Dech. "You record while we sort."

The envelopes contained cards and money, ranging from twenty to a thousand Thai Baht, depending on people's connection with Khun Yaai and their affluence. We would bring the garlands, bouquets, candles, and some pictures to the temple to place around the casket. The photos were mostly snapshots of Khun Yaai and I felt that with every frame I picked up I got another glimpse of the person she had been. I kept smiling back at her. Cataloguing everything was an excellent distraction from my worries, but took longer than expected. They assigned Duen and me to run up and down the stairs to load the gifts in the cars. It felt good to be moving, but I was sweating more than after a kickboxing class at the gym. *When was the last time you did a class, anyway?* I almost missed a step at the reminder. I hadn't swum in ages. *You're getting your body back tonight, so you can pick that up again. Maybe.* And just like that, my anxiety was back.

I caught Aunt May's eye as I came back from putting the last of the gifts in the car. Her eyes were slightly unfocused, but then she tilted her head, asking without words how I was doing. It was disconcerting how easily she picked up on my mood. I wasn't sure I wanted her to know all that was going on with me, yet I felt safe with her.

"I'll have to take a shower. I'm all sweaty."

"Yeah me too," Duen said, fanning her red face.

"Go ahead. One of you can use our bathroom. We'll have to leave again soon to get the gifts into the temple before the prayers," Aunt May said.

Duen and I almost stepped on each other, trying to grab some fresh clothes.

"I'll use Aunt May's bathroom," I said.

Despite the time crunch, I took a moment to look around their bedroom, slightly uncomfortable about being nosey. *She wouldn't have offered her bathroom if she minded.*

The room was neat and pretty plain, with basic furniture and a framed painting of a lotus pond. A beautiful lacquered three-drawer console sat under the window with intricate patterns and flowers carved along the backboard. The piece in itself was beautiful, but the crystal collection on top was truly stunning. It looked like Aunt May had gathered the colours of the rainbow. There were at least one hundred pieces; they all looked beautiful displayed together. All shapes and sizes, none of them looked processed, all natural. I reached out to pick up one but stopped short, not wanting to disturb the alignment.

"Aren't they beautiful?" I hadn't heard her come in, but Aunt May didn't seem offended with me standing in her bedroom.

"They really are. How many are there? Did you collect them all yourself?"

"There are 108 stones and yes, a lot of them I found myself or they were gifts. I started when I was young."

"Beautiful. Do they have some kind of meaning?" I asked.

"Everything means something, Nui." Aunt May laughed.

She picked up a small chunk of deep purple that looked like six-sided pieces of varying sizes glued together.

"Take this. It's an amethyst, and it's meant to bring clarity and wisdom to the owner. Maybe it can help you?" Aunt May closed my hand over the rough crystal.

"Are you sure? I don't want to disturb your collection." I reached out to give it back to her, but Aunt May shook her head.

"Keep it. It's a gift. Maybe there will be a time when you can pass it on to someone else who needs it," Aunt May said. "Now, you better hurry. We have to leave soon."

"Thank you, Aunt May. I hope it works. Oh, and can we talk about the other stuff later?"

"Of course. We'll find time. Now hurry." Aunt May shooed me towards the bathroom.

I rushed through my routine in a haze. This had been a weird day, and the main event was still to come tonight.

56

NUI

WITH MY LUCK, I EXPECTED CHANNON AND KHUN YAA TO BE seated right next to Yumi and me, but it turned out we were a few rows in front of them. The flight wasn't full and Yumi and I had a seat free between us. We'd pushed back from the gate and not even completed the security demonstration when I burst out.

"Did you know that I might have to leave BIS?"

"What? No. Why would you?" Yumi asked.

Her reaction seemed genuine, so Luna hadn't said anything to her either.

"Khun Yaa just told me. My parents have some plans for the shop and need the money from the tuition." Moisture gathered in my eyes, but I was determined not to cry.

"Damn. That sucks. Are you sure about that?"

"I don't know. Khun Yaa said it wasn't final, but my parents have hinted before that it was too expensive."

"Can you apply for some kind of scholarship or support?" Yumi suggested.

"I doubt it. I don't even know if BIS offers something like this, and besides, I'm Thai. My parents will say I can go to a Thai school like my siblings. I hate my life." The first tears fell despite my best intention.

"Hey, it's not the end of the world. You don't even know yet if it's going ahead." Yumi touched my arm. "Come on, don't paint the devil on the wall. Let's see first if it's true, then we can figure something out, okay?"

"Okay." I sniffed, wishing I had Yumi's outlook on life. "It probably means I can't apply for the J-1 either."

"Why wouldn't you? We can look that up later too. I'm sure it's not just for international schools." Yumi leaned back in her seat and stared up front. "Just chill for now. We'll figure it out. You need to think about tonight and the funeral tomorrow. One thing at a time." She closed her eyes.

"Yeah, easy for you to say and don't forget that I still need to lie to Luna's mom, too," I muttered under my breath.

"No, you don't. You can tell her the truth now. What's she gonna do? Come and get you?" Yumi didn't bother to open her eyes. I turned towards the window, not even getting excited when I saw the ground drop away beneath us. For all I cared, I could stay up in the sky forever. Life on earth sucked.

We had barely levelled off when we began our descent into Chiang Rai. Of course, the flight would be super punctual when I wouldn't have minded a reprieve.

"We should probably ask Channon and your grandmother if they want to come with us in the car if they haven't made arrangements," Yumi said.

"Probably. But I need to call Luna's mom and Luna. I can't do this in the car with Channon and Khun Yaa."

"Why not? Channon knows about the switch and he'll get why you want to be here and Khun Yaa doesn't speak English, does she?" I hated it when Yumi was super logical and I had no reason to object.

"It's your grandmother, after all. At least you can do something nice for this one," Yumi added.

I took a step back as if she had slapped me.

"That was low, Yumi. And totally unnecessary."

Yumi looked at me, waited a beat, then nodded.

"You're right. That *was* uncalled for. I'm sorry." She touched my arm in apology, then looked over my shoulder and waved.

"Channon. How are you getting to Sop Raa or whatever the place is called?" Yumi asked.

"Sop Ruak? Krit was going to pick us up, but I told him we'll just use Grab. What about you?" Channon asked.

"Same. Want to share a car?"

Channon turned to Khun Yaa and translated. She nodded with a smile.

"I'll order one," Channon said.

"While we're waiting, why don't you make the calls?" Yumi tapped my phone.

I swallowed the lump in my throat and moved off a few paces for privacy. Who to call first?

"Mom?"

"Why didn't you answer your phone, honey?" Khun Susan sounded out of breath.

"Sorry, I didn't hear it. What are you doing?"

"I'm on a bike. It's so beautiful up here. I wish you had come. What are you up to? Where are you?"

I rubbed my neck and started pacing. Better to just say it.

"I'm…Mom, you're not going to like this, but I'm in Chiang Rai with Yumi. We're going to the funeral tomorrow morning." I held my breath for the expected explosion.

In the background, I heard her call to Khun Mark and Luke to stop.

"Luna, what is wrong with you? Have you completely lost your mind?" Khun Susan whispered it, which shocked me more than if she had screamed. She sounded sad and disappointed. I burst into tears as a wave of guilt and shame swept through me.

"I'm so sorry, Mom, I really am. But I had to go. I can't explain it, but there's something I need to do and I have to be here for that. I promise I'll be back tomorrow afternoon. Yumi and Channon are here too and Nui's other grandmother. I'm fine, I promise." I was rambling and sobbing at the same time. It was as if a dam had finally burst.

"Who's Channon?" The unexpected question disrupted the flood. Of course, Khun Susan had never met Channon.

"He's a friend from the animal hospital. Dad and Luke have met him."

Khun Susan didn't respond. I dug in my backpack for a tissue to blow my nose.

"Luna? I want you to turn around and take the next flight back. No discussion. Just do as you're told." Khun Mark's voice was unyielding. "How could you do this after everything we had to go through these last weeks because of your actions?"

A tissue was useless against the fresh stream of tears. I tried to take a breath, but felt as if a vice was constricting my chest. I jumped when a hand reached around me, grabbing my phone.

"Hello?" Yumi said. "Oh, hi Mr Taylor. It's Yumi."

"I know, Mr Taylor, and Luna and I are really sorry. We

wouldn't have done if it wasn't an emergency. What?" She listened.

"Yes, Dad knows I'm here and he's okay with it. You can call him… I know we should have told you, but I promise you it was really, really important that we come here. And we're only going to the temple and the hotel, then we'll come straight back."

I only heard Yumi's side of the conversation but could easily fill in the rest. It was amazing how she didn't beg or plead but simply stated her points. Of course, it was easier for her to remain detached since she had nothing to lose.

"Okay, Mr Taylor. Yes, she'll explain tomorrow. Do you want to speak to her again? No? Okay, bye." Yumi hung up.

"How bad is it?" I asked between hiccups and wiping my tears.

"Hmm, let's just say I wouldn't want to be in Luna's shoes tomorrow. He was pretty mad and said you're grounded for life. You better prepare Luna for that," Yumi said.

"Thanks, Yumi. I feel so bad about this, but you know I had to do it, right?"

"You wouldn't have had to do it if you guys hadn't pulled that stupid stunt before."

"I know. It just seemed like a good idea at the time."

Yumi snorted and shook her head. She dropped my phone back in my hand and grabbed my arm.

"Come on. Channon's got the car. Let's go."

Channon and Khun Yaa looked at me with concern but didn't comment. I dug out my sunglasses to hide my eyes.

The driver was a cheerful young guy, probably glad to get a longer fare in the middle of the day. Channon took the passenger seat and Yumi pushed me into the middle next to Khun Yaa. I didn't feel like talking at all, and apparently my outburst had a sobering effect on the others, too. Khun Yaa patted my arm a few times. It was sweet of her, but only made me want to cry again. The driver kept talking and asking questions, and Channon and Khun Yaa were too polite to not respond. Yumi didn't understand the conversation anyway, and I was too pre-occupied to contribute.

We were close to Sop Ruak when Channon looked over his shoulder. "We're going straight to the temple. Krit and the family are there and the evening prayers will start soon. Do you want us to drop you at the hotel first?" he asked in English.

Yumi and I looked at each other. I would have preferred to get myself sorted out before seeing my family, but it made sense to go to the temple first for the prayers. Besides, the hotel was only a short walk away, so Yumi and I could leave at any time.

"We'll go with you. We can walk to the hotel from there if necessary. Where are you staying?" I asked.

"Krit and I are staying at a neighbour's house. I think Khun Yaa is with the family."

The driver took us around to the top of the temple so Khun Yaa didn't have to climb the stairs. I caught her looking at Yumi and me as we got out of the car. We weren't dressed for the temple, but it was too late to change now. We'd be able to get away with it as we would be considered foreigners who didn't know better. I handed Channon cash for half the fare, then followed them into the temple grounds. My heart picked up speed, anxious on so many different levels. At the last second, I grabbed Yumi's white Dixie cap and shoved it in her hands.

57

LUNA

T HE DRIVE BACK TO THE TEMPLE HAD BEEN FUNNY. U NCLE Dech kept sneezing because of the cloying scent of the flowers, making his driving slightly erratic until he'd finally had enough and powered down all four windows, letting in a stream of hot air that distributed the pollen even more. Aunt May laughed.

With the boys' help, we brought the gifts inside. Mae and Aunt May distributed the flowers around the coffin and arranged the photos and candles in front.

A few people drifted in, but we still had time before the monks returned. I hadn't checked messages in a while and saw that Yumi had texted to say they'd landed and were on their way. I was excited and nervous at the same time. Only a few more hours before I could return to my body. How would it feel? Would things be different at home? I still didn't know the outcome of the police investigation or why we were to move so soon. Nui had a lot of explaining to do. Should I tell

Nui about the withdrawal from BIS or let her find out on her own? If both Nui and I had to leave BIS, Yumi would be on her own again. I made a silent promise to be a better friend this time and at least stay in touch, even if we moved. Next year she'd be back in the States as well, so we'd be closer again.

Aunt May was too busy to talk, so I moved around the sala to text Yumi and get an update on their arrival time. Before I could hit send, my phone pinged.

'We're here.'

'Where? At the hotel?'

'Temple.'

I walked back around the sala and stopped in my tracks. Khun Yaa, Nui, Yumi and Channon were heading towards us from the parking lot. Heat rushed into my head and a few black dots swam before my eyes. I was ready to faint on the spot. How was I supposed to handle this? The rest of the family moved towards the group before I could unfreeze my feet. I felt completely detached, like a spectator watching a play on stage.

There was a lot of shuffling as everyone said hello. Yumi seemed to take the chaos in stride and simply wai'ed and smiled at everyone. At least she knew Channon and had met Nui's family before. I was glad she was here for moral support.

When Aunt May moved forward to greet Nui, I finally became unglued and rushed forward.

"Luna, Yumi. You made it." I hugged both.

"Nui!" Khun Yaa called. Nui and I instinctively looked at her. Oh shit. We had better be careful what name we were responding to.

I turned to Khun Yaa and wai'ed, which I guessed I should have done first.

"Sorry Khun Yaa. Did you have a good flight?"

She pulled me closer to whisper in my ear.

"I think your friend Luna is very upset. She was talking on the phone and then cried a lot."

"Oh? I'll talk to her, Khun Yaa. Thank you." She pulled me back once more.

"Maybe they should go to their hotel first. They are not really dressed for the temple, are they?"

Seriously? That was her biggest concern? I had to stop myself from either laughing or scowling at her.

"I'll talk to them."

"Nui?" Channon's fingers touched my shoulder. "How are you doing?"

"Oh, hi Channon. Krit said you were coming. That's very kind of you." My voice wobbled.

"Of course. Are you okay?" We hadn't spoken since before the failed switch at Wat Pathum, so I wasn't sure if he meant it as a general question or in relation to the switch.

"I'm fine Channon. Excuse me for one second. I need to talk to Luna and Yumi real quick."

While I was distracted, Aunt May had grabbed Nui's hands and was simply standing there, looking at my face. Tears rolled down my cheek and Aunt May gently brushed them off.

Oh my God. What was going on? What had Aunt May seen? Did she know? I could understand why Nui would be upset though she had never seemed particularly emotional. Why did she have to fall apart now, of all times? And in my body too? Everyone would remember this as me having a breakdown. I shook my head. This was all way too complicated. Khun Yaa was right. I had to get the girls out of there.

I went to grab Nui's arm.

"You alright, Luna? Maybe it's best if you and Yumi go to the hotel first and I'll come and see you later, okay?" With Aunt May right there I should have spoken English, but I automatically defaulted to my current primary language.

Aunt May looked at me and shook her head slightly.

"I think she's right where she needs to be. Come, Luna, sit with me. You'll feel better soon." She put her arm around Nui and brushed past me to walk to the stone balustrade near the Naga stairs. My mouth dropped open.

"What the heck is going on here?" Yumi whispered in my ear. She was rubbing her eyes.

"You tell me. You were with her. What happened?"

"That's not what I mean. I felt really dizzy for a second and could have sworn there were colours around Nui's aunt."

I lost it. It started as a giggle, but seconds later I was full on snorting, laughing and cackling like a madwoman. People turned to look at me disapprovingly, but it only set me off. I couldn't help it. I was officially going mad.

58

NUI

AUNT MAY SAT ME DOWN ON THE STONE WALL FACING THE temple grounds so she could monitor the visitors and timing for the prayers. I'd never cried this much in my life, but I couldn't seem to stop since we arrived at the airport. Aunt May's compassion made it worse. If she knew who I was and what I'd done, I wasn't sure she would still be so supportive though I'd never heard her speak badly of anyone. Her touch helped me calm down, as if she was sending me some of her energy.

"Are you feeling better, Nong Luna? Do you want to talk about it?" she asked.

I shook my head.

"I'm so embarrassed. I rarely cry, but there were just so many things lately and now coming to a funeral. It's all so sad." I sniffed and wiped my eyes.

"That's quite alright. Maybe it was time to let out some of

the sadness so you can move forward again. You'll feel better soon." Aunt May patted my knee.

"I know. Thank you, Aunt May. How are you feeling? I'm really sorry about Khun Yaai," I said.

Aunt May narrowed her eyes.

"You sound like you knew her?"

"I… I kinda feel like I did. Nui told me about her," I said.

"You would have liked her. She was a very special woman." Aunt May smiled.

"I'm sure. That's why I wanted to be here. But I guess I'm not much support to Nui when I fall apart like this." I shrugged, trying to lift the mood.

"Like I said, I think you're right where you need to be. I'm sure Khun Yaai would have loved to meet you."

Her words set off an extra round of silent tears. I nodded, unable to speak.

"The prayers will start soon. Why don't you sit here and listen? Take your time and if you feel better after the first round, you can join us the next time."

"That's a good idea. Thank you so much, Aunt May, and I'm sorry for my behaviour."

"Don't be. All will be well."

We both glanced up when we heard a loud giggle. Luna was bent over, hands on her knees, then she straightened and wrapped her arms around her waist to hold herself upright. What had gotten into her? Yumi stood next to her, looking puzzled and slightly bemused. Khun Yaa had stopped and turned around with a scowl, as if Luna had committed the biggest sin possible.

Aunt May squinted and sighed.

"I better find out what's going on before her mother gets upset." She patted my knee one more time and moved towards Luna and Yumi.

Maybe it hadn't been such a good idea to come here if both Luna and I were on the verge of a nervous breakdown.

Yumi watched Aunt May closely, swaying back and forth as if she was drunk, and rubbing her eyes. *Please don't tell me she's cracking as well.*

Aunt May nodded at Yumi and pointed in my direction, but didn't stop. Instead, she grabbed Luna and pulled her aside. Paa, Mae and some others watched Luna and Aunt May, clearly not happy about the disturbance. At this rate, none of us would get to attend the prayers.

Yumi sat next to me, staring off into space.

"This is all so weird."

"What is?"

"Some weird vibes here. I keep seeing colours around your aunt." Yumi spoke more to herself than me.

"You can see her aura?"

Yumi laughed. "I doubt it. I don't believe in that stuff, but every time I look at her, it's there. Doesn't happen with anyone else, so no, I can't see auras."

"I know Aunt May can, so maybe it's rubbing off on you?"

"As if." She snorted and dismissed my idea with a quick shake of her head.

"So, what do you want to do? You feel better?" Yumi asked.

Yumi's observation had made me forget about my woes for a moment.

"Why don't we just sit out here? We can still hear the prayers, but we don't have to be in the sala. Aunt May suggested it."

Yumi shrugged. "Works for me. It's actually kind of peaceful up here. That is, if one of you isn't crying and the other one laughing like a maniac." She winked at me and bumped my shoulder.

I smiled back at her, feeling more settled.

The temple grounds were peaceful despite the number of people moving about. The sun was setting and cast the last golden rays over the plaza. Yes, this was a good place to rest for now.

59

LUNA

I HAD TO TURN AWAY FROM THE OTHERS, AS EVERY GLIMPSE of them made me want to laugh again. I knew it was completely inappropriate, but I couldn't help it. It seemed as if every person present was playing a role that Nui and I had set in motion as stage managers. I couldn't decide whether it was tragic or funny. The thought almost set me off again. The whole situation was beyond ridiculous, yet it was one hundred percent real and not something I could push aside and ignore. That thought flipped a switch, and I instantly felt like crying. Aunt May saved me when she marched me towards the temple grounds.

"Nui, what has gotten into you? Why are you so hysterical?"

Where do I start?

"Aunt May, what's wrong with Luna? What did you see?"

She looked pensive. "I saw someone in pain who needed support."

Was she holding back? Why? What did Nui tell her?

"Yumi said she saw colours around you." I couldn't look her in the eye.

Aunt May pulled me to a stop.

"Yumi can see my aura? So it's really true. I never had that happen before."

What the…? I stared at Aunt May. Had she gone bonkers too? Was there something in the air in the Golden Triangle that made people act out?

Aunt May smiled.

"I've heard that someone who can see auras can actually transmit that skill to someone who has latent abilities. She might not be able to do it on her own, but my ability can enhance hers. I've never experienced it, but it's good to know it's true. I'll have to talk to her."

I shrugged. There were more pressing issues for me right now. Yumi could wait.

"Aunt May, I'm sorry about my behaviour, but can I ask you something before we go back in?"

Aunt May glanced over her shoulder. The monks hadn't arrived yet.

"What do you want to know?"

"Well, you were talking about having the freedom to make choices. But how do you actually know you're making the right choice?"

Aunt May nodded. "I figured you'd have more questions. Look at it this way: what happens when you make a choice? You simply pick one particular path to follow with what you know at the time, right? And when you're on that path you get to make more choices that lead to yet more choices, right?"

I nodded. "I get that, but how do you know if it's a good or bad choice?"

"Think about it. There is no right or wrong way. You are where you are and you pick one possibility over another, which then opens up new possibilities."

"So you're saying it doesn't matter what I pick? That can't be right." I shook my head. "There must be a way of knowing if you're doing the right thing."

"Let me ask you something, Nui. What did you see when Khun Yaai made her transition?"

I jerked back. "What do you mean? See?"

"Tell me. What did you see?"

Why did I even bother denying it? Aunt May obviously had noticed my reaction in the hospital though I had tried to look solemn instead of fascinated when Khun Yaai passed away. I swallowed.

"I... I think I saw her spirit leave her body." It felt peculiar to say it out loud.

Aunt May nodded. "I thought so. So then, what does that tell you?"

"I don't know. What does it mean?" I asked.

"If you could see that, doesn't it tell you there are two parts to every person? One is the body, and the other is the spirit, and though they are joined, they are independent of each other."

I nodded. That made sense.

"What has that got to do with choices, though?"

"Your spirit is eternal and will return to the source energy where it came from. It's pure positive energy and much wiser than what you consider your mind. More importantly, you inner being is only interested in your wellbeing and, in general, what's beneficial to life."

"That's great to know, but still, what has that got to do with choices?" I tried not to sound impatient.

"It's quite simple. Your emotions tell you where you are

in relations to your spirit or inner being. They are a guideline or you could call it your advice centre. If you feel good, it means you're in alignment with your spirit and if you feel bad, you're diverging from your spirit's take on things. Be honest with yourself, though. The universe knows if you're just saying words because they sound positive but you don't really mean them. The universe can't be tricked that way. So when you have to make a choice, ask yourself, how does my spirit feel about this?"

"You sound just like Ajaarn Anurak." I grumbled, though if both Ajaarn and Aunt May said this was the way it worked then maybe I had better listen.

"Ajaarn, your meditation teacher? He's right, but Nui, you're making too much of it. You can't think your way through this, you have to feel your way. Over-analysing is getting you nowhere. Thoughts are like koi in a pond. One swims into view, but by the time you try to grab it, another swims by. You're making yourself miserable trying to anticipate all outcomes. In your heart, you always know what's right. Just follow that." She took my hand. "Come, we have to go back. Are you feeling better now?" She looked closely at me.

I grimaced. "Yeah, a bit, and I promise I won't start laughing again. Oh, but wait. You never said what the point of all of it is."

"The point Nui is growth." Aunt May tugged me forward. "The point is that with every choice you make you learn and grow and with that the universe expands too."

"What? But how?"

"Come on Nui, we don't have time right now. We'll talk after the prayers."

The monks had arrived and we had to rush to our seats.

Nui and Yumi were still sitting on the balustrade. I wished I could sit with them and hash everything out.

NUI

I was glad Yumi and I stayed outside. We could hear the chants from our perch, and even Yumi seemed content enough to just listen. It was full dark now, with only the sala lit up, and a few lampposts spread across the grounds. I closed my eyes, taking deep breaths. I always liked Khun Yaai's temple. Perched above the village and Mekong river, it seemed a world removed and a place of rest.

"What happens now?" Yumi asked as the monks began another sutra. She was slapping at the mosquitoes, which had come out in droves.

"Shhh, just listen. There'll be a break soon. We can talk then."

Yumi bent to grab her duffle, pulled out some repellent from a side pocket and daubed it over her calves, then held out the stick to me.

"Want some?"

I didn't want to interrupt the prayer, but protection from

the mozzies took precedence.

"Thanks."

"You think your grandma knows you're here?" Yumi asked.

I looked at Yumi.

"I don't know. Maybe."

"What about your Aunt May? Do you think she recognized you? I mean, why would she come up and help you when she's never met Luna before?"

"I don't know, Nui. Can we just leave it for now? I want to listen. That's the whole point I'm here."

Yumi grunted.

"I thought you were here for the switch."

"That too. Geez, Yumi can't you just give it a rest for a few minutes?"

"Fine. But you have to promise I can talk to your aunt later. I want to know what happened. I need you to translate."

"Fine."

Yumi managed to stay quiet for all of five minutes. The setting and chants didn't seem to affect her as much as I'd expected.

"Don't you think it's strange your aunt immediately picked up on yours and Luna's troubles?"

"I'd say Luna's were pretty obvious the way she cracked up. But Aunt May has always been very emphatic. That's just the way she is. Khun Yaai was similar. They always offered to help when they saw someone struggling."

"Maybe you should try to copy them," Yumi said, with a deadpan expression.

"Gee, thanks Yumi. I think you've made your opinion of me quite clear." I automatically went on the defence. "And you've never done anything wrong, have you? Glad one of us is perfect."

Yumi stayed quiet long enough for me to become wary. She was staring at her arms resting on her knees, palms up.

"I didn't say that," she whispered.

Shock ripped through me, my hand smacking my mouth wishing I could take back the words. How could I have forgotten Yumi's pain? The scars on her arms weren't visible as she always wore long-sleeved clothing, but that didn't give me the license to make light of her issues and pretend they weren't there.

"Oh God, Yumi, I'm so sorry." I reached out to take her hand but drew back not sure if she wanted me to touch her. "I didn't think. I am really sorry."

What else could I say?

"Do you want to talk about it? I mean, about what happened?" I asked hesitantly, not really sure I'd be able to handle it. Yumi always seemed to have her act together and I couldn't imagine how I'd help her. Whatever she'd gone through must have been terrible.

Yumi shook herself, then took a deep breath and exhaled forcefully.

"No, I really don't want to talk about it. What is it with this place? Why are we all becoming so emotional here?"

"I have no clue. Maybe it's because misery loves company?" I hadn't meant it as a joke, but Yumi snorted and the heavy atmosphere shifted.

"That must be it! Can't think of any other reason." Her sarcasm was heavy-duty.

She tipped her chin towards the sala.

"Looks like they're done. What do you want to do? Stay or go?"

I sighed, then stood up.

"Let's see what Luna wants us to do. Maybe we should go to the hotel and wait for her there."

61

LUNA

I HADN'T HEARD A WORD OF THE CHANTS BUT AT LEAST FELT more settled, as if a valve had opened up and released some of the built-up pressure. Mae and Khun Yaa would probably read me the riot act later, but for now they were pre-occupied talking to other mourners during the break.

Nui and Yumi wandered over and Nui jerked her head to the side, asking me to meet them away from the crowd.

"Got over your fit, Luna?" Yumi asked. "What you want us to do? What time do these prayers finish?"

"Last night we had three sets with two breaks. Not sure if it's the same tonight. Do you know, Nui?" I asked.

Nui shrugged.

"Normally yes, but they might change it because there's only one full day," Nui said.

"It's up to you if you want to stick around or go to the hotel. I'll try to come over right after if Mae lets me. Not sure what she'll do after my little episode. Speaking of, what did *my* mom say when you told her you're here? Was she mad?" I asked Nui.

Nui cringed and bit her lip.

"Your dad said you're grounded for life," Yumi offered. She didn't sound exactly gleeful, but definitely not sorry either.

"Just great. Damn," I said, then shook myself. No point in fretting over it right now.

"Anyway, what do you want to do? Stay or go?" I asked. "We definitely need to talk."

"Yumi, I really want to stick around. If you want to head to the hotel, you can walk from here. It's ten minutes or less. Just use google maps," Nui said.

"Nah, I'll stay. You guaranteed the booking, right? So we can check in anytime. Uh oh, watch out, here comes the cavalry," Yumi whispered, looking over my shoulder.

Krit and Channon were walking over from the sala. Krit put his arm around my shoulder.

"Feeling better, sis?" Everyone must have thought I'd had a nervous breakdown over Khun Yaai's passing. Little did they know.

"Yeah, I'm okay. What's up?" I asked.

"Khun Yaa suggested Channon walk Luna and Yumi to the hotel. She thought they might prefer to rest." Krit looked at the ground, clearly embarrassed. He sounded like he had done some diplomatic editing of the message.

"Why would she think that?" Nui huffed then translated for Yumi.

"You can tell her it's very kind to think of us, but we want to stay here for Nui. We're not bothering anyone if we sit outside, are we?" Yumi interrupted, not pleased to be told what to do. I silently cheered her on. I didn't appreciate Khun Yaa's unnecessary interference either.

Channon answered in English. "We're just the messengers."

"No problem, thank you. In that case, we're staying," Yumi said, closing the subject. She wasn't the least bit bothered by Khun Yaa's directive.

Just when I thought things were settled, Yumi muttered, "Not again!"

I turned around as Aunt May stepped into our circle.

"How are you feeling, girls?" She spoke Thai but was looking at Yumi.

What an awkward situation. Krit was shifting from foot to foot and Channon crossed his arms then uncrossed them again, aware of his body language. I bit my tongue not wanting to risk another giggling fit.

Nui smiled, and Yumi stared at Aunt May, swaying slightly.

"Are we ready to start again, Aunt May?" I asked to break the tension.

"I wanted to invite Luna and Yumi back to the house with us after the prayers, since they've come all this way for you, Nui."

"But Khun Yaa said…" I stopped myself. No need to start a family feud.

"The girls are more than welcome in my home, and I'm sure Khun Yaai would have been happy for them to join us," Aunt May said.

Krit coughed then cleared his throat.

"I'll leave you to it. Channon, you coming?"

"It's settled then," Aunt May said. "Do you want to come inside or stay out here? We'll start again in a few minutes."

"We'll stay out here. Thank you Aunt May, and thank you for inviting us." Nui wai'ed to her aunt. She didn't confirm if they were coming to the house or not, but I didn't think that was really an option. Had Aunt May asked because she knew something strange was going on between her niece and me, or because she wanted to find out more about Yumi's newly gained skills? How did she even have the time or headspace to think about us, considering we were attending her mother's funeral tomorrow? What was going on with her? Did I have another worry to add to my mountain?

62

NUI

YUMI AND I SPENT THE REST OF THE PRAYERS OUTSIDE ON THE terrace. During the break, I walked her through who was who in the family so she would recognise them at Aunt May's house even if she couldn't talk to them. I didn't know if anyone else was invited or why Aunt May wanted us there. It should have been strictly a family affair, but given the short mourning period maybe they had changed the normal practises. Khun Yaa wouldn't be pleased to see us, but it really wasn't her decision, and I was glad Aunt May had ignored the interference.

The big issue remained though: how and when Luna could get away to meet us at the hotel. Would we manage to do the switch tonight? If not, it would be tough to find a window to meditate before the funeral itself. As long as I was attending, it didn't really matter in which body I was present though I felt I was close to the breaking point with this constant back and forth, rescheduling and vacillating. Some of that had been out of our control, but a lot of it was self-inflicted. We had to find a way, no matter what.

"Looks like they are done." Yumi elbowed me, looking at the sala. I'd spaced out, trying to figure out the timings.

"They'll probably wait for the guests to leave first. We still have a few minutes." I glanced at my watch. It was only seven thirty, plenty of time to make an appearance at Aunt May's then drag Luna to the hotel.

At long last the family was ready to leave. Since not everyone would fit in the cars, Krit and Channon decided to walk with Luna, Yumi and me back to the house.

"Did Aunt May say why she wanted us at the house? What are the plans?" I asked Luna.

"I assume she just wants a quick private memorial and because you came all the way from Bangkok, you're guests of honour," Luna said.

"Guest of honour at a funeral? Seriously? I thought that was Nui's grandmother." Yumi said straight-faced.

I bit my tongue to keep from laughing. Luna playfully punched Yumi.

"Yumi. Stop it. This is serious."

"What? You gonna have a fit again? You girls are all over the place. Anyway, you better come up with an idea on how to make a quick exit. You still have work to do, don't you?" She gave us a stern look.

"Actually, I think Aunt May wants to talk to *you*, Yumi. She was very curious about you picking up on her aura, and she won't get a chance to ask you about that later. So maybe you *are* the guest of honour after all," Luna said.

"Oh. Yeah, that was weird. But either way, we'll have to make it quick. I'm tired of this back and forth. I'm gonna lock you inside the room tonight until you get it done," Yumi threatened.

"Yes, ma'am." I saluted her. "If only it was that simple."

"Why would it be any more difficult than the first switch?" Yumi asked.

"Because things have changed; we have changed," Luna said.

"Meaning?" Yumi asked.

"You know what happened, Yumi. Don't pretend," I said.

"Oh, you mean that Luna's family has to leave Thailand because of the flag on her passport because of the blog you wrote, Nui?" Yumi asked.

"What?" Luna shouted.

The guys in front turned around, but I waved them on.

"Or maybe because your grandma said you'll have to leave BIS when you're back home, Nui?"

"You know about that?" Luna asked, a lot more subdued.

"Or what about you, Luna? Maybe because you don't know if Channon is interested in you or just Nui's looks?"

"Hey! That's none of your business. Stay out of it." Luna bumped Yumi's shoulder.

The three of us stopped, facing each other.

Yumi put her hands on her hips and glared at us.

"You are both so… bad. No, let me rephrase that; you're pathetic. You can't look past your own noses, can you? It's like you have blinders on. Do you still not get it that you take yourself with you wherever you go and that doesn't change just because you look different?"

Uh oh, Yumi was on a roll. Luna and I looked at each other, equally apprehensive as we knew Yumi was right.

"Do you guys really hate yourselves that much? You blame everyone and each other for what's wrong. You, Nui, say people are keeping you from what you want, and you, Luna, complain you have too many options to choose from. Can't you see how ridiculous that is? You are both so selfish it makes me sick. When will you take responsibility for your own lives and actions?"

Yumi didn't wait for an answer, but stomped off to catch up with the guys.

Luna and I stared after her, dumbstruck.

"What in the world…?"

"Geez, what has gotten into her?"

We spoke at the same time, but I didn't dare look at Luna. As much as I wanted to deny it, Yumi had hit the bullseye with her assessment and I felt totally exposed. Did Luna feel the same? How would she react to Yumi's disclosure about the move? Before I could get myself twisted up in thoughts again, Luna linked her arm with mine and pulled me forward.

"She's right, Nui. We have to figure it out."

"I know, but why is it so hard?" I genuinely wanted to know.

"Come on, I'll tell you what your aunt said to me. She's very wise. Maybe we *can* figure this out."

I glanced at Luna. "You're not mad at me?"

"Well, I'm not happy about it, but like Yumi said, we're both responsible for this mess."

As she relayed Aunt May's words of wisdom, I felt tiny pieces clicking into place in my head. First and foremost, I felt relief that Luna and I no longer had to keep any secrets. We both fully understood the stakes.

LUNA

YUMI'S OUTBURST SHOULD HAVE MADE ME MAD OR despondent, but oddly enough I mostly felt relief. Both she and Aunt May had perceived what Nui and I had refused to see, whether out of ignorance or on purpose. It was as if they'd removed a filter from my skewed worldview. While I still didn't fully understand Aunt May's concept of how the universe worked, I felt hopeful that Nui and I would figure things out. This emotional spring-cleaning was draining, and I dragged my feet to the house. The stage was set; all we had to do was escape the family obligations.

Yumi gasped when she stepped on the sala and saw the Giant Golden Buddha's full brilliance. We'd had glimpses of it over the rooftops on the way, but this was the first time she took in the full size.

The house was packed, but I didn't see anyone besides the family and Khun Yaai's best friend. Khun Yaa and Duen commandeered the kitchen. They filled platters and bowls with food for an impromptu buffet. To my surprise, I felt hungry for the first time all day. Letting go of some of the blame and judgment had restored my appetite.

Khun Yaa frowned when she saw us in the doorway. What was wrong with her? She had never struck me as being condemning despite her clear-cut ideas about right and wrong, but this contrary behaviour, both here and at the temple, was odd. Surely it was okay for my girlfriends to be here if Channon was welcome too. I sighed. Aunt May was right. This overthinking wasn't helping, especially when I didn't have all the facts.

I glanced at Nui. Did she see the dynamics in her family differently since she was a part of it and not simply an observer like me? She had a faraway look in her eyes, but even I couldn't interpret the expression on my face.

Krit and Channon stepped around us to pick up some food. We hadn't talked on the way back, both apparently happy to ignore all the emotional upheaval from this afternoon. Aunt May came out of her bedroom and saw the three of us standing on the threshold. She smiled and extended her hands in welcome.

"Come in, come in. You must be hungry. Help yourself to some food." I translated for Yumi. She was the only one there who didn't speak Thai, but she didn't seem bothered. She probably just absorbed it by osmosis and, given her knack for languages, I wouldn't be surprised if she was fluent in a few months.

"So, we just eat and leave?" Yumi asked. "Might actually be a good excuse, since it's just family." Whatever had bugged her before seemed forgotten.

I shrugged.

"No idea what the plan is, but it doesn't look like anyone else is coming by tonight. Let's grab some food. I'm hungry."

The good thing about having Nui and Yumi there was that it would be my duty to host them, and I wouldn't have to face Mae or Khun Yaa just yet. It almost was as if there was an invisible cocoon around the three of us that the others didn't dare to breach. Maybe they were afraid we'd start acting out again.

"Let's sit on the sala. There's no space here anyway," Nui said. We grabbed cutlery and took our plates outside. It was getting chilly, but I figured we wouldn't stay long.

"What time do we have to be at the temple tomorrow?" Yumi asked, biting into some crunchy fried lotus root.

"The cremation is at ten, but I think we have to be there by nine for the final prayers and preparation," I said.

"Okay, that should give us enough time to get back to Chiang Rai afterwards. Our flight is at two. We'll just have to bring our bags with us and go from there," Yumi said.

"So Nui, what is the deal with that flag? What happened? And why do we have to leave the country?" I asked.

Nui choked on her curry and took a sip of water to clear the cough.

"Sorry. I meant to tell you, but there really wasn't time before. You know about the police investigation. They decided to drop the issue, but they put a five-year flag on your passport which means they might not allow you to re-enter the country once you leave for holiday or otherwise. Your parents said it was better to leave altogether. I'm really sorry, Luna. I didn't mean for this to happen." Nui sounded sincere.

A flash of anger swept through me, but I tried to not let it show. All the fighting before had gotten us exactly nowhere.

"And how soon do they want to leave? What about Dad's job?" The last bite of morning glory left a bitter tang in my mouth.

"It's not confirmed yet. Your dad talked to his boss and they are trying to find a solution." Nui's voice was barely audible.

"Shoot. No wonder Luke blames me. I bet Mom and Dad are pretty mad, too."

Nui disagreed. "Actually, they were great about it. You are so lucky to have parents like that. They were totally supportive."

"Yeah, until you lied again and flew up here." I shook my head in disgust.

Damn, my composure was only paper-thin. *Take a breath. Don't flip out.*

"You said you wanted me here, so what was I supposed to do when your mom said no?" Nui said.

Yumi interrupted the looming argument.

"Well Luna, look at it this way: the good news is you won't have to worry about Channon anymore. You'll be gone."

"Yumi!" Nui and I shouted at the same time.

"What? It's true, isn't it?" Yumi shrugged and took another bite. "You weren't sure what you wanted anyway, so now you won't have to decide anything. It's out of your hands."

I stared at her. Why did she always have to be so blunt, even if she was right?

"That's what friends are for, you know. They tell you how it is, even if you can't see it yourself," Yumi said as if she'd read my mind.

"Yeah, maybe, but they can at least be nice about it." I wasn't even sure anymore who to be mad at. Nui, Yumi or myself? I felt the slight tug of a smile. No matter what or how Yumi delivered a message, she never did it maliciously or to make herself look better. I had to give her credit for that, even if the comment didn't sit well.

"There you are. I was looking for you." Aunt May walked out of the house but stopped short before entering the sala. She looked at each of us as if she was taking a quick snapshot of our emotional states. Not too far from the truth if she could read our auras. It gave her a built-in polygraph.

Aunt May nodded to herself then stepped onto the deck and sat next to me.

I glanced at Yumi who was squinting at Aunt May. Nui was studying her feet.

"How are you? Did you get enough to eat?" Aunt May asked.

"Thank you Aunt May, it was delicious," I said, though I'd only eaten half my plate. My appetite had vanished after Nui's news.

"Luna and Yumi want to head back to their hotel soon. Unless there's something else to do, I think I'll walk them back," I said.

Aunt May nodded.

"Tonight it's just us preparing for tomorrow. If you don't mind, I'd like to ask your friend Yumi a few questions. I'm not sure we'll have time to talk again otherwise," Aunt May said.

I translated for Yumi. For once, she didn't seem sure how to respond, but eventually nodded.

Aunt May reached over me and took hold of Yumi's hands. Yumi almost jerked back. I felt trapped in between. Aunt May put her thumbs on Yumi's wrists and closed her eyes.

"Can you ask her to close her eyes slightly and not look directly at me but fix on a point just over my shoulder to the right? And then tell you what she sees."

Nui was staring at us with her mouth open. Yumi did as asked, not even questioning why.

"Oh! This is a lot better. The colours are much clearer now and I don't feel dizzy anymore. I see a lot of purple, but there's also some gold and some dark blue and some really nice green, you know, emerald green."

Aunt May nodded as if she had expected the answer.

"Okay, now ask her to look at Luna and see if she can pick up anything." Uh oh. Nui shrank back in her seat, then stood up.

"Hey! No! Leave me out of it."

Yumi overrode her objection.

"Too late. I see a vague outline but much darker and more red tones and some very dark green. Not totally clear," Yumi said.

"I'm sorry, Nong Luna. I should have asked for your permission. Nui, are you okay if Yumi looks at you?"

"Sure." Aunt May already knew my colours, and I had nothing to hide from Yumi after the last conversations we had.

"Hmmm, I see more yellowish tones, but they appear pale, almost muted. There's some green too, but not as bright as Aunt May's," Yumi said. I translated for Aunt May. She nodded and released Yumi's hands.

"Thank you, Yumi. You have genuine talent. If this is something you're interested in, you might want to consider developing these skills. They are special and they could really help you in life as long as you use them in a positive direction." I translated for Yumi. She grinned.

"That was pretty awesome. And so much stronger than this afternoon. But now I can only see her colours. Yours have disappeared." Yumi seemed disappointed.

Nui stood up. "I think it's time to go."

"But I want to know what the colours mean. Don't be such a spoilsport," Yumi said.

Nui laughed, but it sounded forced.

"You're the one who said it's time to get this over with, so let's go! I'm pretty sure you can read about auras online." Nui turned to wai to Aunt May. "Thank you for your hospitality, Aunt May. I'm sure the family will want some privacy. We'll see you at the temple tomorrow."

"I think you should sit down, Nong Luna," Aunt May said.

She looked back at me.

"What have you girls done?"

64

NUI

My knees gave out, and I fell back in my seat. I looked at Luna for help. She suddenly seemed super interested in the folds of her skirt, straightening the wrinkles. Yumi's head swivelled back and forth between the three of us.

"What did she say?" Yumi asked.

Aunt May waited.

"Girls, I know something is going on and Yumi just confirmed it for me."

Yumi twitched at hearing her name, so I quickly translated for her.

"What did I confirm?"

Luna looked at Aunt May.

"Yes, what did Yumi confirm?"

I didn't know where Luna found the nerve to ask the question. Wasn't it obvious? Luna herself had said we needed to be careful around Aunt May, and now she actively encouraged her to delve deeper? Reckless. Yet, I was curious myself about Aunt May's statement and interpretation. But what would happen after we switched tonight? Wouldn't the change be even more obvious to Aunt May? I didn't think there was any way to hoodwink her.

"You, Luna, have a very similar energy pattern to that of Nui as I know her. And you, Nui, seem to have completely shifted from your previous energy. It doesn't make sense," Aunt May said. She sounded confident about her assessment, but not entirely sure how to explain it.

"Energy patterns change, don't they?" I asked. Luna translated for Yumi.

Aunt May nodded.

"They do, and even change from day to day, but generally the base remains similar over a longer time period and doesn't change as drastically as they have in Nui. Unless Nui had a transcendent experience, I don't believe the energy shift could have happened that quickly from the last time I saw her. It's almost as if an entire transfer took place and your energy, Nong Luna, is actually much closer to Nui's old pattern."

"What? What is she saying?" Yumi asked. "Damn it, this is like watching a movie without subtitles." I quickly translated for her.

"Oh wow. Really? That's amazing, I think," Yumi said.

Luna coughed.

I forced a laugh and leaned back.

"I don't know what to say." There was no way I was going to explain or validate anything to Aunt May.

"You all seemed very upset this afternoon. Is there something I can help you with?" Aunt May asked. Had she decided to leave the aura issue alone? *One can hope.*

"Shall I tell her?" Yumi asked. "Get it over with?"

"No!" I shouted.

Aunt May raised her eyebrows but stayed quiet.

"You can't, Yumi. She's my aunt. She can't know," I said.

"Why not? She already knows something. Maybe she can tell you how to make it work. She seems to be much more switched-on than either of you."

"Yumi is right, Nui. I think Aunt May would understand. And if you ask her to keep it private, I'm pretty sure she would," Luna said.

I ignored both of them and turned to Aunt May.

"Thank you, Aunt May. It's very kind of you to offer, but I'm sure you have much more important things to think about, you know, with the funeral and all. I think it's best if we leave now," I said.

Aunt May nodded.

"Alright! But I want you and Nui to think about something tonight…" Aunt May paused, then inhaled deeply. "Every spirit has a reason for being here on earth and in a specific body. That purpose is unique and can only be fulfilled in that particular combination. Do you understand?" Aunt May looked at Luna and me. We nodded.

"That blend supersedes everything until the spirit returns to its non-physical source."

My mouth went dry. This was too specific for it to be a lucky guess. We didn't have to explain anything to Aunt May. She knew. And she'd given us the key to solve our problem.

65

LUNA

YUMI GRIPPED MY HAND.

"What's going on? What did she say?" she asked.

"She knows. We don't have to tell her," I said.

"And?"

"No 'and'. I think she just gave us the solution to make the switch work." I felt like laughing and crying at the same time. Instead, I turned to hug Aunt May.

"Thank you, Aunt May. Thank you."

She stood up. "Be careful, girls." She looked at Yumi. "Good luck, Nong Yumi. All will be well."

Yumi smiled at her and wai'ed, not even waiting for a translation.

"I'm going to walk Luna and Yumi back to the hotel, okay?" I said.

"I think that's a good idea Nui. But don't be long. We all want to get some rest tonight."

"What's a good idea?" Mae stepped out of the house onto the sala.

"I'm dropping Luna and Yumi off at the hotel, Mae," I said.

"And walk back by yourself? I don't think so." She shook her head.

"But it's not far," I said.

"In that case, I'm sure they can walk by themselves. Or I'll tell Krit to go with them. Say goodbye, then help your sister with the clean-up. Luna and Yumi, thank you for coming and we'll see you tomorrow morning," Mae said.

Aunt May put her hand on Mae's arm.

"Lamai, I think it'll be okay for Nui to walk them back. It's safe."

Mae shook her head.

"This is your house and you can invite whom you want. But Nui is my daughter and I know what's best for her. I thank you for not interfering."

I didn't know where to look, appalled by Mae's reaction, but there was nothing I could do, and I definitely didn't want to get into the middle of an argument between the sisters.

"Don't worry, we're leaving." Nui jumped up and stomped around us to the stairs. She wai'ed to Aunt May.

"Thank you for your hospitality and advice Aunt May. I appreciate it. Yumi, you coming? See you tomorrow, Nui." She deliberately ignored her mother and pounded down the stairs.

Yumi shrugged, then whispered in my ear. "Not sure what that was about, but you better get it sorted. See you tomorrow." She hurried after Nui.

Aunt May shook her head. For a second I thought Mae looked embarrassed, but she simply turned around and walked back into the house.

"Come Nui, let's finish up, then we'll all get a good rest. Tomorrow is a fresh start." Aunt May sighed.

Duen and I cleaned up in the kitchen and at the first opportunity I slipped into the bathroom to brush my teeth and escape to the bedroom.

"You okay?" Duen asked as she joined me shortly after.

I grunted.

"What did you do? Mae seemed angry."

"I have absolutely no idea. I didn't do anything. We were just outside talking with Aunt May."

Duen slipped on her nightshirt.

"I think Mae and Khun Yaa were really upset with you this afternoon. What happened?" Duen sat on the bed looking down at me.

I rolled my eyes.

"Has it actually occurred to anyone that maybe I was upset too and that this was my way of showing it? It was that or crying." I rolled over and faced the wall.

"I'm sorry, Nui. I didn't know." The air mattress shifted as Duen knelt down and stroked my back.

"I think it's difficult for everyone. We just have to get through tomorrow. Sleep well."

She patted my shoulder one more time, climbed into bed and turned off the light.

Yeah, just get through tomorrow. And then what?

I closed my eyes and wiped at the tears. Why did this have to be so difficult? A thought flashed into my mind. If Aunt May's presence had enhanced Yumi's ability to see auras, had she also made it possible for me to see Khun Yaai's spirit leave? I sat up to reach for my skirt and dug into the pocket, retrieving the amethyst Aunt May had gifted me.

I give up. Please help me.

66

NUI

YUMI HAD TO RUN TO CATCH UP TO ME. I WAS LIVID WITH MY mother for interfering in my life yet again. Why did she always have to take this attitude? She acted as if there was only one playbook to live your life by and anyone who didn't do exactly as she prescribed was wrong.

"Slow down." Yumi grabbed my arm. "What happened up there?"

"My mother happened. Like always," I spat.

"What did she say?" Yumi asked.

"She forbid Luna to walk us back. And then she had the nerve to say she knows what's best for me. As if!"

Yumi's laugh stopped me.

"What?"

"You think that's just your mother? All mothers think that. Remember how Luna's mom reacted this afternoon? Same thing, even if she said it differently."

I glared at Yumi.

"It's not funny at all. But you…" I stopped myself, remembering that Yumi didn't have her mother in her daily life.

"You mean, I wouldn't understand because I don't live with my mom?" Yumi asked, not bothered at all. "Why do you think my parents divorced? Both of them were set in their thinking of how things should be done, and in my case, their ways didn't jibe. At least you have parents who agree with each other, so stop complaining."

"Well, they might agree with each other, but they definitely don't agree with me," I countered.

"And that's why we grow up and leave! So you can decide for yourself."

"Yeah, but then they make me feel guilty for not doing things their way."

"You're already feeling guilty, aren't you? Admit it. You're feeling guilty for being angry at them. That's on you and not them. If you feel guilty, it only means you think you should do something different. But if you know it's okay to do things your way, you don't have to feel guilty."

I turned around and glared at Yumi.

"Are you sure we're the same age? You sound like you're a hundred years old, and since when are you a shrink?"

"Ha!" Yumi hooked her arm through mine. "Just lots of therapy and once you hit bottom, the only way is up." She pulled. "Come on, you said Aunt May gave you the key to the switch. So, let's open that door." She grinned. "God, I love silly analogies."

"How?" I asked. "I need Luna for that."

"What exactly did Aunt May say?" Yumi asked. "I missed that part."

"Only that each spirit chooses a particular body and that it always gravitates towards that body."

"Wow, that's pretty specific. She definitely knew what you did, but probably hasn't come across a case like yours," Yumi said.

"Seriously? Do you think that other people have tried this?"

"Oh, I'm pretty sure people have thought about it, but it doesn't really matter. You guys did it, and you need to fix it. Maybe she meant you just have to *want* to move back. Maybe it'll happen automatically if you and Luna simply let it go."

"Well, we've tried everything else, and it didn't work. And now we can't even meditate together, and tomorrow is the funeral." I turned into the driveway of the hotel, swiping at my eyes. This was all so damn frustrating.

Yumi passed me, almost skipping up the steps to the lobby. I envied her carefree attitude. How did she hop from one happy moment to the next, considering her history? Do we really have to hit bottom to change our outlook on life? I wasn't sure I wanted to go that far.

"I'm gonna take a shower and call my dad. He should be home by now."

I followed her into the room, which was quite nice and spacious. Not as fancy as our Bali suite, but still good for a one-night stay. It had twin beds, a small table with two chairs, and a balcony with a view of the hotel gardens. The pathways were lit up by low lights but deserted.

While Yumi took her shower, I sorted out my clothes for the funeral. For once, Luna's conservative fashion style was convenient. A black linen sheath dress that came to mid-calf. I had packed a black and white patterned scarf I could drape over my shoulders in the temple. Flat black sandals, a woven belt to give it a bit of shape, and I would be ready to go from the temple straight to the airport.

Yumi was sitting cross-legged on her bed, scrolling on her

phone, when I came out of the shower. I swivelled a chair to put up my legs on the bed.

Yumi spoke without looking up.

"So, I'm looking up the colours I saw around you guys. Apparently, auras are real and can even be measured and photographed. Aunt May's aura is amazing. All this purple, gold and green means she's very intuitive, empathic and nurturing. It says here that indigo means someone who searches for the truth and can sense other people's energies. Oh, and the gold I saw means she has a high level of spirituality. Apparently, it's pretty rare. How cool is that?"

Yumi clapped her hands in excitement, then looked at me.

"Want to know yours?"

I was curious, but not sure I really wanted to know what my colours said about me.

"Tell me Luna's first." I said, evading the question.

"Ok, so Luna had more yellow and some darker green, mostly. It says that yellow means an optimistic outlook but if it's pale, there's some stress involved like at the start of a particular project or goal and there's a lot of anxiety and trepidation. And that shade of green means the person needs roots and structure, but isn't averse to having fun too. The person is the one most likely to look for reasonable solutions to a problem that has been causing arguments. Man, this stuff is so freaking spot on. Who knew?" Yumi got herself hyped up.

"And I actually saw all those colours. I definitely have to dig deeper into this. This is like having a magic wand." She was almost bouncing on the bed.

"Okay, now your turn. So yours had a lot more red in it. It says here, 'reveals someone who has an inner warrior spirit who can survive any circumstances. They are realistic about most situations.'"

Yumi looked up and smiled. "That's you, isn't it?"

"Pretty much." I felt more pleased than expected.

"Uh oh, you're not gonna like this part, though. It says the dark green shows someone who feels a lot of jealousy and resentment and believes they are never in the wrong. Is that true too?" I leaned back and looked at Yumi's phone rather than her directly. What was the point of denying it? Both she and Aunt May had seen the colours and if the rest was accurate, this one was too.

"I guess," I said. My voice shook slightly.

"Well, the good news is Aunt May said the colours can change daily, and long-term change can happen too, so you can do something about it. Probably takes some work, but if you really have that inner warrior, then you can do it, no?"

I grinned. Leave it to Yumi to see the silver lining. She was right. I could do something about it. I exhaled.

"You know, Yumi, what has been the strangest thing about all this? Everyone expected me to think and be like Luna, but inside I felt completely different."

Yumi snorted.

"And how's that different from all of us? Everyone has a perception of us even if we don't feel like that at all."

"I guess. Thanks Yumi. I think I'm done for today and we have a full day tomorrow."

I climbed into bed and turned off my bedside lamp.

"Night, Yumi, and thanks for coming with me up here. You helped so much. I really appreciate it."

"Oh damn. I completely forgot to ask your aunt what my colours are. Remind me to ask her tomorrow," Yumi said, then added, "I wonder if I can read others' colours too. I'd love to see Channon's."

I rolled my eyes in the dark. Typical Yumi to find a new hobby in the middle of our crisis.

67

LUNA

NO MAGICAL SOLUTION HAD PRESENTED ITSELF DURING THE night. All my expectations and hopes of getting back to normal had gone awry. I felt kind of numb, as if there was a buffer between me and the world. *Just get through today and the funeral.* If I had to return to Nui's home, we would have to find another time and place to switch back. Difficult to do if Nui was under house arrest, but not impossible. Or maybe it was all completely pointless, that we simply had waited too long and were truly stuck now, and I would never get my family back again. *That's not what Aunt May said, and she's been accurate about everything else.* I had to believe she was right. I brushed my hands over my face and sighed. Whatever would happen would happen; it was out of my hands for now.

Duen had already left the room and I could hear noises coming from the main living area. Khun Yaa, Panya and Duen were cooking breakfast for everyone. Khun Yaa looked pale, dressed all in black with an apron protecting her clothing while she bustled about. Uncle Dech sat at the dining table with Paa, drinking coffee. He raised his cup to me, smiled and gestured towards the coffee maker to help myself. Khun Yaa briefly glanced at me but said nothing. At least she seemed more neutral than disapproving today. Duen and Panya were arguing about the right amount of chillies in a Thai omelette. Such an ordinary scene. I poured myself a cup and walked back to our room.

Nui had given me instructions to wear a white dress, but I had also packed a black Thai skirt and white blouse just in case. I had little appetite, but figured I needed something in my stomach to get me through the day. Conversation was sporadic and subdued. Everyone seemed to be lost in their own thoughts, covered in a cloud of melancholy. Krit and Channon's arrival brought some temporary energy back. Both looked very handsome in black pants and crisp white dress shirts.

I offered to walk with Krit and Channon so Khun Yaai's friend could drive up to the temple with the rest. The three of us set out ahead of the group.

"How are you doing, sis?" Krit asked.

"I'm alright, thanks. How was your night?"

"Quiet. We didn't want to disturb our hostess so went straight to bed," Krit said.

"Channon, um, when are you flying back?" I asked.

"At two o'clock. I'll go straight from the temple."

"I think you're on the same flight as Luna and Yumi. Maybe you can go together," I said.

The conversation felt stilted, but I didn't know what else to say. After Yumi's comment the day before, I wasn't even sure anymore how I felt about Channon. Did I genuinely see him as my potential boyfriend, or did I just like the notion of it? Or maybe it was even more straightforward than that.

Since I was in Nui's body, I could pretend whatever I wanted without really having to make a decision. Yikes. *You are not a very nice person, Luna, if you lead him on.*

Climbing up the stairs seemed more strenuous this time. I was breathing hard by the time we reached the top and grateful this would be the last time. I felt 'templed out' after spending three days here. The family was just pulling into the parking area at the back. Lay workers were sweeping the sala where Khun Yaai's coffin stood waiting. I checked my watch. We still had time before the funeral.

Everyone stood around the cars as Aunt May and Mae pulled out stuff.

"Krit, Nui, come and help."

Paa, Uncle Dech and his two boys carried big plastic baskets filled with the weirdest combination of gifts. Packages of dry noodles and rice, liquid soap, toothpaste and brushes, notebooks, instant coffee and tea, candles, incense, dishwashing liquid and laundry soap, batteries and oddly enough toilet paper. Given that the monks couldn't buy anything with money, it made total sense to give gifts directly. Chaiya's arm muscles were straining with the heavy load. Channon stepped forward to relieve him.

Mae handed Duen a set of folded saffron Kasaya monk robes on a pillow, then passed another set to me and a double set to Krit.

"Where do you want us to put these?" Krit asked.

"They go in front of the monks as gifts. Just follow your dad," Aunt May said.

There were still two woven baskets in the trunk filled to the brim with carved wooden flowers. I couldn't fathom what they were for, but figured I'd see soon enough.

"And these?" Duen asked.

"There's a table in the back of the room. Just put them

there." Mae hooked a basket each on Duen's and my arm and we walked carefully to not spill any flowers.

While we were setting up, people arrived. What started as a trickle soon became a steady stream. I didn't see Nui or Yumi. They were cutting it close.

People took their seats, the atmosphere a lot more solemn than during the previous prayers. I still didn't feel much of anything, almost as if I was coming out of anaesthesia, with everything kind of muffled.

"Come on, Nui. We've got to sit down." Krit took my arm and guided me into our seats in the row behind Mae and Aunt May.

The monks filed into the sala and took their positions on the dais. I looked behind me, but the crowd was too dense to see through.

Had something happened to the girls? Surely Nui wouldn't miss her grandmother's funeral even if she had to attend in my body.

I looked at the coffin and the pictures beside it.

Khun Yaai, if you're around, I could really use a sign that things are going to work out. I can't deal with this anymore.

68

NUI

THE LIGHT IN THE ROOM WAS ALREADY ON WHEN MY ALARM rang. I squinted to see Yumi in her nightshirt standing in front of the wardrobe mirror making faces at herself.

"What are you doing?" I croaked.

"Morning. I'm trying to see my aura, but it's not working. I think I need your aunt's help."

I giggled, fell back, and pulled the sheet over my head. What a way to start the day.

Today was Khun Yaai's funeral. I instantly sobered and pushed back the cover.

"You could just ask Aunt May what your colours are if you're that interested," I said over my shoulder, grabbing my clothes and closing the bathroom door behind me.

"Yeah, but where's the fun in that?" Yumi mumbled.

I showered and dressed in record time to avoid thinking. Yumi was sitting on the bed typing on her phone.

"I've already checked us in for the flight so we can leave right from the temple."

I nodded.

Yumi grabbed her stuff and disappeared into the bathroom while I packed the little I'd brought with me. I was checking my messages to see if Luna had anything new to report when Yumi came back into the room. She was wearing wide leg white linen pants with a subtle black floral pattern topped by a mid-thigh long-sleeved fitted cheongsam jacket in matte black. Elegant, distinct, but not over the top. Her hair was in a simple braid down her back, revealing small pearl studs in her ears.

"You look great, Yumi. Want to grab some food before we go?"

"Do we have time?"

"If we make it quick, it'll be okay."

I ordered Khao Tom with chicken, figuring it would hold me through to the afternoon at least.

Yumi had an omelette with mushrooms and cheese.

"What's that?" She pointed at my bowl.

"Similar to congee. Wanna try?"

Yumi scrunched her nose.

"No thanks. That looks like dinner to me." She slurped her cappuccino.

"So, what are you going to do about the switch? You gonna try when we're back in Bangkok?" Yumi asked.

"I really can't think about that now. I just want to be at the funeral for Khun Yaai. The switch will have to wait," I said.

"Again, huh?" Yumi said.

"What do you want me to do? It's hardly my fault that Luna couldn't come over yesterday. Can we please not talk about this now? My head is already exploding."

"You know what's funny?" Yumi asked.

My mouth was full, so I just raised my eyebrows.

"The irony is if you had followed your own advice in your blog you wouldn't be in this situation."

I swallowed.

"What do you mean? Which post?" The blog was a sore subject after the police had shut it down. I had merely put up three posts, but only really recalled the one that almost landed me in jail.

"Spirals. Ring a bell?" Yumi asked. "Here, let me show you." She picked up her phone.

"How can you show me? The site is down." I put my spoon down, appetite gone.

"Ever heard of copy and paste? I liked what you wrote, so I copied it to my notes. Here." Yumi handed me her phone.

Which brings me to my epiphany. If you're looking for negative things to complain about, you're bound to find them. Likewise, if you look for positive things to appreciate, you will also find them. So either way, you can set yourself up for an upward or downward spiral.

Will this work every single time? Who cares? All that matters is you have a wonderful moment that will make you feel better. And once you start that upward trend, it might just spiral you all the way up. Try it and let me know what happens.

"Oh, that one." I sighed.

"Yeah, that one. Not much of an epiphany if you already forgot, huh? You could start today and look for things to appreciate. Maybe that'll get you out of your funk."

I made a face at Yumi. She was way too smart, and now she was even using my own words against me.

"I really hate you sometimes, Yumi. Do you always have to be right?"

"See? Instead of saying you hate me, which you don't,

why don't you just say you appreciate my wisdom?" Yumi laughed out loud.

"Why do you always have to be so bloody upbeat? It's annoying when I'm in a bad mood."

"Oh, it's a work in progress, trust me." Yumi took the last sip of her cappuccino. "What time do we have to go?"

I glanced at my phone.

"Oh shit. We're late. Come on, we gotta run."

We grabbed our bag and sprinted through the lobby and out the door. I was ready to bolt for the road when Yumi pulled me back.

"See there?" She pointed to a tuk tuk dropping some guests off.

I rushed over and didn't even bother to negotiate the exorbitant price. The guy probably thought he could make a quick steal with two foreign looking girls. On the way, I told him we were going to our best friend's grandmother's funeral, and we were running really late and had to hurry. I hadn't expected it, but he must have felt enough compassion to drop the fare to a much more reasonable sum. Dammit, Yumi was right—again!

We still had to climb the stairs as the tuk tuk didn't have enough power to take us up the steep climb to the back entrance. By the time we reached the top the monks were chanting and the sala was filled with mourners. Thankfully, they hadn't started the procession yet. We slipped into the back of the room, trying to regain our breath.

69

LUNA

THERE WAS ONLY ONE PRAYER THIS TIME BEFORE MAE, AUNT May, and their husbands officially presented the gifts to the monks. A few lay helpers rolled in a cart to the open doors, and the monks picked up the coffin and placed it on the cart. The family gathered behind, followed by the rest of the congregation. We walked three times counter-clockwise around the main temple; the monks pulling the cart. I looked back a few times but didn't see Nui or Yumi. The procession then moved towards the crematorium in the back of the temple grounds. Except for the tall chimney, it looked like any other temple building with the typical multi-tiered orange tile roof tops. Stairs led up to a columned open antechamber with a high table in the centre and a large tray underneath.

Mae and Aunt May stepped up to cover the table with a black draping cloth. The monks then moved the coffin on top.

Standing to the side, Aunt May and Uncle Dech said a few words about Khun Yaai that barely registered with me. I expected Mae to speak too, but she was too choked up so Paa took over.

When Paa finished, Aunt May invited everyone to come forward, pick up one of the wooden flowers and place it on a tray underneath the casket.

Ah! This was probably the equivalent of throwing a shovel full of earth on top of the coffin in western funerals. Now I understood why the flowers were made of wood. They would probably be burned with Khun Yaai.

Mourners stepped forward one by one to wai and deposit their flowers. I finally glimpsed Nui and Yumi as they stood in line waiting their turn. Yumi caught my eye and winked. Despite everything, I was glad Nui had made it. The occasion felt too significant for her to have missed it.

When Nui and Yumi came down the stairs, Aunt May beckoned them over to stand with the family. I quickly glanced at Mae and Khun Yaa, but they were both praying with their eyes closed. Krit raised an eyebrow, but left it at that.

After the last person had dropped a flower, the monks stood beside the casket to chant a last prayer. It all seemed to happen quickly now. They picked up the casket and moved into the cremation chamber.

I gripped Nui's hand behind me.

70

NUI

IT WAS REALLY HAPPENING. AFTER THE RUSH OF GETTING TO the temple, the funeral itself seemed to progress in slow motion as if I was viewing it on an IMAX screen, immersed but not really a part of it. Yumi kept me moving during the procession when I would have simply stood there oblivious to what I was supposed to be doing. It was as if the emotional overload had finally short-circuited my brain. Snippets of memories with Khun Yaai flashed through my mind. Some made me smile, but mostly I wanted to cry for what I'd lost. I stood in front of the crematorium and my heart squeezed, picking up its beat. Yumi pulled me with her to pick up a wooden flower and we walked up the stairs to place them under the coffin. My legs wouldn't move properly, as if they were carved from wood as well.

"I hope you're not angry with me for what I did, Khun Yaai. You always said I should follow my dreams, but probably not the way I tried to. Please forgive me. I hope you're at peace and I promise I will do my best to make you proud from now on," I whispered, wiping my eyes.

Yumi lead me down the stairs and over to the family to stand behind Aunt May and Luna. I didn't know why she thought we could join them, but I was still too befuddled to question it.

As the monks finished their prayers and picked up the coffin, Luna gripped my hand. An electric shock went through both of us. I wanted to shake off her hand, but we were fused together, unable to break the bond.

I vaguely noticed Aunt May turn Luna around and grab my other hand. Lightning sparked through me. A roar in my ears blocked out any sound. I felt faint and stood stock still, rooted to the ground. I lifted my head and Luna's eyes locked on mine. She looked just as shocked as I felt; neither of us understood what was happening. If the electrical current running through me kept going, I was going to combust. There was nothing I could do about it and I finally gave up resisting and just let it flow through me.

Immediately, I felt relief.

LUNA

WHEN I TOOK NUI'S HAND, I'D SIMPLY MEANT TO SHOW HER my support. I hadn't expected this visceral reaction. It was as if a giant gong had been struck inside my head and instead of diminishing, the vibrations picked up speed until my entire body felt like a live wire. Aunt May clasped my wrist and turned me around to face Nui. She looked petrified, fragile as a crystal bauble about to be dropped and shattered on the floor. A wave of compassion rolled through me. I felt sad for both of us. She and I had misused and twisted the extraordinary gift we'd been given and turned it into a power play for our own gain.

I'm so sorry Nui. I don't want to be that way. I promise I'll do better.

I wasn't sure if Nui could hear my soundless words, but a look of peace came over her. At the same time, I felt it too. I closed my eyes.

YUMI

WHAT THE HECK? I KNEW NUI HAD BEEN EMOTIONAL ABOUT her grandmother's funeral, but I hadn't expected her to simply faint. I barely grabbed her before she slid to the ground. If she'd been in her own body, I might have been able to drag her a bit further, but Luna was taller and heavier than me, and the best I could do was make sure Nui didn't hit her head. The surrounding crowd was dense, almost suffocating, as we sat on the ground. I heard the monks in the background but saw nothing around us except legs. We needed some space and air. I looked for Luna to ask people to move when finally the crowd backed away. No, wait, they formed a circle, and there on the other side was Luna in Aunt May's arms. Both girls were sheet white and sweating. Something weird had happened. It couldn't be a coincidence that both had collapsed at the same time, no matter how anxious they'd been.

Aunt May said something in Thai, and the crowd parted

further. I tried to pull Nui to the circle but didn't have the strength. She was a dead weight and two people had to help carry her. Someone brought two chairs, and we dragged the girls up into them and pushed down their heads over their knees. A kind person brought over cold towels to place around the girls' necks and bottles of water. The episode lasted a minute, if that. The crowd obscured Nui's family, and I doubted they even noticed the incident. Probably better that way, given yesterday's tension and animosity.

I looked at Aunt May. She was smiling despite the circumstances. Her aura was positively glowing. I automatically smiled back. I wished I could ask her what was going on. Instead of speaking, she held out her hands to me. I took them, unclear what she wanted me to do. She nodded towards Nui and Luna.

Sure enough, the colours were back, but much brighter this time, as if a veil had lifted. Aunt May tugged my hands and urged me more vigorously to look again. What was she asking?

When it finally clicked, I almost screamed. No frigging way!

I looked at Aunt May. She smiled and nodded.

Unbelievable. The aura colours had reversed. Did that mean the girls had finally gotten their act together and switched? I dropped Aunt May's hands and did a silent little victory tap dance, too excited to stand still. Aunt May cleared her throat and shook her head. Uh oh. I'd forgotten that I was at a funeral. I grimaced and wai'ed to her in apology. She smiled.

Holy cow. This was effing unreal. No one was ever going to believe this. Not that I planned to talk about it, anyway.

I looked down at Luna and Nui, wondering if they were even aware of what they'd done. Both were breathing evenly now and colour was returning to their cheeks. Nui pulled the towel off her neck and wiped her face, her eyes still closed. I wanted to shout: Just look! I couldn't wait to see their faces when they realised they were back in their own bodies.

I would have to get used to addressing the real person again, not constantly having to do a mental check that I was using the right name. How would they feel about returning to their own families? Despite their big hopes and dreams, they hadn't really achieved anything except causing mayhem. Perhaps this was the wake-up call they both needed.

Luna rolled her head, coming out of her stupor. I glanced at the crematorium. The family was hidden by the other mourners, but shouldn't Aunt May be there as well? Instead, she had her hand on her niece's shoulder.

73

NUI

I FELT SICK TO MY STOMACH, MY MOUTH WAS PARCHED AND my skin was on fire as if I'd walked over a bed of coals. Why was I sitting in a chair with a cold towel in my hand? The last thing I remembered was the monks picking up Khun Yaai's casket and Luna grabbing my hand. And then a big blank. No, that wasn't true. I remembered having an electric shock, though I'd touched nothing but Luna. I ran the towel over my face to wipe off the sweat. Even if I had fainted, I needed to pull myself together to say goodbye to Khun Yaai. I inhaled deeply and sat up, feeling little pops in my spine as if it was realigning itself. So far, so good. Someone pressed a bottle of water into my hand. I opened my eyes to twist off the cap, then I realised something was wrong. When I lifted the bottle for a sip, I finally made the connection. The fingers were short, and the skin was brown instead of white. How was that possible? I didn't recall having an out-of-body experience. Wait! I slowly raised my eyes and there in front of me sat

Luna, in her own body, blond hair half obscuring her face. My heart skipped, and I jerked back. How did this happen? We had switched back without even knowing it? My hands tingled, and I felt a smile spread over my face. For the first time in weeks, I could take a proper breath. I rolled my shoulders and neck, feeling the muscles relax and tension slip away. Yes, this was how it was supposed to be, no matter what I'd tried to tell myself.

74

LUNA

THIS FAINTING BUSINESS WAS BECOMING REALLY OLD, REALLY fast. I'd had no issues before. I tentatively opened my hands and lifted a foot just to make sure I hadn't locked myself in again. Not that there was a reason for it as I definitely hadn't tried to force Nui from my body. Something weird had happened when I held Nui's hand. Was she okay? I opened my eyes and froze. Nothing had prepared me for the sight in front of me. Nui, in her own body, was smiling at me, her eyes wide and steady, no sign of deception or anger. Oh my God, we did it. I didn't know how, but we'd made the switch back. My eyes immediately filled, my heart bursting with gratitude. I leaned forward to touch Nui to make sure I wasn't imagining things, and we instinctively hugged.

"Welcome back, guys. About time!" Yumi said.

I looked up. She and Aunt May were standing next to us, both smiling.

"How do you know?" I asked.

"You forgot that I'm a wizard at aura readings?" Yumi said flippantly, though I had the feeling she was more affected by the switch than she let on. Her eyes were shiny and her chin wobbled a bit as if she was trying to keep herself in check. Aunt May seemed serene as usual.

"How are you feeling?" Yumi looked from me to Nui. "Any after-effects?"

"How did it happen?" Nui asked. Her English was still impeccable. Had I kept my Thai skills as well?

"You should ask your Aunt May. I think she might know," Yumi said. "You know you guys were lucky we were here. You both fainted and would have had a big bump on your heads if you'd fallen. Not that you didn't deserve it for what you did." Yumi was back to her old self.

I turned to Aunt May. "Aunt May, I don't recall meditating or an out-of-body experience. How did it happen? Did you help us?" I didn't even have to think about speaking Thai, it came naturally. Wow, what a brilliant gift to have come out of all this madness!

Aunt May patted Nui's shoulder. "We can talk about it later. I told you that each spirit seeks to return to its natural body. I knew you were ready, and I acted as a bridge for you and asked Khun Yaai to help with the energy flow," Aunt May said.

"Hey, what did she say? This is not fair. I want to know too *how* it happened," Yumi said.

I translated for her.

"Wow, for real? Amazing. I'm gonna learn Thai now and then I can to talk to Aunt May directly. She has some wicked magical skills."

I translated, and Aunt May smiled at Yumi.

"She said you already have that energy in you, you just have to learn how to access it. And she said it's not magic.

Everyone has it if they know how to use it. Happy now?" I asked.

"I guess it'll do for now." Yumi pouted. "What are you going to do?"

Before I could answer, Aunt May pulled up Nui from her chair.

"Come Nui, we have to say goodbye to Khun Yaai."

They stepped through the crowd in front of us to the crematorium. It was time for Nui to resume her family duties.

"Come on, Yumi. Let's pay our respects to Khun Yaai. I want to thank her. We can talk about it later when we're on the plane," Luna said.

"Go ahead. I'll wait here."

NUI

I FELT CALM YET STRANGELY NUMB, ONE STEP REMOVED FROM the affairs of the people around me. I hadn't expected the switch to happen naturally. Aunt May must have been right that our spirits were linked to particular bodies for a purpose, and if so, I was in the right place at the right time in the right body. All I had to do was figure out what my purpose was.

Little pinpricks of energy ran down my spine and into my arms and legs as if they were reconnecting pathways that had become dormant while Luna occupied my body. It felt like internal acupuncture, neither unpleasant nor enjoyable, just something that had to happen. Aunt May's hand held steady on my shoulder, anchoring me.

Back in my body I had lost Luna's height advantage and I could only see the elevated antechamber to the crematorium. Khun Yaai's casket was gone. While Luna and I had been recovering from the switch, the monks had moved the coffin inside the burn unit. The crowd parted to let the monks pass back into the temple proper, finished with their service to Khun Yaai. I caught a glimpse of my mother. She was shaking, with a tissue pressed to her face. I squeezed my eyes shut. Mae had always been the stern parent, rarely allowing herself to show emotions. Had I been too harsh in my criticism of her? Had I been too blind to see there was another side to her? What else had I missed in my years of railing against my circumstances? A deep sense of appreciation swept through me. The switch with Luna might not have given me the exact outcome I was looking for, but overall, I had no reason to complain. At least *I* had my life back as I knew it, whereas Luna would have to face the consequences of my actions. I felt guilty about her pending punishment, but even deeper remorse about the changes I had enforced on her unsuspecting family.

LUNA

I FELT BUOYANT, AS IF MY ANCHOR CHAIN HAD SLIPPED AND I was ready for take-off. My cells were clicking back into place like millions of tiny Rubik cubes. Instead of praying, I kept running through a mental checklist, my hands twitching, wanting to verify that yes, these were my arms, my nose, my feet. More than a few times, I caught myself pulling at my hair feeling the different texture and length and checking the colour. If we hadn't been at a funeral, I probably would have used my phone to look at my face. Above all, I felt as if a vast reservoir of negative energy had been emptied into a void, leaving me more hopeful than I had felt in recent weeks.

"We have to go, Luna," Yumi whispered in my ear.

I nodded. I didn't want to disturb the proceedings more than we already had, so I simply wai'ed and bowed one more time, then turned away.

Yumi was standing at the back parking lot with Channon next to her. A car was waiting with the doors and trunk open.

"Do you have my bag, Yumi? Hi Channon." I felt awkward. It was the first time speaking to him as myself.

"Yup, let's go." Yumi slipped into the backseat.

"Oh shoot. Wait. Is my phone in there?"

"I think so. Why?" Yumi asked.

"I'll be right back." Nui would need her own phone. I quickly called up my text history with Channon and deleted it. Too bad I wouldn't be able to read the messages again, but it was better than sharing the private content with Nui. I slipped back behind Nui and pressed the phone in her hand, pointing to the exit. She nodded.

I wai'ed to Aunt May and turned to leave but she grabbed my arm. Again, I felt the stillness that emanated from her.

"Before you leave, Luna, I want you two to think about something in the future."

She pulled Nui closer, so we couldn't be overheard.

"I hope you realise what you experienced today was a gift. Make sure you treat it that way. There are no coincidences in this universe. Everything has meaning and no matter how small or bad an experience is, it has the value to teach you something. Do you understand?"

Nui and I nodded, and I for one, truly meant it.

Aunt May smiled. "And tell your friend she's welcome here anytime."

"Thank you so much Aunt May, for all you have done for us. Nui, call me when you get back." I wai'ed once more and walked back to the car.

"See, that wasn't so hard after all." Yumi winked at me.

"Aunt May said you're welcome any time and that you're an ancient soul and there is not much she could teach you."

"Ha. Just wait until I got this aura thing down and speak Thai."

I grinned.

NUI

WE STAYED UNTIL THE CREMATION HAD FINISHED BUT WOULD have to return later to collect the ashes. Some we would scatter at the temple, but the majority over the Mekong River to officially release Khun Yaai to the afterlife. I always thought it was a nicer way to leave earth than being buried in it.

Aunt May claimed she needed to stretch her legs and suggested I walk with her.

"How did you know about us, Aunt May?" I asked.

"I didn't exactly *know*, it was more an intuition. There were little things that seemed odd in your, or I guess Luna's behaviour, like she didn't belong where she was. And, of course, your auras. What happened in the first place?" Aunt May asked.

I cringed.

"It was kind of by accident. We both had out-of-body experiences and somehow connected and switched." I shrugged as if it was no big deal.

Aunt May looked at me, silently analysing how true that statement was.

"What are you not telling me, Nui?"

I winced. No point in varnishing the truth for Aunt May.

"Well, we had played with the idea, but we didn't *really* expect it to work. That was a surprise."

"Why would you even consider it?" Aunt May asked.

"Because…. Wait, are you going to tell my parents?"

She raised her eyebrows but didn't speak. Would it matter if she did? I cringed, imagining how they would react to having had a stranger in their home.

"Because I never get to do anything. The family always expects me to repeat what they have done, but they are so short-sighted. I want something different. And now it looks like my last option is gone too. Khun Yaa said that I'll have to leave my school because they need the money to expand the store. Nothing ever works out for me." I felt embarrassed by my outburst, my earlier serenity gone. Why was it so hard to be content with what I had?

Aunt May hooked her arm through mine.

"Let me ask you something. How do you think you managed to switch back?"

"You said you and Khun Yaai helped us."

"Yes, we added energy, but we didn't initiate it. That had to come from you."

"What do you mean? I didn't do anything. I just let go."

"Exactly! Once you let go of resisting, it had to occur naturally."

"But what has that got to do with my future life?" I asked.

"Nui, are you deliberately refusing to see what's so obvious?" Aunt May's tone had sharpened, jolting me.

"I… I don't know."

"Think."

"You mean, if I don't block what I want, it will happen? How?" I threw up my arms. "It's not like money can magically appear, can it?"

"It's the way the universe works. You, of all people, should understand that everything is energy that can transform into anything you want. If it wasn't malleable, you wouldn't have been able to switch. You just have to let in what you want and not block it. As for the money issue, there might be a way to work it out. You'll have to wait until Khun Yaai's will is read," Aunt May said.

I stopped and stared at her.

"Are you serious?"

"You'll see." Aunt May smiled. "Come now, let's go home."

I followed her like a puppy, millions of new thoughts racing through my head.

What if…?

78

LUNA

THE RETURN TO BANGKOK WAS UNEVENTFUL. YUMI bombarded me with questions, but I told her I needed time to process and focus on my return home. I kept glancing at Channon on the other side of the aisle. He, of course, didn't know I was back in my body and simply treated me with his usual polite manners. I was still ambivalent about whether I wanted to think of him as my potential boyfriend. It was cowardly, but I didn't want to bring up the subject with other people around.

"How are you going to tell Channon?" Naturally, Yumi jumped right at the subject I most wanted to avoid.

"Don't know," I said.

"I have an idea." Yumi grinned.

"What?"

"Not telling you. Channon and I are going to the shelter. Why don't you come for a bit?" Yumi jutted out her chin, daring me.

"I need to get home. Mom and Dad will be furious."

"They don't know what flight we're on. We only said we'd be back this afternoon."

I owed Yumi, so perhaps a few extra minutes wouldn't make any difference. Besides, who knew how long my house arrest would last and when I'd get another chance to see the dogs?

"Fine." I grumbled, but felt secretly relieved to get a reprieve before facing my family.

<hr>

WE GRABBED A TAXI FROM DON MUANG TO THONG LO. I'D been to the shelter many times, but never in my own body. It felt odd walking through the familiar corridors but not having my volunteer pass with me. It was late afternoon and a couple of people were prepping the cages for the night. We walked out into the run area where most dogs were resting after a day of play. Chone stood out with his size, grey fur and a black bandit mask around his eyes. Next to him was LaTe, the puppy I'd rescued from a soi dog attack.

Chone sprang up to welcome us but stopped a few metres in front of us, his head swivelling between Channon and me.

"Chone," I mouthed soundlessly.

As if released from a rubber band, he sprang forward and raced straight to me, jumping up and licking my face, making me laugh. I caught the look on Channon's face and laughed even louder.

"See?" Yumi said, pleased with herself. "I knew it."

Chone ran figure eights between Channon and me, unsure who to settle down with. Meanwhile, Yumi scooped up LaTe.

"I think I'll adopt this one if Dad lets me. He's just the cutest little fellow." She nuzzled his head.

I finally looked directly at Channon but spoke in Thai to give us some privacy.

"You know why Chone reacted this way?"

"I can guess, though I'll admit I never really believed it." Channon rubbed his neck. "Wow. I mean, that's crazy!"

"I know. Listen, I get that it's a lot to digest, but let me know when you want to talk, okay?"

"I'm, eh, yeah, sure. I think I need a bit of time," Channon said. He kept blinking, as if he didn't trust his eyes.

"Fair enough." I gave Chone a last rub and turned to Yumi.

"You know, Yumi, you should become president instead of a fashion designer. You always have the best ideas and find solutions." I really meant it.

"Who's saying I couldn't be both?" Yumi winked. "Imagine that, the first female president who can actually dress herself." She laughed out loud at her own joke.

My hands shook when I rang the doorbell instead of using my keys, feeling like a visitor who needed to be invited in. Mom opened the door and her eyes immediately teared up. She pulled me into a tight hug.

"Oh, thank God."

I burst into tears. "I'm so sorry, Mom. I really am."

"I'm just glad you're home and safe. Don't you ever do anything like this again."

"I won't, never ever."

"Yeah, but you're still grounded." She smiled through her tears.

79

NUI

I BARELY HAD A MOMENT TO THINK AFTER WE RETURNED TO Aunt May's house. There were many details still to be taken care of before we could fly home. Everyone got drawn into clean up duty, sorting gifts and writing thank-you cards, delivering excess food to the local orphanage and flowers to the hospital where Khun Yaai had passed away. In the morning, we went back to the temple to collect Khun Yaai's ashes and scatter them over the Mekong river. Oddly enough, I expected everyone to be most upset at that point, but I could almost hear a collective sigh of relief from my family once the ceremony was over. Perhaps that's what it meant to release a loved one into the next life cycle. For me, it was comforting to know Khun Yaai was still with me in spirit. There was no doubt in my mind that Luna and I wouldn't have managed the switch without her and Aunt May's help.

The entire time, Mae moved around like a robot, happy for Aunt May to take the lead in whatever needed organising.

It was scary to see her that way and though I understood why, I almost would have welcomed back her bossy attitude. I hadn't realised how much we all relied on her to keep the family affairs running smoothly.

It was good to have Krit back, though I'd had a few uncomfortable moments with him when he asked me about Channon. I didn't know how much Krit knew about Luna's dating situation or, more importantly, if Luna had talked to Channon yet to explain the change in circumstances? Regardless, I had little choice but to nip Krit's probing in the bud, even if I sounded mean. I had zero interest in going out with Channon to keep up appearances. They would have to figure this out.

By the time we said our goodbyes, everyone seemed eager to get back into a normal routine. If people wondered why I hugged Aunt May far longer than necessary, I didn't care. I hoped I'd be able to visit her again soon. She was the one person I felt would never judge me no matter what strange path my convoluted thoughts or actions took.

We arrived home to a boisterous welcome from Joey who must have felt abandoned with only Khun Bpoo keeping him company the last two days. Mae had said nothing about school, so I assumed I'd go back the next day as normal. Even Duen was unusually quiet and everyone retreated into their rooms pretty quickly. I took Joey on his evening walk through the neighbourhood. Though my world had shifted in the past months, everything appeared to be the same.

"Nothing ever changes here, does it, Joey? At least I know *you're* glad I'm back. Do you think I should tell Mae about the foreign exchange thing? She's really not doing well right now." I sighed and Joey looked up at me. "Nah, you're right, this can wait."

Back in the house the oddest little things kept tripping me

up. There were now three of us sharing the same bathroom and it kind of bugged me having to wait my turn. Walking into my bedroom and seeing Duen in bed already reminded me how little privacy I would get from now on. It was lovely though to have Joey curl up by me again. I had missed him.

My mind was still swirling with Aunt May's revelation and what it meant for me. The reading of Khun Yaai's will was still a way off and I was crossing my fingers it meant I could continue at BIS, but there was nothing I could do about it now. It was time to get my head back into studying and learn as much as I could while I still had the chance. Yumi was right. Even if I couldn't stay at BIS, I had the option to forge my own path afterwards.

80

LUNA

THE FIRST NIGHT HOME, I FELT LIKE A GUEST IN A HOTEL. Everything seemed new, and I walked around touching and rearranging my things and taking the longest shower ever with my own soaps and lotions. Mom thought I'd lost it when I changed the bedsheets and towels, something Khun Bo would normally do, but I wanted a fresh start all around.

Luke was a complete brat, making snide remarks to me until I finally reminded him of some of the past transgressions that I'd covered up for him. In fairness, they weren't as life-changing as what Nui had done, but I had no patience for putting up with his attitude. It helped that he seemed impressed by my courage to simply fly off against the express wishes of our parents. Maybe he fancied himself a bit of a rebel too, but he clearly enjoyed his moment of gloating when Mom stood firm on my house arrest. She insisted I come home right after school on Monday instead of hanging out with Yumi. At least she didn't object to me going swimming. Being back in the water and cutting laps through the pool made me feel like I was shedding my old skin as Nui and coming back into my own. It was ironic that Mom didn't realise I actually enjoyed simply staying home in my room or hanging out with the family. Both my parents had been fairly mellow about the trip to Chiang Rai, and the house arrest seemed more a formality than something that would go on for too long. Sure, eventually it would get old, but in the overall scheme of things it could have been worse. I could have ended up in prison, thanks to Nui.

Nui was back in school on Tuesday. We hadn't talked since I left Chiang Rai, and I was curious about how the rest of the funeral had gone. We finally got the chance when our last lesson was cancelled.

"How did it go, Nui? Everyone okay at home?"

The animosity of recent weeks was gone, but there was a cautious awkwardness between us, as if we had to figure out how to talk to each other again.

"Yeah, all good," Nui said, but then she sighed. "Well, as good as can be expected. Everyone is so quiet, not at all like they normally are. I'm really worried about Mae. It's like she's running on autopilot, but not really there."

"It must be hard for her. Give her some time. How are you feeling?"

Nui sighed. "I don't really know. Odd. Kind of like a misfit. I can't shake this feeling that something is missing."

"Missing what?"

"That's just it. I don't know. It's like an itch I can't scratch. Or maybe it's just that I need to get used to being in my own body. Everything seems so small. What about you? All back to normal for you?"

"Yeah, pretty much. Except that I have house arrest. Thank you very much."

"About that, Luna… I've been meaning to apologise to you and your family too. Seriously, I don't know what possessed me to start the blog. It was so stupid and I feel terrible that you have to move because of that."

Nui's apology felt sincere.

"Yeah, it's too bad we can't stay, especially now that Yumi is here, but maybe a fresh start isn't such a bad thing after all. I mean, at least for me, not so much for my family." I cleared my throat. "You know, Nui, I've been meaning to ask you. Had you planned this all along when you first suggested the meditation? I mean, the switch and then the blog?" I knew I was risking getting into a fight again, but I wanted to know.

Nui jerked back, then laughed. "Oh, come on, Luna. How could I have planned that? Did you honestly believe we could switch spirits?"

"No, not really, but still. What the hell *were* we thinking?"

"Clearly, we weren't, but for what it's worth, I am grateful we got to do it. I don't mean the blog and all that, but I think living your life for a little while has given me a whole new perspective. I suppose I got an idea of what could be, even if nothing has *really* changed for me yet."

"True, but I think we took this whole 'walking in someone else's shoes' a bit too literally. Did you wonder what would have happened if Aunt May hadn't been there?"

"Yeah, I'm so glad she figured it out and knew what to do. Guess you can't hide from someone who's really tuned in. Speaking of, how's Yumi's aura reading going?"

I snorted. "Yumi is Yumi. She marches to her own drumbeat. It wouldn't surprise me if she and Channon started dating for real as soon as I'm out of town, or maybe even before."

"What? Are you serious? How do you feel about that?" Nui seemed upset on my behalf.

"You know how Yumi is. If she sets her mind to it, Channon won't know what hit him. She's been pretty open about fancying him all along. And I'll be gone anyway, so it's not like she'd be poaching."

"Did you talk to Channon? I mean, did you explain to him what happened? Krit keeps asking when Channon is coming around."

"Sort of. He knows about the switch, but he said he needs some time to think about it. Don't worry, I don't think he's gonna call you."

"So, that's it? I thought you wanted to date him after we switched back." Nui raised her eyebrows.

I blew out a breath and fiddled with my scrunchie to keep my hands occupied.

"Yeah, I thought so too, but if I'm honest, it's more that I liked the idea of someone being interested in me. Channon is such a great guy, you know: super kind, always helpful and never asking anything in return. He's pretty much a saint and I think I need to get myself sorted out before I can think of dating someone like him.

"Wow, you're pretty cool about that," Nui said.

"Come on, Nui, let's be real. I think Channon and Yumi are a much better match. With her, he'll always know where he stands. You should be glad, by the way. Can you imagine if I hadn't told him and he'd wanted to move to the next level?"

"Yuck, stop it." Nui waved her hands in front of my face. "Can we change the subject, please?"

I grinned. "Fine. So what's the latest on your end? Are you staying at BIS? Any updates?"

Nui sighed. "Nothing yet. But we only got back

yesterday. Aunt May said there might be something in Khun Yaai's will that would help."

"Did you know that Khun Yaai made it possible for you to go to BIS?"

"What do you mean?" Nui asked.

"Khun Yaai's best friend said she sold some fields to give your parents the money for the school and she talked to your mom about it. You didn't know?"

Nui's mouth dropped open. "No, I didn't, but that would make total sense. Oh, gosh I missed so many things that were happening behind the scenes and I just assumed the worst." Nui shook her head. "I really screwed up, didn't I?"

"No comment," I said.

"I suppose, as long as we learned our lesson like Aunt May said, that's all we can do."

"You mean, go with the flow and the universe will deliver to us what we focus on?"

"Yeah, but also that we can't judge people from the outside. We don't know what's going on in someone's head."

"Ha, or who's in the body? Maybe not the rightful owner." I elbowed Nui in the side.

She giggled.

"Or maybe it's as simple as what your mom always says."

Nui and I spoke at the same time.

"It is what it is."

We burst into laughter.

81

YUMI

Lumpini Park was crowded with joggers and families out for a Sunday stroll. The clouds had finally cleared after a massive thunderstorm earlier in the day and steam was rising from the wet pavement around the lake. I was standing on Aldrin Bridge when my phone pinged.

'Hey Yumi, how are you?'

'Hey Lu. All good here. How's life in San Francisco?'

'Ok. We're settling in and school starts tomorrow.'

'Have you heard from Nui?'

'Yeah, she arrived, and she said her host family is really nice. She starts next week.'

A wet nose touched my hand. LaTe was getting impatient and wanted to move. He knew his best friend was coming.

'Sorry, I gotta run. I'll text you tomorrow.'

'Ok, take care, let's talk this week. I have some stuff to tell you.'

'K. Bye.'

I'd barely put my phone away before LaTe pulled me forward, eager to get to his buddy Chone. They immediately started wrestling and nipping each other. I never tired of watching them play.

"Hey, sorry, I'm late." Channon handed me an iced matcha latte, then wrapped his arm around my waist and kissed me.

THE END.

TO MY READERS

Thank you so much for choosing to read Taang-Leuk, whether you have been waiting for Luna's and Nui's story to continue or you have stumbled across this book by chance. If you enjoyed reading Choices, perhaps others would too?

Recommend it: Just a few words to your friends, your book groups, and your social networks would be wonderful.

Review it: Please tell your fellow readers what you liked about my book by reviewing Taang-Leuk on Amazon and Goodreads or on whatever site you bought the book from. If you do write a review, please send me a note at maria@mariakuhnbooks.com so I can thank you with a personal email. You can also stop by my website www.MariaKuhnBooks.com to keep up to date with future books. Simply sign up at the following link. As a gift you will receive a free bonus chapter that is not available through commercial channels.

Thank you for your support. I hope to see you next time!

Maria Kuhn

GLOSSARY

Ajaarn - *Teacher (title)*
Farang - *Foreigner*
Kha (female version) Khrup (male version) - *commonly added to a sentence to make the sentence more polite and formal*
Khor towd (kha) - *Excuse me*
Khun + First name - *Form of address i.e. Khun Susan, Khun Mark, Khun Bo etc*
Khun Bpoo - *Grandpa (paternal grandfather)*
Khun Yaa - *Grandma (paternal grandmother)*
Lèse Majesté - *A crime. Any person who defames or insults the monarchy can be imprisoned*
Mae - *Mom*
Nong - *Form of address for a younger person*
Paa - *Dad*
Puen sa-nid - *Best friend*
Rawang noi sii krub - *Watch out*
Sabai di - *I'm well*
Sabai di mai kha? - *How are you?*
Sawasdee khrup/kha - *Hello/goodbye*

Soi - *Street*
Soi dog - *Feral street dogs*
Talapad - *Ceremonial fan used by monks*
Tuk-tuks - *Three wheeled open-sided motor taxis*
Wai - *Hand gesture (hands together in prayer form in front of the body) as a greeting or show of respect*
Wat – *Temple*

STAY IN TOUCH

Readers Club Offer

FREE DOWNLOAD

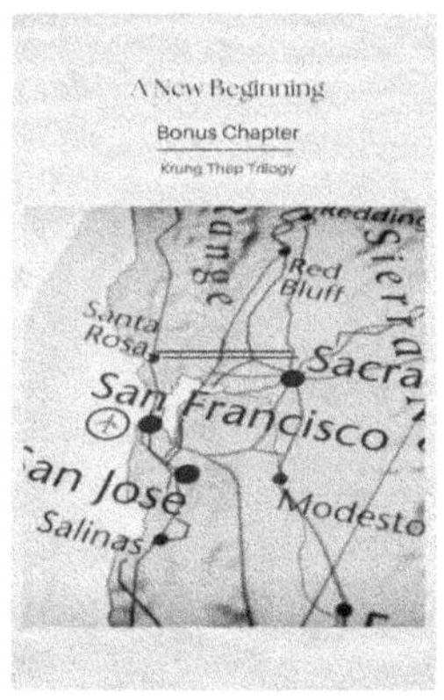

I hope you enjoyed Luna and Nui's journey. If you'd like to find out what happens after Bangkok, simply go to www.MariaKuhnBooks.com and sign up for my Reader's Club. As a gift you will receive the free companion story 'A New Beginning'. I will also let you know when the next book, a Young Adult Mystery, is coming.

ACKNOWLEDGMENTS

Back when I started Plyan, I didn't expect the story to turn into a trilogy, but here we are. I hope you enjoyed the journey and the sometimes unexpected detours as much as I did. Luna and Nui have come a long way and I'm pretty sure Yumi will indeed end up President one day.

I was fortunate to have a lot of help along the way, including my lovely critique group who diligently and rigorously took the chapters apart and helped me put them back together again. I couldn't have done it without their comments, criticism and sometimes flat-out crazy suggestions, always delivered with a sense of humour. Yet again a big thank you to Nikki who corrected and suggested better Thai phrases and made sure I didn't step over cultural boundaries. Khob khun mak kha, Khun Chanida. A big thank you to Laura and Manu for their patience with my ever changing requests for the cover.

As always, thank you to my beta readers for the early feedback. Every single comment helped. The story has developed over time, so any remaining errors are, of course, entirely mine.

ABOUT THE AUTHOR

Maria grew up in a tiny village in the German countryside. Today, she calls London home (for now) after more than three decades of globetrotting and working in luxury hotels. Along the journey, she's befriended colourful characters, tasted more cuisines than she can count, and immersed herself in diverse cultures and awe-inspiring landscapes. Each adventure merits its own tale—eventually.

Taang-Leuk is the conclusion of the Krung Thep trilogy.

ALSO BY MARIA KUHN

PLYAN-SWITCH

(Krung Thep Book 1)

EEK-DAAN - THE OTHER SIDE

(Krung Thep Book 2)

www.ingramcontent.com/pod-product-compliance
Lightning Source LLC
Chambersburg PA
CBHW072044190726

48294CB00005B/1392